The Seven Ages

Eva Figes was born in Berlin and came to England with her family just before the outbreak of the Second World War, where she has lived ever since. She is the author of eight novels, including *Waking* and *Nelly's Version*, and four books of nonfiction.

D1335106

Eva Figes

The Seven Ages

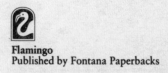

Flamingo
Published by Fontana Paperbacks

First published in Great Britain by
Hamish Hamilton Ltd 1986

This Flamingo edition first published
in 1987 by Fontana Paperbacks
8 Grafton Street, London W1X 3LA

Flamingo is an imprint of
Fontana Paperbacks, part of
the Collins Publishing Group

Made and printed in Great Britain by
William Collins Sons & Co. Ltd, Glasgow

For Günter Grass
. . . from Sophie

One

I can hear the silence, and through it individual sounds. I had forgotten how total it is, the dark, and the stillness, each sound distinct in the silence which surrounds it, the dark which holds it. It is a bit unnerving at times, after so many years in the city. I must have lived against a constant background of noise without realising it, so that fused sounds were the norm, a din which became a different kind of silence, a steady hum to which ears and pulse adjusted, as vision adjusts to a night which is not dark at all, but a fusion of artificial lights puncturing pools and puddles of night, to merge in a murky red sea above the tideline of roofs.

But here, at night, you can hear a pin drop into infinity. The dark is an echo chamber, it rises and rises above my head as I stroll to the gate for a breath of fresh air and lift my face to a black sky with its pinprick of distant stars. It makes me feel solitary, feeling dark space fall away from me on all sides, the earth falling away below my feet, space above me, the land slipping and sliding. Stars recede at the speed of light. We are small objects whirling in infinite space.

It is different during the day. Then there is so much to do that I hardly notice my solitude. I go down to the village to shop, or try to clear my small garden of weeds and dig up the cabbage patch. And the cottage itself takes some getting used to: although my few bits and pieces are in place nothing is quite settled. It takes time to know just where a chair or bed should stand, and whether I need some shelves here or there. I am still bumping into corners, feeling a small shock of novelty at the steep angle of the narrow stairs. And when I have had enough of deciding where to store potatoes or put a hook for the oven cloth I shut the door behind me and walk. Out through the lanes, skirting the hedges and ditches of my childhood, exploring the fields of memory. This corner where the

1

old barn once stood; the edge of the wood where we loitered with our bunches of bluebells and Ada sang at the top of her voice; the stile on which we sat and told each other stories. Past, present and future merge in the contours of this unremarkable landscape.

I have been down to the river and tossed twigs into the water, to see them eddy downstream. And sat on the ruins of the castle walls to follow the shadows of clouds passing over the patchwork of fields below. I have watched sparrows settle on the telegraph wires and even, when the road was quite empty, put my ear to one wooden pole to listen for messages humming through. And always, on my return, I look in hedges and ditches for enough wild flowers to fill a jar on the kitchen table.

It is not easy. There seem to be less than there were, but once you begin to look hard in the long grass you find them easily enough, small blue flowers, yellow or white. Star-shaped, or cupped like a bell. Single or clustered. And I hear forgotten words coming into my head, I hardly know from where, whispered on the night wind like a sigh: stitchwort and mugwort, archangel and milfoil, cinquefoil, calamint and bugle. I find myself pottering round the kitchen muttering words like a charm or incantation, trying to remember how and when I first heard them, conjuring up images to go with the sounds. Vervain. Fumitory. Mullein and mouse-ear hawkweed. Eyebright and periwinkle.

Some of the words I heard from Granny Martin, who taught us the names of many of the wild flowers and grasses we brought back. She told us how her grandmother regularly made cowslip wine, but even then they were hard to find, and I have not seen one this summer. But there is a scent of honeysuckle on the night air, and a whisper as a sudden night breeze rises and falls, shuddering through the trees, and small creatures stir in the dark, bark, cough, while an owl hoots in the distant wood, and I hear her voice saying how at that time, the dark time, we lived surrounded by forest, vast, impenetrable, a huge ocean of dark which closed in on us like the high night sky round a slither of new moon, so we lived surrounded by fear, and night closing in. For at night the wolves prowled beyond the edge of the forest, to forage, it was said, not only for a stray sheep but any child foolish enough to be out of doors, and men, too, had been hunted in packs and cleaned to the bone. We could hear them howl on a clear moonlit night.

Her voice got deeper, rough and husky, as I tried to light a few twigs in the hearth and smoke billowed into the room. Coughing, I got up and opened the window, to get rid of the stink of woodsmoke and soot, and cool air blew in, bringing a scent of earth and grass. I saw a new moon rising above the woods, emphasising their black intensity. And my grandmother, said the voice, who was called Moruiw, was feared by many, because she was born on the fifth day of the new moon, signifying that she would become a herborist. I, Emma, born with the magic veil, have gathered strength from her powers.

The feeble fire had died in the grate, but the room was still very smoky. Where did the voice come from? I tried to recall where and when I had heard of Moruiw, who might have had healing powers, rummaging in the confused memories of childhood, legends of the neighbourhood, a dim mist lying over the fields of the past, blurring edges, mingling with things read and images conjured up by the old folk in their stories, larger than life, a permanent part of it. I knew about Emma's Mound on the high ground beyond the church where the earth cured warts on midsummer eve, and girls gathered once a year with rushlights to see into their future.

Her voice continued now, husky with years and smoke. I could imagine the circle round her, a smell of animal fat and hide mingling with woodsmoke, and two bright stars visible through the hole in the roof. It was a time, she said, of black winters and hard frosts, and war, always war. Twice, in two following summers, the settlement had been burnt to the ground and the harvest plundered. Cattle had been taken, and young children had died. In the year my mother Medhuil was born, she of the dreams, it had been foretold that if midwinter fell on a Tuesday there would be an evil winter of hard frosts, a damp and rainy spring, and that many women would die, and sheep also. And only Moruiw kept her child through that year, though whether it was because she laid it on the roof at new moon, or passed it through the hollow stone we all know to this day, I cannot say for sure. But it was also rumoured that it was not so much her cunning which kept her own child alive as evil words and deeds which caused the babes of other women to fall sick and die.

All of which would have been enough to put her through the ordeal by water, since evil gossip against Moruiw was rife amongst the neighbours. But the lord Edwin had a wife, the lady Aethelfrida, who could not be brought to bed of a living child, and it was my grandmother Moruiw, with her girdle of adderskin and the twelve grains of coriander seed which she tied to the lady's thigh, who brought her to bed of a living daughter, after potions and blood-letting on the first day of the new moon and a fine amulet of amber had all failed. Then the lord Edwin was mighty pleased with my grandmother, even though he had wished for a son, and made her a gift of cattle and enough wheat for a twelve-month. He also saw to it that those who accused her of witchcraft were themselves put to the ordeal by water as a trial of falsehood, and after a couple of duckings the gossip died away entirely.

Two bright stars shone in the dark sky, timeless, glimpsed from an age far beyond knowing, across a black ocean of space. I could sense, now, that the voice in the smoke was not intended for me. Dimly, I made out other figures, huddled together for warmth under the hole in the roof. The old voice of Emma was speaking to them, no doubt about it. Hear me, the husky voice told them: hear this and remember.

Moruiw had one more child after Medhuil, and a hard time she had of it. Her own man had been killed in battle the previous winter, and some said he had been dead too long to have sired her son Oswiu, known all his life as Oswiu the Black on account of his swarthy looks and fierce fighting spirit, and that his father was one of the attackers who had raped and pillaged nine months before. Moruiw kept her own council, but a difficult birth she had of him, and after he slithered out between her thighs and the women saw that not only his head but his entire back was covered in black hairs gossip spread among the women who attended her that he had been sired by no man, but a wolf from the forest.

Perhaps this was why, in their consternation at the boy's appearance, they forgot to remove the eaglestone tied to her thigh to draw out the child, and the womb was drawn out after. By the time they found out their mistake it was too late, and though they sat her on hot coals, hoping the foul smell of burning rags and feathers would drive it back up, and anointed her burning vulva

4

with oil of thyme after pushing her organs back in, and applied water in which mallow and hollyhock had been boiled, they could not hide from themselves or the whimpering mother that things looked bad, and Moruiw who, in spite of her pain and her great fatigue, knew more than any of them, asked to be left alone with her daughter.

Medhuil was still only a child then, as different from the newborn baby as night from day, fair-haired, gentle and mild, a dreamer, where the black baby was fierce even in his first cries, which began when he was swung by his heels and slapped on his slimy hirsute back still wet from his mother's womb, and rarely stopped thereafter, day in day out, as an insatiable hunger seemed to shake his small fierce frame, to grow big and strong and fighting fit. He could not grow fast enough. Go, said Moruiw to the child Medhuil, who from that time on became her eyes and ears, and told her of a place near the river where she would find a bramble with both ends growing into the earth; go before dawn, when the first light glimmers over the brow of the hill, speaking to no one before you leave, and do not look behind you as you go. Using your left hand, cut off nine shavings from the newer root, then come back here and boil them with mugwort and betony, feverfew and cinquefoil, bugloss and periwinkle, as I shall direct.

Medhuil did as she was told, and Moruiw lived on to a great age, though from that time on she could not walk more than a step or two, since her falling womb was bound up with plaster of hemlock and pitch. So those who needed her help came here, to consult her at her own fireside. And now it was always Medhuil who scoured wood and pasture, meadow and riverbank, for the herbs and roots and berries she needed for her skill. Moruiw told her where to look and how to pick, the white archangel near riverbanks in summer and autumn, yellow stonecrop on walls and rocks and in sandy places, sorrel in damp pastures, nightshade in places where the sun does not reach.

This last was said to memorise. It came back to me, as the night wind whispered the words through the leaves of the trees at the back of the house: archangel near riverbanks, sorrel in damp pastures, nightshade where the sun does not reach. Hear this and remember.

5

The days of Moruiw were still the days of the old religion, and times were hard, harder even than now. In winter falling storms bound the earth, and the men sang boastfully enough, in the great hall, to the clink of the mead cup, told of the killing of monsters in the great wood, spoke of the singing corselet and the ringing sword as the liquor flowed. The women had no part in it, the singing, songs of the heroes, for they might have told another story, if they had been heard in the great hall. For though in winter they heard the bard sing of old heroes, the killing of dragons, of defending our settlement from the dark terror which lurked in the wood, with the coming of spring and the sad cry of the cuckoo came death for us, working in the fields, and our barns burning. Whilst those hired to defend us were doing much the same elsewhere, no doubt, destroying crops and slitting a few noses.

Each spring unbound the terror, and Medhuil, though only a child still, began her dreaming. At night she saw a moon suffused with blood which would grow to the full even as she watched it, and make her cry out with fright. And though Moruiw instructed her to search for the white poppy, and brewed her a warm drink from it, she could do nothing to erase her dreams, though the moon now appeared as though under water, and she did not wake.

But when emissaries who came bringing gifts of peace tried to kill our lord Edwin after being feasted in the great hall, and two of his thanes were killed in the scuffle, Edwin swore a terrible oath, that if he should have revenge on his enemy, and the new god prove more efficacious than the old, he would turn to the new faith, and his followers with him. And so it came about that he laid waste the lands, not only of the lord who had sent to kill him, but also those of three other lords, so that the air was filled with keening, reeking of blood and smoke, as crops burned and cattle were slaughtered.

On his return his priests agreed that the new god did indeed appear to have more power than any of the old gods hitherto, and so it came about that Edwin and his lady Aethelfrida and all their followers were baptised. And he ordered a church to be built of wood, and that his daughter Hilda, born of the magic of Moruiw, should be baptised and given to God.

There was a lull, a rustling of bodies stirring, and Emma's voice reached a new pitch. Hilda of the holy bones, she said. In the last years of her life no meat or drink passed her lips, she survived on a few drops of holy water each day, and a single wafer. Till her skin became brittle as paper and the flesh thinned into mere cobwebs and no one knew when to administer the last rites. And I have heard that a man once tried to steal her skull and was struck dead on the spot, and the water in which the bones are washed each year has cured men of the falling sickness and restored light to the blind. But that occurred long after, for before that the lady Aethelfrida had given birth to a son and decided to join her daughter in a life of religious seclusion. For the birth of a son had caused her lord much rejoicing, but made her weary of the world. And when she could neither eat nor sleep for weariness she would send for my mother, Medhuil, who brought herbs and potions.

And afterwards it was given out by the priest that my lady had seen a vision in which a stranger came to her, his garment bathed in light, holding a white bird in his hands which suddenly flew heavenward, and spoke to her words of such import that the lady was struck dumb with awe of the holy spirit and did not leave her chamber for three days and nights, and spoke neither to the lord Edwin nor to her attendants. But she told Medhuil, who brought an infusion of bishopwort and marjoram for her head, for the thoughts that would not leave it, that she was sick at heart that her lord was always fighting, and had she brought a son into the world for this?

And so she rode away to join her daughter, who had been given to God in perpetual virginity, taking with her a gift of much land, pasture and forest rich in venison, and twelve cartloads of chattels, including gold and silver, fine linen and furs. All that she had brought on her marriage.

I sit at the window, unwilling to stir, listening to the night. The whole earth shudders in a sudden breath of wind, and I remember following Ada on such a night to the high ground above the church, hearing my heart thumping with fear as I saw the beam of her torch swing to and fro. What was it we were trying to find out, stumbling into the dark future? She brought two white feathers, and a candle which we stuck on a boulder, and as the feathers

7

began to rise above the flame she recited some sort of mumbo-jumbo and I had to join in the chorus, something about DILEMMA PIPEMMA repeated three times very fast under our breath. Only one of the feathers dropped into the flame, which Ada said did not count, as it curled and turned brown. The pungent smell of a burning feather. As it happened, she was wrong, but at the time, as I stumbled after her through the dark, I thought she knew everything.

If cattle be privately taken away, chanted the voice, then sing on the foot spoor, and light three candles and dip on the hooftrack the wax thrice, and no man shall be able to conceal it. And if it be a horse sing on his fetters or his bridle: that which I have I will not cease to hold, neither plot nor ploughland, neither turf nor toft, of wood nor of water, of sand nor of strand, be thou with thine and leave me with mine.

These words my mother taught me, after she had married Eric, bastard son of lord Edwin. For my father that was to be had been falsely accused of horse theft, and in denying the charge he chose the ordeal by iron, not simple but threefold, and carried the hot metal the length of three men. And when, after three days, his hand had not festered, he was cleared of the charge, but his marriage to Medhuil so shortly after started a rumour of healing by witchcraft, that she had used more than red nettles and leaves of green marche pounded with egg white and oil to soothe the burning, and that he had married her as part of the bargain, or to stop her mouth. But if she used witchcraft it was of a different kind, for in truth he had long been under the spell of her grey eyes and gentle manner, and the hair that was pale as sunlight without being washed in lye of mistletoe to make it fairer.

He had seen her first picking roots and grasses in the field by the river, and if his eye was caught by her hair gleaming like flax, his mind was full of what he had heard of her cunning, not only the dressing of wounds and the brewing of healing draughts; for it was said she could speak to the bees as no one else could, and though they would hum and argue about it, they would not leave once she had hung beewort on the hive and thrown gravel as they swarmed. And I have heard her myself as a child, sing Sit ye ladies, sink, sink

8

to earth. Never fly wild to the woods, and her voice, like her hair, must have made them think of honey, for we never went short. And it was known that she could put a grown man to sleep with a drink of wormwood, radish and hemlock before stitching an open wound so fine that it left no scar.

But the dreams of Medhuil gave her no peace, either before or after her marriage, and a full year before his father was killed in battle she dreamed of a black horse galloping riderless through the trees, and told her lord that Edwin would die. And he took to watching her toss and turn in the night, with her eyes moving under the closed lids, though she was blind to the flickering candle he held near her pale face, and as he lay beside her in the dark he could hear soft murmurs, muttered words and sometimes a low moan, as though she communed with an unseen spirit, and it put fear into him, but also desire, the long slow burn he had felt ever since the day she had soothed his scorching palm with her cool ointment. And though he took her while she slept, she would not wake, but whimpered a little, and frowned. In the morning she rose with dark rings under her eyes, and a great weariness in her body. And if she spoke at all it was of those dreams, of black ravens gathering, and a stag attacked by hounds, and a broken roofbeam under a threatening sky. And in the seventh month she was brought to bed of a stillborn child, a boy born with eyes closed and a mute mouth, as though the dreams had sucked him under.

Then Moruiw, who was still living, though unable to leave her own fireside, told her to rise at dawn and, having eaten nothing, to sip the milk of the cow of one colour, run to the brook without looking behind her and spit it into the running water with the words

> May this be my boot
> Of the loathsome late birth

then scoop up and swallow some water, using the same hand she had used to take the milk, and run to a neighbour's house without looking behind her to break her fast. And afterwards she went to the graveyard and stepped three times over the child's barrow, saying

> May this be my boot
> Of the heavy swart birth

9

and picked up a handful of earth, wrapped in black wool, and sold it at the crossroads for a farthing, handing it over with the words

> I it sell
> Or have it sold
> This swarthy wool
> And grains of this sorrow.

So the black dreams of her dead child were carried over the hill, and far off.

And so, said the voice, I was born, Emma-of-the-caul, signifying that I should have healing power. And I have it still for the luck of my line, and it will pass to you, and you, and you. For, as it protects the child from drowning in its mother's womb, so it protects the traveller by water. And though it brings misfortune if it be black, mine was red as a rosebud, so it was known that my eyes, when they opened, could seek out pain under the skin, and my mouth, when it learned to speak, would seal a parted wound so the skin knitted in silence.

And when I was still only a child my mother taught me to find marche and periwinkle, brownwort and vervain, pennyroyal and lupin, how to make a circle round them at dusk and sing over them at dawn, how to know which worts must be sung over and those that belong to silence both coming and going. And she told me of the red flowers that stop blood from flowing, and the yellow blossoms which cure fever and sickness of the liver, since pestilence comes in a yellow cloud which sweeps across the land and a man sick with his liver will turn yellow. And she showed me the virtue of worts that grow on dead men's graves, on roofs and high rocks, how to ward off snakes with vervain and southernwort, cure snakebite with a salve made from adderwort and elder, and that bishopwort is held by many to be a cure for monstrous night visitors and frightful dreams, though her own dreams continued, no matter what she took.

For she saw the wooden church burning before it was razed to the ground, and the lord Edwin lying under the earth, and though she did not know that Oswiu the Black would kill her husband in a drunken brawl and die himself of a festering wound before he could pay for his life, she had dreams which made her cry out in the

10

dark and shiver from head to foot if his name was spoken. But Eric slept, and held no candle to her restless eyelids. After a few years of marriage he was used to her, and ignored her oddities.

And she dreamed, too, of the unborn child stirring in her womb, how he would be taken from her to serve God. For when the young lord Wilfrid succeeded Edwin he aimed to please God, having taken heed of the warning sent to him by his mother and sister. For Hilda took to fasting after her father's death, and the lady Aethelfrida sent her son a poem she had composed, together with a gold ring to be laid in the earth with her husband's mangled corpse. Broken are the bonds, she wrote, and blood flows into the earth. Thus man, who does not mind the spirit, shall come to nothing. The wolf will howl, the raven circle above, and the sad cuckoo will cry in the spring. Nothing will save them. The castles will crumble, and the roofbeam fall into dust. Brambles will tug at the buildings of men, binding them into the earth. The grip of the earth will hold them, and soon they will vanish under wild grass, seeds taking root. Knotgrass and kneeholm, brownwort and madder, ravensfoot and comfrey, groundsel and celandine. So ends the anger of man.

There was a long silence, broken only by the hoot of an owl echoing through the wood and the night wind sighing through dense foliage.

This was the dream of my mother concerning her son Edmund, as it was to come to pass in future years. For she foresaw it clearly enough in the dark months before his birth, after his father had been laid in the earth, and in later years, when her memory of the small boy had grown dim, and only the dream remained vivid, she would murmur the words by the fireside, soothing the old pain. For though she had lost him he was not dead, and the glory she foresaw in her dreams during those months was to comfort her in the long years ahead. Better thus than the battlefield, she would say, knowing the fate of the sons of women.

I saw in my dream, she told us, that I was carrying a boy, who would be born on the first day of a new moon, signifying that he would be wise and book-learned, though endangered by water. And here the old grief would well up in her, swimming in her eyes, for it was while he was minding geese by the river that the bailiff had come to take him away, when he was barely seven years old. And Medhuil was to see in her dream, many times, the monastery that the lord Wilfrid, fearful of his mother's admonitions, had built for the good of his soul. She saw a forbidding, gloomy place, surrounded on all sides by swampy marshes, a place to which no free man would go of his own will. Airs of pestilence rose from the swamps, and she saw that sunlight only rarely penetrated the mists that enclosed it, and then but dimly. The punt carrying her son vanished into the white mist, and did not return.

I remember him as a small boy, said the voice, playing sticks by the river. And that winter before he was taken we took turns in minding him when the cough would not leave him, nor the low fever, not for fennel and sage, not for honey and lard, not for any number of Paternosters, and virgin honey with seed of marche and seed of dill, and holy water in everything. And Medhuil murmured Mattheus Marcus Lucas Johannes Deum patrem Deum filium Deum spiritum as she had heard the priest say the words over sick cattle, and I think she loved him the more because of the trouble she had with him, and so her grief was deeper, and would not fade. And in after years she would take comfort from the prognostic of those born on the first day of the new moon, that if he escapes the danger by water he will be long in life. And during the long nights of his sickness, when she heard him coughing under the skins, and the longer nights of his absence, she remembered her dream from before his birth.

For the dream was a dream within a dream, for she had seen beyond the mists as they closed round the small boy who loved nothing so much as to float sticks in the river and ride piggyback on our old sow, and whose mischievous tongue would stumble over the words she tried to teach him, bishopwort and cinquefoil, bird's tongue and agrimony, and whose face, she could see, was tear-stained as the punt skimmed through the reedy marsh and vanished into the mist. For she saw a bearded man in a monk's habit surrounded by written scrolls which she could not decipher, having learnt neither to read nor write, but legends came out of his mouth so that in the air above his head she saw the lord Edwin visited by a white dove who promised to slay his enemy if he turned to Christ, and afterwards, as he sat in the darkness outside his hall, troubled in mind and gazing up at the evening star whilst his followers, drunk with beer and victory, made noisy riot within, an unknown stranger came to him from out of the darkness with an eerie light about him and placed his hand on his head saying: When this sign shall be given you, keep your word to God. Whereupon he vanished, leaving a burning mark on his forehead which did not cease to trouble him night and day until he was baptised, when the bishop's hand and holy water quenched the burn. And she saw, illuminated, the great church he would order to rise on the spot.

And as she got older, and told of her life by the fireside on winter nights, her dream of Edmund and his dreams became more vivid as other memories faded, and she told us how many had been cured at the tomb of the lady Aethelfrida, a child with Lenten fever, who sat by her tomb all night, and a man foaming at the mouth and gnashing his teeth who calmed miraculously. And how her body remained as the day it was buried, free from decay and uncorrupted. And Hilda too, how her bones multiplied, until each church in the neighbourhood had at least a fingerbone, and how before death, since she had touched neither food nor drink for a great number of years, it was possible to see right through her, and a light shone from her skin. But after death both hair and toenails continued to grow and, being cut once a year, the trimmings were put in water and drunk by the sick, and so many were cured. All of which was to be recorded by Edmund as his black beard turned grey and then white, and his skin turned the colour of parchment he wrote on, and he saw, through the murky mist which surrounded the dark walls which enclosed him, a riverbank, and sunlight rippling on water, and heard a soft voice murmuring of eyebright and adderwort, speedwell and fumitory as she touched him with her fingers of soothing sleep.

And she saw in her dream that he would write no word of this, of geese cackling on the riverbank, and sticks floating downstream, of the smell of drying wool by the fireside and the hot mulled drink soothing his aching throat when he was flushed with fever, or her fingers rubbing salve into his scalp to get rid of the lice. But she saw, too, that though he spoke in a strange tongue and

13

eschewed the company of women, being enclosed with monks like himself, and studied all manner of ways to deprive himself of sight and sound, smell and taste, yet when he closed his eyes at night he heard his mother's voice crooning a lullaby, and felt her hands tucking him up tight for warmth, and he tasted seed of dill and seed of marche running in honey on his tongue and saw the bees swarming at her call and sunlight gleaming on walls and leaves and water as he had not seen it shine in a lifetime.

And though the names of Medhuil and Moruiw did not figure once in those pages, beside the saints and the killings, she saw in her dream that their seed would be everywhere, though no one knew it, would multiply with time over hill and dale, meadow and pasture, just as the wind blows foxglove and parsley, nettle and clover, their strong roots binding the earth. As she saw that though roofs would have fallen, and castles crumbled, leaving only a few words, and some dark deeds blowing in the wind, and though the bones of Hilda would give birth only to more bones, yet the daughters of Moruiw should people the land without knowing, as henbane and red nettle grow unregarded on Edwin's barrow, eyebright and fumitory cover the forgotten spot where Eric was slaughtered. Who knows where to find the yellow flower of the mouse-ear hawkweed, or toothwort, stitchwort or brook-lime speedwell? And yet they continue to grow and multiply, in ditch and pasture, on coastline and riverbank, clifftop and gully, and the ruined buildings of men.

The voice stopped quite suddenly, and I woke up. Or, at least, I imagine I must have woken up, since I could only have been dreaming. Nothing else would account for it. I felt stiff and cold, because the window was ajar and cool night air blew in, bringing a faint whiff of grass and honeysuckle. I suppose I will get used to being alone here at night, this dark silence sucking me in. Once I have put up some curtains I can shut it off in a normal fashion, if I am in no mood for infinity, but now I am fully conscious of the night sky rising above my head, lifting my heart with it in something like awe. And the dark silence that surrounds me is full of possibility.

Two

I have acquired a second-hand bicycle, and I am gradually getting used to it, though I tend to swerve on corners and wobble rather self-consciously if I meet anything coming the other way. I have not ridden a bike since my early days as a midwife, when women still had babies at home, and after thirty years or more my calf and thigh muscles tend to ache afterwards. But it is fun, and becoming more fun as I gain confidence. I had forgotten how high one sits, looking over hedgerows, into front gardens, with the air rushing past. At first I felt quite giddy, but my slight sense of vertigo was spiced with exhilaration. Now I ride every day, unless it rains, and I no longer feel absurd: instead it gives me an immense sense of freedom.

Kate telephoned last night. She has just come back from a conference on foetal monitoring, where they were shown the latest advances in the new technology. As usual, there are administrative arguments about priorities at a time of cutbacks in expenditure.

Sounds a long way from my old tin trumpet, I said. Maybe it's as well I retired.

I can afford to sound humorous: by now I am used to having a daughter who knows so much more than I do. Ever since she got into medical school. Even before that, as she was such a high flyer at school.

Not a bit of it. We need more people like you. Her voice sounded depressed. I keep seeing women who can't afford to eat the right food, and who live in appalling conditions – damp, overcrowded, you name it.

Plus ça change, I said.

Still, we can see what we've got these days, she said glumly. I

15

suppose that's something. And we can always opt to abort. No good having a world full of cretins.

It was a typical Kate remark, the kind that got her misunderstood by those who do not know her as I do. I could imagine it not going down well with male colleagues, particularly now that she stands in authority over quite a few of them. Her sister, even now, might have stormed at her for a cold heart. I knew otherwise.

So, she finished up, what are you doing with yourself down there? Not bored with country life yet?

She had been against the move when I first brought it up, full of dire statistics about retired people who drop dead for no reason, having cut themselves off from their near ones and dear ones, or who try to move back into the city. I resisted the temptation to point out how rarely I saw either of them, unless Sally happened to need a baby-sitter in a hurry. I am against resentful mothers, on principle, and there are times when I find it a relief not to be saddled with my offspring. When she saw I was not to be moved from my decision she began to make helpful suggestions, and even found the time to come down to help with the move.

We must find you something to do, she said. How about starting a family planning clinic in the village?

I laughed. No thanks. I've retired, remember?

Meals on wheels, Darby and Joan, mobile library? Although she was joking, there was a serious undercurrent to her teasing. She did not believe in my 'doing nothing', as she called it. Or anybody else, for that matter. The bossy older sister, always getting Sally to tidy up her room or do her homework. Sally resented it, still does come to that, but I would hardly have managed without her. From a very early age it was Kate who stopped things from sliding into chaos at home whilst I was out working. I relied on her, knowing I need not worry. Just as now, I am sure, those women with their swollen bellies relaxed under her hands in the ante-natal clinic, trusted her when she said everything was fine, and stopped smoking because she told them to. She would walk the corridors of the hospital, wearing her white clinician's coat like a shining armour, of reason and authority. Kate rarely bothers to argue, being empirical to her fingertips, but when her sister accuses her of liking power she says that the world cannot be changed without it.

16

All right, she conceded. I'll let you go back to communing with nature. Only don't start talking to the trees.

I replaced the telephone receiver and went back out of doors to do a bit more weeding before it got dark. My little patch of garden is quite overgrown with nettles and chickweed, but I hope to be able to plant a few seeds by next spring, if I can clear the ground and dig it over by then. My predecessor has left a few woody cabbage stalks, a couple of straggling rosebushes, and mint and parsley which has run wild over most of the vegetable patch. God knows whether I shall succeed in growing anything to speak of, and I am rather afraid of making a fool of myself. So I tend to sneak out in the evening, when I am less likely to find a critical eye watching me over the gate. You want to turn that soil three times with three days in between, some old codger advised me as he watched me trying to get a fork at the tangled roots of nettles: then let the frost get at it. No use trying to grow nothing before that. Sing to it, that's what my granny used to do, and her granny before that told how they used to smuggle wafers out of church at communion to kill the caterpillars, till the vicar found out and preached a sermon on the blasphemy of feeding the body of Christ to crawling insects, and made them swallow it before his eyes.

Sing to it, said Ada, popping the tiny seed into the furrow. And then you have to skip over it three times – once with your legs crossed.

I did as I was told, though I never knew how much she had thought up on the spur of the moment. I fell headlong and grazed both knees.

The days grow gradually shorter, and dusk catches me out. The horizon flushed pink and gold, outlining what is left of the old woods, mile upon mile of it, stretching back into our dreams, the leaves of long ago underfoot, rich and dark, nourishing roots and soil in diminishing layers of humus. Footpaths thick with brambles, mushrooms and spotted toadstools, the first white snowdrop among brittle leaves, a wintry sky among bare branches and row upon row of receding trunks, so many, you are first giddy, then

17

lost. But always something to be found, pine cones and acorn cups, leaves like skeletons and the brown triangles of beechnuts which crunch underfoot and have hairy insides. And, with the return of fine weather, comes a low-lying mist of bluebells.

Once it gets too dark to work in the garden I stroll down the lane for a bit. I feel the night wind going through me, all things through me: scents, sounds. I am a harp in the wind, stringing tight, senses tuned to every subtle modulation. Small insects flit in the fading light before they too are swallowed up in the gathering gloom to become no more than a light touch on the skin, a buzz and a whisper, a whirring of wings in the dark. I can feel them whisper, the ghost voices coming out of the hidden land, light as a moth they touch me, as unseen leaves and grasses murmur, chickweed and fumitory, wild thyme and clover, in the healing tangle of time. For the whispered charms that run through them have held their voices for centuries, so now the dark ocean of grasses sings not only of itself but of those fingers plucking their roots, searching them out, how Moruiw gave birth to Medhuil, whose dreams still lie here, under the earth, the fossils of white bone. And even now those nightmares come up to haunt us, ditches that smell of sudden death, the rank odour of killing, the cry of agony coming from the night wood. Fingerbones come out of the soil, so heavy with loss one would think the plough could hardly turn it. Ears lopped off, noses slit, hands and feet pollarded like stunted branches of willow, cuts so deep that no silk stitches could mend the damage, and no amount of celandine mixed with a woman's milk cure the hurt. For a witch can cure the Devil's work, but not man's, so ran the old adage, running through the grasses since Emma's time, when the old woman refused to fetch out her amulet for a man who had had his eyes put out, though her granddaughter begged for her to help him. The blind man with his listening face heard the words, and Judith never forgot them, passing them to her child and so down the ages as the grasses now whisper them back.

But down the hill the stream sings a different song, it gurgles in the dark of a drowning, a ducking that somehow went wrong. *Bedda* bubble the pebbles, and even now on a moonlit night if you look carefully you will catch a glimpse of her reflection in the

18

water, for her dark beauty was such that the river held her image and would not let it go, and it was in the flowing water that Judith would come to catch a glimpse of the mother she could not remember, and, since she was not unlike her, what she saw was the truth.

Beauty is a snare, sang the river.

Beware, sighed the reeds. And she saw how her image was trapped forever from too much gazing, so the reeds held her hair down under the water, and frogs croaked a mocking chorus not unlike the cackle of wives she heard as she went under.

There had been rumours of deadly love potions, and wax images under the threshold, and a jealous wife throwing a fit from which she never recovered, or at least not the use of her right hand with which she had struck her on the cheek. And when they found the crimson mark on her left shoulder it explained everything: the sick cow and the ailing child, the thunderstorm which, though they rang the church bell, lasted for three hours, and flattened the fields in a downpour of hail; the wilfulness of men who followed her about, haunting her door, though their wives scolded and brewed and consulted on love potions to win back what was rightfully theirs, so that when Will Fletcher choked and turned purple and gave up the ghost nobody blamed Meg and the foul concoction of hemlock she had put in his beer, and of which she had said not a word to anybody, being quite convinced that it was Bedda who had buried hairs from his beard and his nail parings under her threshold and said words over them which held him her prisoner, wherever he went, and any attempt to break the spell would result in death. So when they found the scarlet mark on her shoulder the truth burst with such clarity that their hearts sang with relief, the relief of all things made visible, all shadows banished. Once more the evil in their midst had been rooted out, hearts lifted, a cloudless summer sky lifted, clear and blue as the forget-me-nots which grew on the riverbank, and as they marched in procession a skylark sang, high above the meadow, sustaining its joyous solo like a benediction.

Free, free, sang the skylark, almost invisible in the blue sky that was almost white, high above the heads of the procession.

Free, free, it sang, above the dark head of Bedda reflected in the water, gazing mournfully up at her daughter with those lustrous eyes that would get them both into much trouble. And neither Bedda nor Judith recognised the voice as for them.

For when they ducked her in the water the end of the rope came loose miraculously, and when they pulled it in her body had vanished. So they knew that the water loved her, and the river had received her innocence into its own. So she was free, free, and now the skylark's eerie song had a mocking tone, for if she was free of them they would never be free of her. Her spirit and their guilt, one or the other would cause havoc: to livestock, their ailing children, to barm in the brewhouse and butter in the churn.

Free, free, sang the skylark, as they made a search for her body, skirting the riverbank, and by now the grass was humming with crickets singing the same song. They pushed a loaf out from the edge, with a lit candle stuck in the middle, to see where it would stop as it floated downstream so they could dredge the spot, but they found nothing, and when the loaf suddenly sank, dousing the candle, it was known that her spirit was alive down there, and hungry with it, even if her body was nowhere to be found. And on a clear night such as this, when there is a new moon rising, it is sometimes possible to see more than the shadow of her face reflected in the dark water. A small silver light, flickering like an unearthly candle flame, moves across the surface of the water, or rather, just beneath it.

And so, said Ada, they think her spirit is still down there, haunting the place. We could ask her to help us.

It's a long way from the river, I said doubtfully, though I remembered Ada's attempts to float a loaf with a candle stuck in it when a neighbour's dog went missing. The dog turned up next day and we had to forgo supper as a punishment for wasting good food in wartime. But I was not hungry anyhow, being sick with the worry and excitement of it, from the moment we stole the loaf out of aunt Doris's pantry to the time it began floating downstream with the candle flickering and got stuck near the far bank against what looked like a bundle of old clothes, when we took to our heels and did not stop running until we were almost back at the farm, gasping for breath, legs trembling.

20

If she notices the bread, said Ada, we took it to feed birds. Wild ducks or something.

It's a long way from the river, I said doubtfully.

It's where they found the body of that airman, whispered Shirley, and Dorothy told her to shut up in a quaking voice. It was creepy enough up here, above the churchyard, sitting in a ring on Emma's Mound in the dark. Ada had brought a torch, but she would only flash it occasionally so as to spare the battery. The trees round the churchyard formed huge, impenetrable shadows. Sounds, but no lights, came from the village below.

My gran says girls used to drown babies down in the river when she was a girl, whispered Joyce.

I couldn't do that, squeaked Dorothy. Why would anybody do that?

I could hear us breathing in the dark. Then a sudden gust shook the trees. Nobody knew how anybody could do such things. The future, grownups, such things were as dark and incomprehensible as the night.

All right then, said Ada. We could ask Agnes. She's close enough.

Only a stone's throw from us was the spot by the church where she had been walled up for thirty years. The vicar was fond of telling us about her at Sunday school, how she lived in the north wall of the church with an open grave at her feet and only a small cat for company, though travellers came from a great distance to hear her, and through her tiny window with the black curtain marked with a white cross she heard all the troubles of the village, large and small, broken promises and washing stolen from the yard, broken jugs and ailing babies, beatings and gossip and rumour.

I didn't think nuns were supposed to know about ordinary things, objected Shirley.

I think we were all a bit uneasy about the procedure. The church wall loomed eerily close in the dark. There were those who declared that if you put your ear to the church wall at midnight you could hear her voice praying very softly, and then sobbing. And though it was much earlier, you never knew what might happen.

21

Of course she did, Ada said firmly. Anyhow, her sister was the wise woman of the village. Gran says she brought all the babies into the world. We can ask them both.

Ada produced a small kitchen knife and now we took turns to pare some rather wormy windfall apples we had collected during the day, with Ada holding the torch. Dorothy's paring broke halfway, since she was a bit clumsy with the knife, and Ada said it was a bad omen and she would probably die young. But when she began to snivel we found a spare apple and peeled it for her.

Your husband's name will begin with C, announced Ada, flashing her torch on the spot where the paring had landed in the long grass. Only Ada was able to decipher them, but then she also kept firm control of the torch.

Charlie Parker, suggested Joyce. Dorothy spluttered, and put her hand in front of her mouth.

I don't want to get married at all, said Shirley, flicking her blonde pigtails over her shoulders. I'm going to be a film star. But she took the knife when Ada passed it to her, and tried to find an apple without any wormholes in the skin. A muffled titter of derision had greeted her remark, since nobody could stand Shirley when she was being stuck up, and giving herself airs as though she was different from the rest of us. It rather threatened to disrupt the aura of solemnity and push back the shadows. However, Ada flashed her torch and revealed a long smooth curl of appleskin hanging from the spiked tip of a bushy grass stalk. This, she announced, was shaped like an S, and stood for STAR, because it was hanging and not lying on the ground.

Says you, sneered Joyce.

She's going to marry old freckle-face Simon Carter.

Smothered giggles rose in the dark. Everyone knew that moony-faced Simon was always hanging round the school gate when it was time to go home, and followed her around like a silly dog. Shirley was clearly annoyed, and pushed Dorothy, who was giggling louder than the rest of us. Then somebody objected that it was a daft game anyhow, and that Ada was making it all up.

I am not, said Ada.

This is boring, said Shirley contemptuously. I'm going home. And she stood up.

I know another game, Ada announced hastily, before the others could follow her. Shirley yawned, hesitated, but sat down again.

And that was when it happened. Not right away, of course, and afterwards nobody was quite sure just what had happened, or if we had simply imagined the whole thing, as Joyce made out, though she was as scared as the rest of us at the time.

Ada had told us to hold hands with our eyes shut. Be very quiet, she whispered, though I could feel a tremor down my arm which I knew was Dorothy trying not to giggle, and I found the temptation to look, if only for a moment, almost too much, so I had to squeeze them very tight. Ada said we were not doing it properly, and that we had to sit still enough to hear our own breath going in and out, and gradually we calmed down. I could hear the wind stirring in the branches of the oak tree, and a dog bark at the far end of the village. A burst of men's voices in the pub died away, leaving only the creak of a branch easing in the wind and a humming susurrus of insects in the grass all round us. And then we heard it, a sound so eerie that at first it did not seem like a human voice at all, but it went on and on, a high scream carried on the wind in an unending wail, so thin but full of pain that it seemed to come through a dark void and fill it. It went on and on, drawing itself out in a high-pitched thread of desolation that had no need to stop for breath but wound itself round the church tower and threaded the trees with its piercing agony and died away over the dark rooftops, to lose itself in the far off sky like an echo.

W-what was that? stammered Dorothy. Her fingers had been clutching mine so tightly that my hand was quite numb.

Nobody knew what to think. Even Ada was oddly quiet, and when she switched on her torch I saw that her face was very pale.

It came from the church tower, whispered Joyce, her voice shaking.

No it didn't.

Then where?

Ada flashed the torch about, so its feeble beam touched bits of the church, the trees, and the roof of the vicarage, till Joyce reminded her that she could be signalling an enemy aircraft, and did she want us all shot?

23

I think about it now, as I did then, but now I know I have heard it many times since. It took a while for me to make the connection. What does a child, what did any of us understand then? We went our separate ways in the dark, and Ada was unusually silent as we walked back to the farm, and I had trouble keeping up with her, as she flashed the torch beam on the rutted lane. She said not a word, neither of us did, when aunt Doris demanded to know what we had been doing out so late. She sent us up to bed with a scolding, and without hot drinks.

I thought about it then, lying in the dark, and I think of it now.

It must have been Agnes, whispered Ada from under the bedclothes, as we lay unable to sleep. Imagine being walled up for all those years, not being able to run around and do things. I'd go barmy, wouldn't you?

Yes.

Ada thought for a bit. Perhaps she wanted to shout and scream all the time she was alive, and couldn't. So now . . .

She did not finish. I heard the bedsprings squeak as she turned over. The unfinished thought hovered between us, making sleep impossible. Somehow neither of us uttered the one word uppermost in both our minds, as though we had crossed into a dangerous world where ghosts were no longer to be taken lightly. It occurred to me to ask Ada what game she had begun when she made us close our eyes and hold hands, but I decided to say nothing.

But it won't do, our childish vision. Agnes chose her confinement within the north wall of the church. Ada did not choose to be kept behind after school, even for an hour, and so she visualised a sort of lifelong detention. But Agnes chose, insofar as a human being can choose. And so it becomes necessary to ask why she opted to be buried alive, seeking the voice of God in a quiet spirit, looking each day into her future grave.

I think about it now, and it occurs to me that the scream was responsible. She must have heard it many times, just as I have done

24

since. Mary, mother of God, help me! would go the cry, and perhaps it seemed to her that they had left it too late, with their bellies swollen to bursting, gasping for breath with the sweat coming off them. As a child she must have seen it, or, if not seen it, heard it often enough to know what being given in wedlock meant, that within nine months they would call on the mother of God to help them, and that sometimes even she could do little enough. So was it any wonder that at the first sign of blood coming from her she began to throw fits, and hear voices, and speak in a tongue that was not hers, so it was thought the girl was possessed by the Devil, until the priest took to visiting her and pronounced her, after long hours of praying and private talk, to be called by God to a life of perpetual virginity.

That is how I see it now. And if people talked in after years of the miraculous change in her, since in earlier years she had been wild as a tomcat, spitting and throwing pots on the floor if her father so much as laid a hand on her, nobody broke her will, she chose freely, though it was the priest who persuaded her father that he was blessed, not cursed, in the gift of such a daughter, so the beatings finally stopped. Though some say he only stopped trying to thrash her into marriage when his right hand was turned to stone, and no amount of holy water could cure it.

The legends have of course multiplied. The vicar, in his little pamphlet, left on sale in the church to help restore the roof, where the old beams have fallen prey to deathwatch beetle, is careful to separate known fact from fiction. He mentioned what he regards as the latter, being a very secular vicar, because it is colourful, and because the known facts would not fill even such a slim pamphlet.

The current pamphlet says nothing of a sister, almost as famous in her day as Agnes, since she was the village wise woman and brought every child into the world. But I know about her, just as Ada did when we were children, though I cannot recall our source, except that it was not Sunday school. I suppose it must have been the same underground spring which Ada, having been born in the neighbourhood, had been hearing since birth, a sound which sang children to sleep, murmured through sickrooms, a brook of gossip

25

bubbling through kitchens and wash-houses, rattling with the butter churn and running off with the greasy dishwater into a gurgling drain.

She was the seventh child of a seventh child which, together with the inherited caul, gave her special powers, so that nobody felt safe unless Margery was called in when their time came. But Agnes felt safe only in her little stone cell, because she knew the history of those births, and understood what kind of luck was involved.

Margery told the story at the lying-in of her daughter Joan, which was a lengthy business. That in itself had become a custom, since Margery had heard it from her mother when Joan started pushing her way down the birth canal, and she thought that Maud had probably been told in much the same way by Judith. I cannot imagine myself using such a story to divert one of my expectant mothers, but then my function was rather different. I have to imagine so many things. Margery, for a start. Put myself in her place, with a few herbs drying on the roofbeam and an old cooking pot in which to brew some dark and foul-smelling concoction, bitter with the crops of meadow and riverbank, and the sour earth of the graveyard. Horrid smells habitually came from her hearth, but then everyone knew that foul smells had a power of their own, and could drive the womb back into the body when it threatened to drop out after birth.

And then there is Joan, little more than a child herself, with her thin face showing the strain, suddenly dropping the pot she was carrying so that milk spilled over the kitchen floor, as she clutched at her swollen belly with a cry that brought Margery running, and after her a whole flock of women clucking round her. What is there then but words to take the mind off the lull that is only an interval between spasms, and lift it beyond? How else can the body bridge the long tedium of waiting for the next agony? Margery understood this, that however much faith she might have in her arsenal of potions and amulets, it could never be enough, particularly for a first birth. And so she had become a skilled storyteller. Her narrative powers helped to divert not only the unfortunate victim, but the attendant women, who were less likely to question her methods on occasion if suitably entertained.

The seventh child of a seventh child, Margery was saying, lifting the heavy iron pot to the centre of the floor, where the wooden tub stood. Steam billowed up from the dark greenish-brown water, bringing with it the pungent meadow smells of mallow and southernwood, linseed and mugwort. The thread of her mother's story was lost in a cloud of hot vapour as half a dozen hands helped Joan to lower her cumbersome bulk into the tub and she sat, dizzy with weariness, with the brackish water lapping her huge stomach as though she had been dipped in a hot pond. But the heat was oddly relaxing, and the steamy aroma, pungent with wormwood and fennel, reminded her of being sick with a feverish cough as a small child, and Margery dosing her with remedies as she lay by the fire. So when they lifted her from the tub, wrapped her up, and began to rub her genitals with ointment she did not resist, but stood submissive as a sleepy child. Which, for the moment, she was.

The seventh child of a seventh child, said Margery, wrapping a blanket round her: and every one of them a girl. The pride in her mother's voice was unmistakable. It was, after all, the badge of her profession, the foundation of all her skills. And, if she chose this moment to tell the story, it was not only to reassure her daughter, going through her first ordeal, but because she had a wider audience too, in the neighbourhood women who had come to assist.

Joan, sniffing the drink put into her hands, felt sure that the child now lying inside her must be a girl too. Nobody in the family had given birth to a boy since the days of Judith, her great grandmother, whose story they were about to hear, though not for the first time. It was her seventh child, Maud, who in turn gave birth to Agnes and Margery.

Costmary and mugweed, said Margery, seeing her daughter grimacing as she sipped at the mulled wine. Drink it all, there's a good child. It will speed things up.

Joan tried to do as she was told, though even the smell of the hot liquid made her gag. In between cautious sips, as she forced it down, she watched the other faces round her. Granny Mason, as usual, was fussing round the room, getting in everybody's way as she made sure things were done in the right order. Just now she was scolding Annie Carpenter, newly wed and a few months younger than Joan, for putting the bolster down the wrong way and thus increasing the likelihood of a breech birth. Annie retired to a corner, biting her nails, and watched nervously as Goodwife Tyler, herself nearly seven months gone with her fifth child, knelt by the fire and began to pump the bellows.

Aaaah screamed Joan, hearing her voice as from a great distance, her head swimming with the concoction she had just drunk. A ring of women's faces floated round her, attentive, solicitous. Matthew Mark Luke and John, bless the bed that she lies on, muttered Granny Mason, and Joan felt the pain fade away as though it had never been.

Margery tied the eaglestone round her daughter's thigh and patted her hand reassuringly. There, she said, that will help draw it out. Never fails. It took years, she went on, going back to the beginning of her story, to build the castle as it stands today. My grandmother Judith saw with her own eyes how the walls went up, stone by heavy stone, and the moat was dug. A hundred oxcarts came and went each day from the quarry over the hill. You could hear the forest ringing with the sound of axes felling trees, and horses dragged the huge trunks away and up to the building site. Day by day a little more sky appeared between the branches overhead, and a few more clearings to be searched for firewood before the land was ploughed. Judith, little more than a baby in arms when the work began, watched the forest fall and the towers grow tall as she herself got bigger, heard the ringing sound of iron on stone and saw a thick cloud of dust obscure the sun at noon. The village was suddenly full of carvers and carpenters, joiners and painters, masons and smiths, who found lodgings in the neighbourhood or camped on site. At night they crowded into the alehouse, money changed hands as never before, and women were careful to bar the doors after nightfall when they heard their voices laughing and singing in the dark.

That, said Margery, was how Judith got with child for the first time. There was a pause, and everyone waited attentively, while Margery lifted her daughter's shift and ran her hands over the swollen belly, prodding and poking at the tight skin, so you could

28

have heard a pin drop if it had not been for the fire crackling and Joan saying Ouch in a not very loud voice, whereupon Margery slapped her wrist reprovingly and told her not to fuss, and that she was only making sure the child was lying in the right position, which it was, so she ought to be thankful.

Now, she said, suddenly aware of the expectant silence around her, and pulled down the shift. Where was I? Oh yes. Nobody knew why Judith was old Emma's favourite. Right from the start. Some say it was because she listened more attentively to what her grandmother had to say, never taking her eyes off the old woman's face, which was lined like a walnut, so that the wise woman knew she would be a good learner. And others said it was because, even as a child, Judith looked like the ghost of her mother, with her white skin and the huge dark eyes staring out from under the mane of thick black hair; so that the child's haunting beauty reminded the old woman of her daughter, Bedda who drowned in the river, Bedda who had perhaps used her magic foolishly, but who vanished so entirely that her name was never mentioned without fear. So that her children grew up knowing little or nothing of the mystery, though they had heard whispers of the floating loaf with the lit candle which carried on down the empty river and found nothing. But they were little more than whispers, so that young Edgar, still in his cradle at the time, grew up half believing that it was blonde Medhuil, the older of his two sisters, who, having cared for him almost since birth, was in fact his mother. Whilst Judith was dark and wild, and something of a tomboy as a child, Medhuil was soft and fair and gentle, and the boy would run to her for comfort if he was hurt, and cling to her skirt whenever he was frightened.

But I, said Margery, giving the fire a poke under the iron pot, so that flame-red sparks flew up the sooty chimney, I think Emma chose Judith as her successor because she was brave. Some people might call it foolhardy, as her mother was said to be foolhardy. And Margery picked up a spoon to taste the brew in the pot before going on. But Judith did not know the meaning of fear, not since the day she put her hand in the fire to pull out a plaything when she was but two years old, and somehow the flames did not burn her. By the time she was five years old Judith would go anywhere, or do anything. Judith was not afraid of the dark. She was not afraid of the new moon, or the sound of wolves howling in the woods. Thunder growling beyond the hill could not scare her, nor ghosts in the graveyard at midnight. By the time she was ten years old nobody could hold her. She would go anywhere, do anything, even near a newly dug grave after dark, and warnings only made her laugh. It was as though she regarded the land as her natural birthright and that, from Emma's point of view, was a distinct advantage, since the most potent worts invariably grow in spots which are difficult to reach, and often involve danger in the picking. So if Emma sent her into the woods at midnight or down to the river at sunrise she would go without a murmur. My eyes and ears, Emma called her, now that age and her terrible infirmity kept her indoors: my eyes and ears and nimble fingers.

But there was more to it even than that. For Judith had a good memory. By the age of ten she knew every one of the thirty herbs which must go into the ointment known as gratia dei, and by the time she was twelve she could also recite the thirty-five essential roots and grasses required to make save, a drink which heals all manner of wounds without plaster or salve.

Vervain violet and knapweed

she would sing, throwing pebbles on the ground and jumping after them on one foot to pick them up.

Red nettle comfrey and soapwort

she chanted, throwing her wooden ball against the wall of the cowshed and catching it with great dexterity.

Sorrel chickweed and crosswort

she whispered under her breath as she jumped over the swinging washing line. And when she was sent down to the river to mind the geese there was no holding her:

Scabious heart's tongue and clematis

pulling at grass stalks, jumping and skipping,

Celery woodruff and camomile

she chimed, watching a white feather eddy down river, and by the time she got home at nightfall, by the time she had eaten her soup and said her prayers and blown out the candle she had recited every one of them, from alleluya to zedoary.

Perhaps the fact that her mother was dead had something to do with her lack of fear. Certainly her sister made no attempt to control her. Most of Medhuil's rather desultory attention went on improving her own appearance, and she spent many hours making her skin even whiter and more spotless with powdered beanmeal mixed with lily root and soaked in vinegar, or washing the fair hair so like that of her namesake in lye of mistletoe to make it blonder still, and the time that was left over from these self-improvements and household chores went exclusively to petting and spoiling little Edgar, her baby now. Medhuil's placid good nature was not given to finding fault or scolding: she kissed and cuddled the baby and allowed Judith to do much as she pleased, as long as she did not make him cry.

So Judith would run wild at her grandmother's behest, like a bird flying from the falconer's wrist, over hill over dale, and when she returned to old Emma's fireside it was never empty-handed. She would spread them on the hearth and into Emma's lap, little green heaps of fresh-smelling brooklime and darnel, dandelion or briony.

A workman fell as the north tower was being constructed and, since the wound in his head looked ugly, they carried him to Emma's hearth, where she stitched the wound and sang a charm and sent Judith hurrying off to find pimpernel and bugle to lay on afterwards with egg white and flour. It was almost dusk when she set out, skipping over muddy cart ruts, jumping over puddles. She skirted round the edge of the churchyard and climbed to higher ground. Here, since the land had not been sown and ploughed, grasses and wild flowers grew in profusion, and she knew she would find the plants she was looking for.

Come bugle come

she sang

And I'll take thee home.

Startled birds flew out of the grass as she ran, and the earth was full of a summer susurrus of insects all round her. She laughed in the long grass as it swished round her, but then a large black shape suddenly lurched out at her, black as a crow but bigger, much bigger. It fell on her as no wild beast had ever done, tearing at her clothes, biting and snarling, and though she fought and struggled, using every inch of her body that could still move, which was not

31

much, to kick and scratch and spit, the looming shadow came between her and the open sky, his weight was on her so she could not run, and a hand came over her mouth so she could not cry out. Her mouth was open and his palm tasted of sweat and dirt and bacon fat so the taste and smell in her mouth and nose made her want to gag and as his weight pushed up between her legs and she felt the burning pain shoot up inside her teeth finally closed convulsively on a morsel of hard stinking flesh. She could feel the blood running down her chin as the black brute let go, howling with anger and hurt, before he got up and ran off into the night. Judith sat up and spat, shuddering. Then she tore up handfuls of grass and stuffed them into her mouth.

It was almost midnight when young Judith returned to the house. She stood on the threshold with scratch marks on her white face and blood running down her legs. Medhuil stifled a scream when she saw her, would have punished her there and then, but something about her expression stopped her from hitting her round the head and shoulders or screaming blame and abuse. Instead she pulled her sister indoors without a word, and brought her to the fire. Judith was shivering uncontrollably, with teeth chattering and fists clenched. But when they unwound her tight fingers they found crushed scraps of bugle and pimpernel in the palms, which were stained quite green.

While Medhuil wiped her face and took off her torn clothes and picked the bits of grass out of her wild black hair, old Emma put the pot on to boil. And when the water began to bubble she threw in savin and madder, hyssop and wild thyme, ivy and laurel leaves, rosemary and calamint, and also some fennel. And when the bitter fumes began to rise from the pot they set the child on a hollow stool with her legs wide apart and the pot below so that the fumes could rise inside her and do their work. But though they did this each night for days and then weeks, her bleeding had stopped. Nothing, it seemed, would bring back the flowers of her girlhood. In the months that followed Judith became first thin as a ghost, since no food would pass her lips. The least morsel would taste like the sour and rancid flesh of a man's palm in her mouth, making her gag and retch and heave up half her stomach juices. And then she began to swell, and you might have thought there was nothing inside her but wind and the little blood of her own flowers, but as summer turned to the burnished shades of autumn she took to wandering the countryside on her own, skirting the hedgerows, stuffing juicy black brambles into her mouth, and hard scarlet rosehips too; or walking into the woods to scour the forest floor for beech burrs and mushrooms. And when the snows of winter came and a hard frost kept her indoors she would take nothing but a little milk and sour cheese, though there was bacon smoking in the rafters, enough to last the season through. And so, before the snows melted and the icicles began to drip from the eaves, Judith gave birth to her first. A daughter, they say, born with a full head of hair, red as a flaming torch.

Margery paused for breath and looked at her daughter, who had become quite sleepy during the telling of this story. Oooh, she now cried, somewhat feebly, conscious of all eyes turned expectantly on her, but Margery put her hands to her daughter's belly and shook her head.

It don't want to shift, she said. Time to try a fumigation. Spikenard and root of costmary. She made sure the eaglestone was still in place. Granny Mason pushed young Annie out of the door to fetch more water, and took the pail from her when she returned. Between them they filled the cauldron and set it back on the trivet. Cakes and ale were handed round, whilst Margery started rubbing dried leaves into her lap.

Building the castle took years, she said. The old lord, William that was, had the work started whilst Lord Robert was still but a lad, torn from his mother's knee so he could learn how to be a man, till he could push a lance, wield a sword and swing a battle axe against all comers, as well as jousting and hunting and playing a fine game of chess. So he comes back, as proper a young lord as ever sat astride a horse or broke a man's head in combat, just as the masons were putting the topmost stones on the south tower, and his father's coffers were all but bare. Still, they do say the fine new castle soon paid for itself, as Lord William and his men took to the road with a will. The dungeons could hold any number of unwilling guests, so large they were, and spacious, with stabling

33

enough for their horses too. So the price of the ransom was set rather high, to include the cost of food and good clean straw for the many months it took to free them, since a messenger would face similar hazards on the road, going and coming. And in no time the coffers were full, hoards of gold and silver in the strong room, and the great hall resplendent with luxury, rich hangings and trestles that groaned under the weight of food and wine.

Margery took her daughter by one arm, Annie Carpenter took the other, and together they pulled her great bulk off the bed and set her on the hollow stool. Ouch, said Joan, but it was not because the pains were starting again: her foot had touched the hot iron cauldron which Granny Mason had placed underneath. The fumes going up between her legs were soothing. Granny Mason dabbed a little butter on her scalded heel, and the eaglestone tied to her thigh, being pregnant too, rattled when she moved her foot forward. Margery wrapped the coverlet round her shoulders to keep the fumes in.

So, said Margery, where was I? Oh yes. When young Robert could tilt his lance with the best of them, it was thought fit that he should have a bride. And it was with this in mind that his father had built a lady's chamber up in the north tower, overlooking the river and the fields beyond, with every creature comfort in it, a fireplace with its own chimney to take out the smoke, and hangings on the walls fit for a queen. A golden cage with a talking magpie hung from a perch, and the curtains round the bed were stitched all over with leaves, acorns and flowers of the forest. Two iron dogs lay in the hearth, where a fire burned winter through, and the oak coffer was richly carved.

And it was said that Lord Robert, right from the start, would think of no one but the Lady Blanche, whom he had first seen as a child when he went to serve in her father's hall as a page. At the time she was no more than a child herself, and though she was comely enough, with her clear grey eyes and nutbrown hair, and could weave garlands for her head as prettily as the next child, it was not for her looks that he relished her company. She would laugh at him if he dropped a trencher whilst serving her father at table, and run races with him and win, and beat him at backgammon. But when an enraged dog bit him she did not laugh, but took

34

cress and wild thyme and seethed them in water for him to drink, and laid clean leeks soaked in milk on the wound. And she knew stories from old books about distant lands beyond the sea, and at night she could read the stars in the sky as easily as any book, and sing sweetly in foreign languages. And Robert, who could handle a hawk and keep his seat in the saddle, who as he grew older could fight and parry in full armour, could stand in his stirrups to swing his two-handed sword whilst charging the foe at a gallop, or use his long-sword in one hand whilst wielding a mace with the other, who could cut down a man with his battle-axe or unhorse him at speed with his lance, was felled by a single look from her cool grey eyes.

And the reason was not hard to find, and had nothing to do with love charms or potions, or even, perhaps, with the fact that as she grew tall she grew comelier, with a lilt to her walk and a curve to her figure under the falling velvet trimmed with fur, and a new hint of gravity in the grey eyes. No. The fact was that Robert, for all his manly virtues, his seat on a horse and his hand with a sword, had no head for book-learning. An hour with the chaplain would have him reeling and confused, and when he tried to follow the argument of a book with his index finger the letters seemed to leap about like hares in an Easter meadow. As for Latin and foreign languages, it was as much as he could do to stammer his way through the Paternoster. It was Blanche, he knew, who held the keys to a secret garden, as surely as any châtelaine, and he could not unlock the door without her.

Blanche knew the meaning of dreams, and that if an eagle settles on your head in a dream, that betokens much honour, but many eagles at once mean plots and assaults from enemies. She knew on which days to bleed, and how the moon influences healing. She could relate the wanderings of Ulysses, and tales of star-crossed lovers. She could brew potions for any ailment that might afflict a man, and catch thieves in a basin of water. And when, as her father's squire, Robert injured his leg whilst out hunting, it was Blanche who prepared the plaster of wheat flour and white of egg, and it was she who brought him the juice of knit-wort to drink, once, twice, but no more, for at the third time it unknits. And for nine days she came to his chamber with a drink of juice of comfrey,

35

daisy and royal fern seethed in stale ale, and whiled away the tedium of those nine days by telling him the story of Tristan and Iseult, and how Rosamond cured the wounded knight Elias, and brought him spiced wine to drink when he could not sleep. And when it was time to remove the plaster it was she who soaked the linen in colt's foot and hound's tongue, red fennel and peritory, and prepared a fresh plaster of brooklime and chickweed and bound the leg up once more on its splints so the bones would knit, and anointed it daily with good wine.

And so, by the end of thirty days, when he could hobble once more, though all his life he would walk with a limp, and his gait slightly crooked, young Robert knew that neither Iseult nor Rosamond had half the charms or the healing gift of Blanche with the nutbrown hair, with her cool fingers and smooth young brow and the clear grey eyes that looked at him so winningly. And they do say that when she rode to the castle with her retinue she brought with her twelve acres of forest, two manor houses, and a silver gilt dinner service large enough for forty persons, with a dozen ewers and six salt-cellars of solid gold. And largesse was scattered a-plenty to the beggars and crippled who gathered along the roadside to see her pass, so much that for years afterwards the wedding of Lord Robert to the Lady Blanche was remembered as the time when it rained pennies from heaven.

But that was only the start of the rejoicing. Nobody had ever seen such goings on, such feasting and revelry. On a single night, I have heard tell, the guests at the castle were served in the great hall with a hundred sides of venison, eighty roast rabbits, a dozen peacocks with tail displayed, seven swans, sixty pigeons, and numerous quails and woodcocks. And the feasting continued for ten days. Each night six baskets of trenchers rich in gravy were given out at the drawbridge, and on the final day twelve barrels of ale found their way to the castle gate.

And this, said Margery, is where the trouble started. For the ale was strong, and plentiful, and some had more than was good for them. And though the curfew rang, and the fires went out bit by bit, the night was strangely disturbed. Nobody had heard such sounds coming through the dark, from shadowed meadow and wood. Was it an owl screeching, a vixen yelping? Nobody could be

36

sure, lying sleepless in the small hours, whilst dreaming dogs whimpered and cows moaned in the straw, and a thin sound, was it song or sobbing, drifted from castle walls to the misty valley below. It was as though all indoor things had fallen prey to nightmare, whilst out in the wild night creatures were tense and watchful as never before, ears pricked, eyes alert, as the frenzy of hunting and hunted was turned to a new pitch, so the night air stank of blood and high sounds of pain and terror echoed now and then from copse and field and hollow. Perhaps it was only the wind, a marauding fox or polecat, but when dawn came and Judith rose to fetch water she was caught coming back from the spring by two black shapes who leapt out at her from a ditch and dragged her down, kicking and screaming, and took it in turns to have her there in the ditch, with her head in a puddle of mud and her feet tangled in thorns, whilst they held her down and stifled her cries. She bit and kicked and struggled, so that one lost an eye that day and the other a finger, and when she dragged herself back to the house at last she was smeared with their blood as well as her own, and no water to wash it off.

And although old Emma made her eat hot and piquant relishes, such as pepper and mustard and cresses, and though she gave her draughts of ale in which artemisia and polypody had been boiled, which sometimes caused her to be very unhappy, and sometimes very angry, and sometimes made her merry, but in a frantic sort of way; and though she made her walk a great deal, and work hard from dawn to dusk, and eat and drink heartily, the flowers did not come back, and nine months after the wedding at the castle Judith gave birth to a second daughter, large and strong, with a birth mark on her left shoulder and hair as black as pitch. At exactly the same hour as the Lady Blanche almost died giving birth to a weak, puling boy they named Roger.

Margery stopped, seeing that Joan had begun to sag against her, a dead weight in their arms. The girl's face was white with strain, showing up the sprinkling of freckles on her nose, and under her closed eyes. Granny Mason dashed cold water in her face, and the girl suddenly opened her eyes, and whimpered.

Bled on the wrong day of the month, muttered Margery grimly.

37

For all their Latin and book-learning.

There was a general tut-tutting of disapproval, not unmixed with gratified self-righteousness, at such malpractice on the part of a learned doctor of theology. And Margery seemed to grow in stature, with her broad bosom and hefty behind, as they lifted the exhausted girl from the stool and helped her back to bed.

Margery brought her a cup full of dark liquid.

What's this? Joan wrinkled her nose as she sniffed at the nauseous drink.

Don't ask, girl. Just drink it up, said Margery, and went back to the fire.

She took one sip of the bitter concoction, and felt her gorge rising.

Dittany, she heard somebody say. And she took another sip, holding her nose this time.

Hyssop, she heard someone hiss in the huddle round the fire. The urge to retch was very strong, but she managed to swallow another mouthful.

Costmary and mugweed, added Granny Mason, as she took several deep breaths before attempting to swallow a bit more.

Bull's gall, added Margery firmly, bringing a bowl. Joan vomited.

Goodwife Tyler had washed her face and hands, and Annie Carpenter brought her a little spring water to drink. Joan lay back, face pale as the sheets, and felt a great urge to drift off to sleep. She heard her mother's voice coming as though from a great distance, as she continued her story. Something about huntsmen, after his marriage Lord Robert lived in the saddle, always riding to hounds. She knew what it meant, of course, as she heard her mother's voice drift through the mists of sleep, having been told as a child to hide, hide everything, herself included, if hunters came storming by, demanding free quarter of the poor. Three men at the door, she heard, and woke with a start. Medhuil had time to crouch behind the wood pile, taking a flitch of bacon with her. Old Emma, rooted to her seat by the hearth, mumbled a curse as they pushed their way in, and the children began to scream in a chorus of terror. Get out, said Judith, picking up the poker from the hearth: you can see we are poor, with too many mouths to feed.

Well, said Margery. She was brave, and she would have used the poker, but she could be no match for three of them at once, in their boots and spurs and leather gauntlets, and no doubt they decided to try a different sport, since stag and boar had eluded them and hours of riding had brought no greater diversion than a few downtrodden fields of barley and a blind beggar mauled by the hounds.

Afterwards they bathed her and put her to bed. Medhuil, weeping with terror when she crawled out of the woodpile, old Emma rubbing her bruised shin and mumbling a thousand curses under her breath as she found strength from some forgotten source to hobble. They smeared her black eye with May butter and blew the powder of a burnt eggshell up her nose to stop the bleeding, and Judith lay with clenched teeth, cold and stiff as stone, and would speak to nobody, though her child with hair black as pitch cried in the cradle and would not be comforted, and the older one crouched in a corner with her grey eyes round as pebbles and her thumb in her mouth, watching, as she had been doing all along. And when her purgations did not come they cut her big toe, and bled her on the legs below the calf, and cupped under the nipples, round and dark as the colour of crushed blackberries. And though each month they drew off as much blood as she could not be cleansed of the child quickened and grew to full term, and was born with a harelip and six fingers on one hand. Another girl.

Joan was persuaded to sip a little hot broth. She had scarcely swallowed two mouthfuls when she felt a huge hand squeeze her belly hard, as though it was no more than a bag of curds. She spilt her broth, and let out a lusty yell of shock and protest. Margery came to the bedside as the girl lay panting, lifted her shift, and pushed a finger into the orifice. She shook her head, untied the eaglestone and put it at the very top of her thigh.

Holy Mary bore Christ, she murmured, Holy Anne bore Mary, Holy Elizabeth bore John, Holy Cecilia bore Remy, Sator Arepo Tenet Opera Rotas Amen. Oh infant, whether alive or dead, come forth.

*

Then, said Margery, there was the feud that broke out between Lord Robert and a neighbouring baron, Lord Harville, I think it was. Ordinary folks never did find out what started it, though some say it had to do with a prize falcon, or some sort of wager, and most thought that Lord Harville had taken a mind to the Lady Blanche, and that since she was already another man's wife he would remove her by force. Be that as it may, they came suddenly, without warning, and when the drawbridge was drawn up almost no one hereabouts had had time to take refuge inside, to say nothing of livestock. So the castle was defended well enough but men working in the fields had their hands chopped off and nothing but gory holes left for eyes, and the standing corn was set ablaze, and barns and byres too. And some say Lord Robert and his men had gone hunting, and others that a minstrel had drugged the wine, but while Lady Blanche was safe within the castle walls, and could hold them against all comers, those on the outside had a different story to tell. Though they do say it took four men to hold down Judith, and she kicked three of them so hard in the groin that none of them would father another child, and the fourth got a bloody nose for his trouble, and a crack on the head that felled him utterly, for young Edgar was quite a lad by now and crept up unawares whilst three were clutching their privities and the last was at it, and afterwards the two of them buried him as best they could beyond the cabbage patch since his companions left him behind.

But her sister Medhuil was safe, for her ladyship had taken a fancy to her when she came as a messenger from Emma, bringing potions to keep her sickly infant from dying, when neither her own skills nor the prayers of the priest seemed enough. And since then she had lived in the castle, with her fair skin growing paler and her long blonde hair more like flax, and her ladyship kept her always by her side for her soft voice and winning ways, and her skill with the needle. For she could sew silks on a hanging with such artifice that all who gazed on it it swore that the roses gave off perfume and closed at dusk, whilst birds' feathers stirred on the spreading branch, and their gleaming eyes moved.

But that night, whilst her sister sat safe, though trembling, in the north tower of the castle, Judith was left to fend for herself after

40

the terrified infants had been put to bed and Edgar had filled in the grave beyond the savin bush. She had bruises all over and her lip was split, her black eyes had grown blacker and she had lost a tooth (one tooth for each child, they say), but by now she knew what to do. So she took the roots of fennel and parsley, wild carrot and celery, and the leaves of savin and calamint, and cooked them in vinegar until all was well boiled. Then she poured the liquid through a cloth to strain it, added honey, and boiled it all over the fire. This she drank cold for seven days, mixed with water in which madder had been boiled, before taking a herb bath. But though she was often sick, and grew thin, and found it hard to keep her food down, a child came feet first into the world, after a labour lasting three days and nights. It was a girl, blue but breathing, so barely alive that the midwife, who had only been stopped by Judith from hauling it out piecemeal, christened it on the spot. But it survived.

Joan heaved an audible sigh, and Margery left her seat to come to her daughter. She prodded the bulging shape on all sides.

You've got a long time to go yet, she declared. Don't you feel no strong pains coming on? Must be near on twenty minutes.

Joan shook her head, her lips trembling. Tears stood in her eyes. Will it come feet first? she asked, her anxious voice scarcely above a whisper.

Lord no! Margery let out a great guffaw. Whatever put that idea in your head, child? Head's lying just where it should be. She put her ear to the swollen belly. And it's not dead neither. So why the eaglestone don't shift it, I can't think.

Annie Carpenter offered to go and fetch a horse's hoof which her mother owned, but her words went unheard in the general pother surrounding the lifting of the steaming pot from the trivet. Goodwife Tyler held the cloth while Margery and Granny Mason poured the green liquid through it. Finally a sodden mass was left in the centre of the cloth, and the women twisted it at both ends to squeeze out the excessive moisture.

Pull up your shift, said Margery, and she slapped the dark green pulp between her thighs, spreading it up to her navel. Joan gasped with the shock of it, and the sudden heat.

That will help draw out the child, she declared, looking down at

41

the girl. Her eyes had a determined glint which her daughter had not seen before. So long as we don't leave it on too long. Don't want all your innards coming out after.

Joan's dark pupils grew larger. She had seen nothing between navel and knee for a month or more, but she could feel the plaster hot and wet at her bottom end, and a few drops of liquid trickling on her skin. Then the muscles tightened, she could see the mound of her belly change shape, become more acute, and then the spasm took her breath away, so that she cried fit to burst her lungs.

That's artemisia for you, said Granny Mason, with obvious satisfaction, rubbing her hands at the foot of the bed. I don't hold with these Latin charms and the like. We got by without them in my day.

Now, said Margery, settling down by the fire with a fresh mug of ale, they do say, and she lowered her voice to a conspiratorial whisper, that the Lady Blanche had more secret reasons for keeping Medhuil by her, which had nothing to do with her looks or her skill with the needle. She may have begun by favouring the wise woman's grandchild to keep her baby son from dying, but after his birth she had other reasons.

Margery paused, and glanced meaningfully round the room. Three heads came closer to hers and Joan, who perhaps was not meant to hear, lifted herself on her elbows to catch every word.

Some say she was fearful of childbirth, after that first time. And others that it hurt her, whether because of the birth or his love-making, I do not know, though perhaps she never had any great liking for it. Anyhow, be that as it may, she decided that enough was enough, and who among us would blame her, for no pleasure, even if pleasure it be, is worth the price, as you and I know well enough. And though she had tried putting vervain under his pillow, and lettuce seed into his wine, and had given him a topaz ring to wear, out of love, so she told him, though she meant to produce chastity, yet his lust was as strong as ever.

Alas, she said, a second child will surely be the death of me. And sent Medhuil down to the village with a gift of butter and eggs to consult her grandmother.

Old Emma was near to death by this time, and could neither

42

move nor speak, though she would signal with her eyes in ways that only her family could understand. But between them the two sisters had learnt most of the remedies she knew of, and the gift of butter and eggs was more than welcome with so many mouths to feed. So they put their heads together, and Judith looked into her grandmother's face to make sure the left eye was not blinking, which was a sure sign of disapproval, and Medhuil went tripping back to the castle.

Colewort, rue and St. John's wort, she whispered. Dried, powdered, and strewn in his food. And give him an amber to wear.

Then Medhuil came back a second time, bearing the gift of a fine woollen cloak. It would warm Judith all winter, as she walked abroad, and cover her children at night. Again the girls put their heads together, under the frozen gaze of their grandmother. And Medhuil returned to the castle.

The testicles of a cock with its blood placed in his bed, she whispered. Henbane juice smeared on his privates, and columbine, and vervain rubbed on his laces secretly.

But when Medhuil returned a third time with a purse full of small gold coins Judith looked long and hard into her grandmother's eyes and fetched a green glass vial stored in her coffer and held it in front of her for a while, turning it round, to see if there was any movement in the old pale eyes. But she did not blink or stir, and though Medhuil held her right hand in both hers, knowing she would occasionally respond to questioning by a slight movement of thumb and forefinger, the hand remained frozen.

Tip it into his wine, whispered Medhuil, pressing the vial into her ladyship's hand, and that night her husband did indeed fall into a deep sleep.

But when Lord Robert failed to wake next morning, and continued in a profound slumber for three whole days and nights, so that none knew if he would live or die, and the priest came and went to pray at his bedside without result, then the Lady Blanche did not know what to do for terror, for the whispers turned to murmurs and the chaplain, when neither holy water nor a spate of Latin words would wake him, said a charge of witchcraft must be brought, and denounced her ladyship. And some of her women, including Medhuil, were also locked up under guard, whilst her ladyship knelt in silent prayer and the chaplain, fearing his lord would never wake more, brought holy oil and performed extreme unction. And as he continued to breathe those round him waited for a sign, to know the meaning of it. And who should live, and who die.

But the sign, when it came, was a strange one. On the third day he began to stir, and murmur strange words to himself, and when he at last opened his eyes his attendants saw him stare fixedly at a corner of the chamber, and cross himself, and smile with a look of pure beatitude. I have had such visions, he murmured happily. I have seen the Holy Cross.

Chosen by God, said the chaplain, falling on his knees, and though some, including my grandmother, privately surmised it was the henbane that did it, there was no doubting that Lord Robert was a changed man.

Before any food or drink touched his lips he would take the sacrament and hear mass, and though he looked and spoke as before and seemed sound of mind and limb, he had lost all his desire to go hunting, and neither hawk nor hound could please him. Instead he spent much time praying, and fasted on Fridays, and all his thoughts were fixed on one thing only, to reach the Holy Land, and drive out the infidel. Some of the silver gilt cups which the Lady Blanche had brought as part of her dowry he gave to the monks to be used as chalices, and he gave them too the use of three meadows for masses to be said for his soul in perpetuity. And then, at the head of fifty fighting men, with cooks and carpenters and smiths to attend to them, with bakers and grooms and every skilled man for miles around who would go, with minstrels and chaplain and a fingerbone of St. Hilda welded into the hilt of his sword, Lord Robert rode off into the sunrise for many a long year.

And so the Lady Blanche got her wish after all, though in a wondrous fashion, and slept alone. And old Emma looked wise, but said nothing, not so much as the wink or blink of an eyelid, and Judith took the cow of one colour and the ten pieces of silver that her ladyship sent down with Medhuil as messenger. And they ate well that winter, and none of the children took sick.

And a great change came over the neighbourhood as the Lady

Blanche took charge of the estate. During the cold weather she sent food and firewood to all those in need through age and infirmity. And by the time of the spring sowing she had sent for her bailiff to inquire about each field and farrow, every stick and stone of the estate, every tree and barn and byre, meadow and mill. And she knew every soul in her charge, and kept a strict watch on what was owing, but no more, so the days of rich pickings were over. For she kept her own tally, and hired her own man to hear complaints and watch over the bailiff, who was known to take more than was owing, and grew fat and powerful on the proceeds, since he had his own henchmen to demand money or crops with menaces.

Now it so happened that the young steward hired by her ladyship to root out injustice had taken to meeting Judith secretly at dusk, by the riverbank. He came to her first because no one had so much courage in telling what she knew to be true, and many a tale would find its way to her door that would otherwise never come to his ears, for fear of what might follow. But Judith had no such fear, just as nothing could deter her from stepping outside her door after the shadows had lengthened on the hillside and night gathered in the woods beyond the river once the last red glow had died away in the sky, so that if the young man took to meeting her with a single purpose, he continued to come to the riverbank as midges swarmed in the dusk for quite another, for the sound of her husky voice and the night shadows gathering in her eyes and hair and the curve of her limbs in the twilight. And it was there that they fell upon him, one night, the bailiff with his four henchmen, three stabbed him to the heart and threw his bleeding corpse in the river whilst two held Judith down. And after it had vanished into the dark water four held her down, one by each limb, whilst the fifth had his will of her. And so they took turns, as her struggles grew feebler, and left her body, as they thought, for dead.

Foolishly, as it turned out, for she crawled back to the house at dawn, and bore witness against the murderers, who fled into the forest and beyond to escape capture.

And afterwards Judith made a suppository of the root of yellow iris, fastened with a thread round her thigh so it could not go up into her womb. And when no blood came she sat in a bath of savin, pennyroyal, furze and laurel leaves for many a long hour, and afterwards put in wild celery, all green, and root of lupin smeared in clean honey, and acorns too. And though her bruises faded and she could soon walk as before the blood would not flow and she felt life quicken inside her, though she took no food and looked haggard and thin, with dark shadows under her eyes. And at seven months the head came through so small, with bluish skin and eyes closed, that the midwife took holy water and said the words of the christening while it was still only half out between her thighs and she knew not what sex to call it, or whether it was living or dead. And although this daughter was born so small, and of a dreadful colour, as though she too had been battered before birth, yet when the midwife slapped her she survived, and began crying, a thin wail which continued day and night for months on end, so that Judith had no end to her grieving, but heard it in the small hours, and at daybreak. But the child's eyes never did open, and when she had washed them in water in which fennel had been boiled, and anointed them with her milk mixed with aloe, and laid on eyebright and celandine, she knew that the child was blind.

Joan, clutching the jasper in her right hand, tightened her grip as though hoping to squeeze liquid out of it. The spasm reached its peak and faded, receding gradually, as the room swam back into focus. She was very tired, felt herself sinking, when suddenly someone was slapping cold vinegar on her hands and feet. Then the stink of burning feathers under her nose brought her sharply back to full consciousness.

Here, said Margery, arranging a snakeskin girdle across her navel. She patted the brittle strip, murmuring as she did so:

> As the snake sloughs its skin
> So bring this child from within.

The women sitting round the fireside began to argue the fabled merits of other girdles: that of the Blessed Virgin at Westminster, used by queens and great ladies; the red silk girdle sent out by the nuns of Abbeville to women in labour, which had belonged to St. Anne when she gave birth to Mary. And Granny Mason swore she had seen miraculous deliveries with the green girdle of Aethelfrida, which once belonged to Mary Magdalene, till it vanished without

46

trace a few years back. But Margery stood by her snakeskin, which had been handed down through the family since before old Emma's time. Eve had used a snakeskin when she gave birth to Cain and Abel, and though she did not go so far as to say hers was the very same, it was known to be almost as old, and just as efficacious, even if it had helped to deliver nothing but girls in recent years. But then it had brought no murderers into the world either.

So, said Margery, for seven years the Lady Blanche had no fear of childbirth, but nursed her son through his feeble infancy till he grew stronger, and kept him always by her side. She taught Roger always to be kind to birds and small animals, and never to torment God's creatures for the sake of doing hurt. And all the ladies of the castle made a great fuss of him, and taught him songs and games, and his mother told him stories of ancient times, and gave him a caged bird that sang in his dreams. And my great aunt Medhuil, who was then young and fair, gave him an amulet to wear, which would keep him from sudden death.

And during those seven years whilst her lord was in the Holy Land the Lady Blanche found new and cunning ways to manage the estates, so that many had cause to bless her name. After the death of her young steward, for which she blamed herself, uttering prayers of contrition and letting nothing but bread and water pass her lips for thirty days, she became thoughtful for a time, and disinclined to laughter or light diversions, and deaf to her child's babbling. But then she ordered an immense tapestry to be stitched, to be hung in the great hall finally, and welcome her lord home. It was to depict a hunting scene, with horses and hounds and Lord Robert astride his horse in the act of killing a wild boar, and to do this immense work, with a thousand stitches needed to depict each leaf on a tree, and a thousand leaves on the branch of a spreading oak, to say nothing of the flowers of the forest stitched under the horses' hooves in a colourful carpet, each petal and leaf and bud distinct on the green ground, to do this immense work she brought in women from miles around to work with her and her own ladies. And in this way she heard rumours of trouble still a-brewing, rumblings of a coming storm, and gossip of evil-doing before it was done. Stitching at the rich caparison on her absent lord's white horse, she heard about stolen chickens, cows that would give no milk, straying husbands, and images buried under the threshold to harm a neighbour. But she heard of other things too, hints of extortion, of suffering and hardship, tales of violence and misappropriation which would not have surfaced otherwise, for fear of revenge, or lack of someone to speak. But the gossip of women stitching, year in, year out, as the huge tapestry took shape oh so slowly, revealed all things to her with eyes wise enough to see and ears sharp and cunning enough to hear, as the birds took shape in the trees and her husband's favourite falcon appeared on the falconer's gauntlet, and work began on the border of flowers and leaves, yards of garlanded oak leaves entwined with acorns and eglantine which would keep a dozen women busy for several years more. And though the Lady Blanche said little as she stitched at a clump of primroses under the hooves of her husband's horse, behold, some were banished, or sent naked on horseback to have their crime exposed to public mockery, when none had been found to denounce them, whilst others suddenly made restitution by bringing food to the needy, or firewood to a widow's door.

Her ladyship, it began to be said, was a seer, had knowledge of the black arts. It was whispered that she could see all that men did by gazing into a basin of water, in which images appeared, as in a glass darkly. Others thought she had a silver mirror in her chamber which revealed things far off. And that she saw her husband's return after seven years plain enough to have the tapestry finished and hung.

Few of those who had set off seven years before came riding back, and Lord Robert himself was like a strange apparition, bleached dry as a bone by hot suns and desert winds, and his skin like parchment. His hair had turned to the colour of white gold, and his pale eyes, deep in their bony sockets beneath beetling brows full of highway dust, seemed always turned to the far horizon. He did not see the great hall with its tapestry, nor hear the minstrel singing at the feast. He did not see the peacock dressed in its feathers come to the table with beak and claws gilded, nor remark on the page boy behind his chair. Some say even his grown son, whose head now reached to his elbow, could not stir him, and that he did not know his own wife among the women who stood at the gate to welcome him.

He had a wound in his thigh which would not heal, though he did not seem to feel it. The Lady Blanche bathed it in spring water to which harefoot had been added, and made for him the drink save, which will heal wounds without plaster or salve if you use anise and eyebright, meadowsweet and root of mayweed, juice of cowslip and devil's bit scabious, and bathed it in wine and made a tampon of gratia dei and afterwards laid on a plaster of egg white and flax.

And at night he could not sleep, and though the Lady Blanche prepared him a potion of poppy and lettuce seed in warm wine he tossed to and fro on his pillow, muttering strange words, and sometimes he would rise in the night and pick up his sword, flailing it wildly in all directions, shouting, and leaping on furniture. Once he killed an attendant who tried to disarm him, and it took several men to restrain him at last. Lady Blanche lay in her chamber with a man across the threshold, and Medhuil, who shared her bed, knew she scarcely closed her eyes before dawn.

And then came news of a campaign to be waged against the French. For the first time since his return from the Holy Land Lord Robert's vague pale eyes, as though half blind from sand and sun, seemed to focus on the things around him. He ate heartily, slept soundly, and was up at dawn with a sense of purpose in everything he did. For miles around, every man who was fit to fight was mustered, archers and spearmen, and a whole company of knights who had grown to manhood whilst he was absent, thinking themselves doomed to jousting for coloured ribbons since they had been born too late to go with him to such a great war, a holy war, and above all a war, and now rejoiced at a fresh opportunity. Once more cooks had to be found, and carpenters, and smiths to mend swords and armour. If the land was left untended, so much the worse. Labour services were dispensed with for rent in money, which bought horses, and harness, and more men. And if the treasure chest was almost empty, no matter, since the promise of pillage was enough to stir men's hearts if the smell of blood was not enough.

So they rode away to war, after a feast in the great hall during which too much wine and ale was drunk, so that two men lost their lives without ever crossing the sea or seeing a foreigner; and next morning, bleary-eyed and with heads aching, they heard mass, made confession and dedicated their souls to God.

Lady Blanche was left to manage the estate once more, with the coffers empty and too few hands for the plough. Even the minstrel had gone to war, and the great hall was dark and empty, bereft of laughter and song, with only the huge new tapestry glowing in the shadows. Ploughshares had been turned into swords, cups into vizors, and breastplates beaten out of dishes, platters and ewers. At night there was silence over the valley, after the curfew bell had rung, though some could hear a hum in the dark and misty air from a thousand chantry masses sung for the souls of the dead, year in, year out, for ever and ever amen.

Somehow the harvest was reaped in that difficult year, roofs mended, meat salted, feathers bedded and dues paid. And though her own women still met in her chamber to spin and sew, and wove fine linen from flax, no work was begun on a second tapestry to hang opposite the first. Lady Blanche had no heart for it, and the women no time. Cows had to be tended, and the cabbage patch, firewood and water fetched, and the pot kept on the boil. Double the labour in half as many hours for most of them, as the winter set in.

The winter was long, and wolves came out of the forest, leaving their prints in the snow. The ground froze too hard to bury the dead in the churchyard, and the river turned to ice. No traveller had come through the valley since the snow began to fall, and an icy stillness, like death, hung over the snowbound fields. Only the shrill cry of birds wheeling high in the sky for prey broke the silence, and from the north tower the land looked a blank white sheet spread out ready for the future to be inscribed. But if, as some claimed, the Lady Blanche tried to see the future or read the course of the war in a bowl of water it turned to ice as she gazed, whilst her silver mirror had become a web of frosted ferns.

But when the thaw revealed black earth and bare branches, and the first traveller arrived at the drawbridge, he brought no news of a homecoming, nor promise of rich booty. The vision of French gold, of furs and hangings and velvet and good red wine had kept

50

hope alive and put warmth into many a chill fireside, but now it faded. For the traveller brought an unmistakable message: Lord Robert was captive, and the ransom required immense.

The sum demanded was so vast that a special tax would not pay it off in one year, or even in two. So although Lord Robert was richly entertained by his French captor during his long stay, with feasting and revelry and much good sport, those who worked his land had to give up the few coins they had and more of their hard-earned harvest. Lady Blanche, having mustered such silver and gold as still remained to her, including her own rings, having written to her brother for help, but to no avail, since he was in debt too from the French wars, was forced to go on levying a special tax, year in year out, till the sum was paid in full.

During the years it took to pay his ransom Lord Robert was kept right royally, and nursed with great care when he took sick of a fever, since only a living lord could fetch back his keep. He was bled copiously according to the advice of his host's astrologer, and fed only the most delicate morsels. But many of the men he had taken with him, and others of their sort, now began to drift back across the sea, and travelled the countryside in small bands. Having grown accustomed to a life of plunder and booty-hunting in time of war, they saw no reason to change their habits in time of peace, or go back to the plough. Rumours of brigand bands who roamed lawlessly through hill and vale, pasture and forest, taking what they would and absolving their sins with goods stolen from others, since they feared the fires of hell but not much else, terrorised the countryside. It was a shame, seeing that we paid our dues to be protected by the very men who now murdered and robbed at will. Doors were barricaded, coins buried, bacon flitches hidden in straw, and fine coverlets more often under the bed than on it. And they do say some women thought nothing of risking bell book and candle, and forty days' penance on bread and water at the very least, by dressing themselves or their daughters as men.

Judith kept a pitchfork by the door, and a cur that would snarl at all comers and took food only from her hand. Her five daughters were taught to be watchful as hawks, and as cunning as vixens, running to ground at the first sight or sound of trouble. And they do say that the girl who was born blind had second sight, and even whilst still in her cradle would begin to cry if someone with evil in his heart came near the house. And the child with flaming red hair could utter sixty curses in a row without stopping for breath, whilst the girl with the harelip and six fingers could run on all fours, keeping close to the ground, so that no one might catch her. But one day, as all five lay sick of the Lenten fever, Judith left the house at dawn to fetch fresh spring water, and by the road she saw six brigands riding towards her, armed to the teeth with swords and knives and axes. So instead of running back to the house, she had cunning enough to run in the opposite direction, across the open fields and towards the river. And they followed, needless to say, impelled by a woman's fright, the sight of a skirt lifted and a clean pair of heels, and though six of them had her, or went through the motions, grunting and laughing and egging each other on whilst five held her down, when they rode off to fill their stomachs and bags with such booty as they could find, it was downhill and farther off. And though the blind child was crying in its cradle as she crawled back bruised and bleeding, with her gown torn and two teeth missing, though the cur whimpered and the fire in the hearth had gone out, and the older children babbled with fever and fright, the house stood unharmed and with everything in its its place.

After Judith had cured her daughters of the fever by giving them a drink of wild celery and feverfew boiled in water and strained, she took four eggshells full of hyssop roots, and four of iris, savin, rue and savory, and two of seeds of bishop's weed, dittany, catmint, fennel seed, and boiled them in clean running water, and drank it each morning with ale. But the blood would not flow, her belly quickened, and the child that was born had a twisted foot, it coming out first and being pushed back by the midwife.

Joan let out a long, agonised cry which had all the women round her in a moment.

Holy Mary, Mother of God, she gasped. I'm going to die, I know I am.

No you're not, said Margery in a matter-of-fact tone of voice, rubbing butter on her fingers before prodding around in the orifice. Isn't a woman born who didn't think that with her first.

Or her last, come to that, added Granny Mason dourly.

I can feel the head right enough.

She wiped her fingers on the hem of her gown and put finger and thumb on her daughter's nose, pushing the nostrils together. The girl began to pant through her mouth, her childish eyes wide with alarm as her gaze shifted from Margery's face to the others looking down at her, and back to her mother.

So the spirits help push it down, she said.

But then, said Margery, still holding her daughter's nose, came the great pestilence. Some said it was brought by ship, and others that it came in a great yellow cloud, bearing the wrath of God. But come it did, and the land became like a country of ghosts, returning to wilderness. Cattle were left to roam through the standing crops, and died untended in ditches. Ripe corn rotted in the fields, and there was no one to mow the lord's own meadow. Soon untilled land went back to the wild, and the roofs of empty houses collapsed in the first bad weather. Those who survived fasted on Fridays and walked barefoot round the parish church, carrying the relics of Hilda in procession. Meanwhile the Lady Blanche lost all hope of paying off the ransom, with land untilled and rents sinking. And though the heirs of dead tenants paid over heads of cattle as before, the price of livestock slumped as heriots multiplied. Even the mill had ceased to make a profit, with little or no corn to grind, and no travellers came to pay tolls on the deserted highway. Besides, half the bridge had collapsed, and no hands found to repair it. Even her ladyship's garden, where she grew such sweet herbs in happier days, and flowers too, became a tangled wilderness. The dovecote stood rotting, strangled in ivy, and the fishpond stank with green slime.

Judith did what she could, but it was not enough. She sprinkled the floor daily with vinegar, and put feathers to burn in the fire. For each of her children she made an apple stuck with pepper, garlic and rue and hung it round their necks before they went out of the door. But it was not enough. One by one her children were taken, the youngest first, and each time she was still numb with the shock of bearing the small still body to the graveyard and seeing earth thrown on the pit without ceremony, since the priest was one of the first to go, when the signs showed on another child, the bad breath and blotches under the skin and boils coming up, and the death agony started. And a kind of heaviness came over her, a sullen weight which bore down her shoulders from the day she first stumbled into the churchyard, a weight which was not that of the child, still oh so light with the twisted foot now limp, and a numb cold in her heart made her mouth go dumb, so she spoke no word and shed no tear but moved like a grey shadow, bathing their hands and faces in vinegar several times a day before they took sick, bled them when their heads began to ache, fed them spoonfuls of feverfew and put plasters on the boils after they had been cut and cauterised. It was as though she was deaf to their cries, deaf to the cry in her own heart during the days it took for them to die, nor did she know, afterwards, how many days had dawned and darkened during that time.

And when the last died, her firstborn, the body was too heavy for her to lift, and she would perhaps have sat in the stench of her empty house, waiting dumbly for death to take her too, if Medhuil had not chosen that very day to leave the isolated safety of the castle, showing a surprising kind of courage, one that nobody would have expected, could have expected at a time like this. But come she did, holding a smelling apple of camphor and gum arabic to her nose.

Medhuil, always pale of skin, was paler still from being shut up for weeks, but even more so from having been bled every four days, and keeping to a frugal diet of figs and filberts and eggs in vinegar, to ward off the pestilence. She came bearing a gift of powdered emeralds and pearls, dissolved in quicksilver with an ounce of gold and with water of borage added, and when she saw her sister standing there, pale as a wraith of winter sunlight in her fine clothes with the fur-trimmed hood, thin from fasting, and from fear too, with a manservant holding her palfrey at a safe distance, then poor Judith, wild Judith, black Judith, Judith of the far fields and open sky parted her lips at last and let out a cry. And it was not a cry like sobbing, or grief, but a harsh sound, so eerie it could freeze the blood in your body and send fear into any man that heard it, so hard and strong it could shatter a pitcher more than a stone's throw away. The horses shivered and twitched when they heard it, and her sister dropped the precious vial in fright, sending drops of quicksilver running in all directions.

It was the first sound that had come out of her since the dying began, and now it seemed to go on and on, echoing round the bare hills and empty sky, and the forest creeping nearer. The dreadful sound would have made folks shudder if there had been souls to hear it, but there were few left in the wasteland, and those that survived were stony and beyond fright. The manservant took to his heels and Medhuil, knowing that no words could reach her, rode off to get help. It was she who found two men to bring the child's corpse to the graveyard, but Judith did not follow the bier. She sat at her fireside staring into space, muttering words to herself, as though she was crazed or bewitched, whilst the dog at the door whined and howled for food, till the whine turned to a whimper, and the whimper to panting, and this in turn to stillness.

Afterwards she left her cottage and took to wandering aimlessly through fields and pastures, eating roots, picking herbs and grasses only to drop them on the ground, as though she had no use for them, neither mugweed nor St. John's wort, herb Bennet or red nettle. No one tried to reason with her, or stop her. The land was too empty, deserted. She saw, if she saw anything, only unreaped barley flattened in the furrows, or a rotting carcass caught in a thorn hedge. She ran wild in the stillness unbroken by any church bell, as she had done once as a child, but without seeing. If she saw anything it was birds of prey wheeling, or hovering in an empty sky; if she heard anything it was only the wind, or silence. If she spoke it was not to any living soul, but to something under the hard ground she would lie on, mumbling with her face in the dirt. Only the night cold drove her back to her house after dark.

It was a wandering friar who found her, whilst looking for lost souls. They say he had come into the neighbourhood, knowing our priest was dead, and that he was quite fearless, would enter the hovel of death without flinching, or holding his nose at the stench. The sound of his little bell bringing extreme unction to those about to die brought, not terror, but comfort, a promise unexpectedly kept. No doubt he saved many a poor soul who might have died cursing instead of asking forgiveness, and confessing their sins.

55

The friar found Judith sitting in a ditch with her black hair dishevelled and a wild look in her eyes, mumbling inaudibly. He understood her story, and spoke gently to her, as he picked the bits of dried leaf out of her hair and took hold of her shaking hands. It was as though he had all the time in the world, to wash her mudstained face in clean spring water, and pull the thorns out of her fingers. He heard the broken syllables that came from her mouth, and spoke words of his own, soothing words, not so much the words of God he had acquired as a novice but those he had first heard his mother speak to him long ago, and which Judith had heard too. Words which turned to touching, as a child needs to be held for warmth, and comfort. Touching which turned to tenderness, which being received, was given, and being given was further balm to wounded mind and body, and as such, must be accepted.

So his touch, being gentle, stirred her, and when his mouth found hers she opened to him, as naturally as the parched earth to water, as hungrily as the starved seed to sunlight, or the March bud to warmth. She felt a sweet spring rising in her, welling up in her as never before, and when he entered she took him, really took him, as though she would never let him go. And all the time she held him she knew she would bear a seventh child, and that this time she would do nothing, absolutely nothing, to stop it being born.

Ohohohoh cried Joan, ignoring the end of Margery's story. Goody Tyler was wiping her forehead with a damp cloth.

Won't be long now, crowed Granny Mason, peering over Margery's shoulder as she parted her daughter's legs. She grinned encouragingly at the girl, showing the black gaps in her teeth.

Dear God Dear God, gasped the girl. Holy Mary Mother of God.

It's time to try the pepper, announced Margery, having seen the state of the child's head at one end, and her daughter's flushed face and exhausted condition at the other. It was rather an expensive item, and rarely used, so her words were heard with expectant awe. She tipped some ground pepper into her palm, held it under the girl's sweaty nose, pursed her mouth and blew hard.

There was a pause, a moment of stillness during which the only sound to be heard was of firewood crackling in the hearth. The women waited, crowded round the bed, intently watching the girl's face. Joan felt a tickling sensation in her nose, which grew, and grew, until it was so strong that she let out an enormous sneeze, and even as she felt her head exploding there was a dreadful rending, burning sensation down below.

The head is out, said Granny Mason, just as Margery smeared fresh butter on her fingers and helped draw out the rest of the infant, slithering fast in its mucous skin, slippery and bloodstained.

It's a girl, of course, she said loudly, even before cutting the cord.

Three

I have finally got round to doing something about my crates of books, now that shelves have been put up along every spare bit of wall. But I am still in something of a dilemma, since there is no question of being able to keep everything. The rooms are much too small, and in the past I never threw anything out, so now I find myself sitting in a somewhat bemused state of indecision, surrounded by heaps of paperbacks, forgotten novels, antiquated editions of midwifery and nursing textbooks, some of them going right back to my student days, and even a few of my favourite childhood classics. How odd they look now, with their inset colour plates of knights in armour and long thin ladies, and on the verso of the title page a lion couched on an open volume: BOOK PRODUCTION WAR ECONOMY STANDARD. 'This book is produced in complete conformity with the authorised economy standards.' Thick pulpy paper with little flecks in it, like tiny bits of straw.

There is my signature on the fly-leaf, awkward letters scratched with a steel nib, then flowing more confidently with a fountain pen. The old surname, then the new. Well, it seemed very new, and rather strange, for a year or two. As much part of my history, my personal odyssey, as the old clothes and shoes I threw out years ago, and the snapshots stuffed into a bottom drawer. They only tell me what I wore, how I looked, but these forgotten books remind me of what I was thinking, what I was. The prayer book aunt Doris gave me when I was confirmed, the binding coming unstuck from the leatherette cover, and her writing on the fly-leaf. A thin little book on the interpretation of dreams, price one shilling and sixpence, in which you could look up what it meant to dream of losing a tooth or getting a letter. Why, for instance, did I suddenly feel compelled to try and grapple with the theory of nuclear physics twenty years ago? I could not have got very far, obviously. Books on radio astronomy, the expanding universe, and plant life. A hefty psychological study, price three guineas, on the meaning of dreams, in which there are no good omens, and everything is transformed into something bad: anxiety, neurosis, wish-fulfilment as a last resort. Such a long accumulation, going on almost unnoticed over the years, like the growth rings within a tree. Only remarked upon when the trunk is cut.

My attempt at ruthless sorting was getting nowhere. I was constantly surprised by what I found, and would start to read. Or, having firmly decided that a particular book was of no interest, I would skim through a few pages just to be sure and become unexpectedly intrigued. Luckily I was rescued from this impasse by the arrival of Kate and Sally, who were rather surprised to find me sitting in this mess. I had quite forgotten the time, when I heard Kate sounding her horn outside the gate. A moment later there was a babble of voices as Sally opened the rear door and the two children slid off the back seat.

Did you forget we were coming? asked Kate, when she saw the mess on the living room floor.

Of course not. I tried to push a pile of books nearer the wall, so that it was slightly easier to move about. They've been lying around for days. I've been trying to decide what to keep and what to throw out, but it's very difficult. I just hate the idea of throwing any of them away.

Perhaps you could get something for them second-hand, suggested Sally.

Wouldn't get much for this lot, scoffed Kate. Good lord, have you still got this old thing? She waved one of my old midwifery textbooks in the air, and began to laugh. Throw it out, mother. Or better still, burn it on bonfire night.

But Emily had already found an illustrated storybook and was sitting crosslegged on the floor, pretending to read out the contents to Adam. She pointed at the pictures, then ran her index finger under the words, telling a story that was half memory and the rest her own inventive power. When I came through with the tea tray the two of them were quite absorbed, little Adam with two fingers in his mouth and eyes round and dark and dreamy.

After lunch we walked for a bit, the children finding berries and old man's beard and chestnuts, and shuffling gleefully in drifts of dry leaves. Our hands and pockets were soon full of their discoveries, given to us to mind whilst they ran and slid and shuffled. Kate picked some dried teazle to take home, and a neighbour came to her garden gate and gave each of the children an apple. At the moment everything is soft: light, air, everything. Sunlight glows, a blue sky slightly misty, with a smell of burning always in the air from unseen bonfires. A dying incandescence in the trees, falling now, bit by bit.

But Kate and Sally have begun arguing, as usual. Home versus hospital deliveries. Sally has a friend who wanted. Had a terrible fight on her hands. Doctor's attitude was. Kate said sharply that most of her women lived in places not fit to live in, let alone have babies. Ineffective heating, damp. How about an emergency on the fifteenth floor when the lift is out of order? You're just being alarmist, argued Sally, because it's your job. Doctors think they have a right to control our bodies, our minds too.

To my surprise the girls asked me to arbitrate. After all, said Kate, you've thirty-five years of practical experience as a midwife. And, added Sally, you've done a lot of home visits in your time.

I liked visiting people in their homes, I said. On the other hand, having to ride a bike in the rain was no fun.

It's not a question of what you like, objected Sally.

No, I suppose not.

What's best for the patient, insisted Kate.

It was rather like trying to find a point of balance on an unused bicycle, without swerving too much one way or the other.

Most births are quite safe at home, provided those at risk are brought into hospital.

You see! Sally was jubilant.

I had to avoid running her down. Of the two, she was far more accident prone, more obviously vulnerable. My front wheel positively swerved as I tried to proceed very cautiously.

On the other hand, there are always unforeseen risks. And there is the question of manpower.

Precisely, Kate agreed firmly. One midwife bicycling round the back streets is hardly cost efficient.

Trust you to talk about cost efficiency, sneered Sally. But her voice had risen slightly, in a way that made me worry for her. Having a baby is the most important event in a woman's life, and you want a production line. As though we were battery hens!

To tell you the truth, I said, knowing it was not quite the whole truth, but as near as I could get to it, I think it almost always boils down to a question of money. In my time I've seen the pendulum of opinion swing both ways, but medical theory had very little to do with it really. When I started work only first babies were delivered in hospital as a general rule. But not because home births were thought to be a good thing: there simply weren't enough beds. And now, I suppose, there aren't enough domiciliary services, because everything is so organised round the hospital, as a sort of vast technological machine.

Nobody spoke for a bit. Ahead of us the children were running around in loops and circles, stopping to look at things. Emily found a curled white feather in the hedgerow and blew it up into the air.

I don't think individual choice has ever come into it much, I added.

Kate grunted, and kicked at a pebble.

That's what I mean, argued Sally, with a hint of triumph in her voice.

I hoped I had restored harmony for the time being. For Sally's sake I forbore to mention that in my day most women would do anything for a hospital bed, and I said nothing about how I had used my staff privilege, all those years ago, to give birth to Sally in the hospital, when the norm for a second child was a home delivery.

Who's arguing about choice? said Kate, frowning at the horizon. That's not at issue. Ordinary people don't choose. That's for the rich. In the bad old days they chose to have their babies at home, quite rightly. And nowadays they have them in hospital, just as rightly.

Don't say you've started approving of private wealth too, raged Sally.

Did I say anything of the sort?

To be fair, she didn't, I said, stepping into my old familiar role as peacemaker and referee.

When they left, the boot was loaded up with branches of copper leaves, apples and sweet chestnuts, as well as Kate's teazle stems. I offered them some of my old books, and Sally took a few storybooks for the children, but Kate simply shook her head and laughed when I pointed to the pile of medical textbooks I had been accumulating since my days as a student nurse.

I'd burn them if I were you, she said. You couldn't give them away. But they'd make a good bonfire.

It is very quiet now they have gone, but the hours pass quickly. Each day the night draws in a little sooner, making the daylight hours more precious. And they are particularly so just now. A soft sunlight that does not burn, and mild blue skies rising, slightly misty, above glowing trees in an atmosphere smelling constantly of wood smoke. This should be called a grandmother's summer. Almost every day I can see smoke rising beyond the trees or somewhere down in the valley, and I have been raking dead leaves into a pile at the back of the house. Either I must burn them or leave them to rot as compost. Two possible theories of evolution here. Burning is tidy, and more fun, yet could be a bad idea in the long run. But everywhere I see smoke rising, destroying a harvest of leaves and stubble.

The generations come and then go, tenuous as the leaves now falling. A little bit of humus in the soil, or a thin wisp of grey smoke rising. Only a few short seasons ago it was aunt Doris running the farm, and Ada growing taller with each spring, and now such names, and so many memories, are only a breath on the wind and my own time is nearly done and it is Emily who will outstrip us all. A few more names chiselled in the churchyard, and the earth underneath fed, as I feed my compost heap in the corner under the trees and let the leaves lie.

Only the spirit, sighs the wind, as I rake leaves into a heap.

Flesh is grass, whispers the brittle pile as I sweep them from the

63

path. Only the spirit.

Ashes to ashes, crackles the bonfire, as the smoke rises, making my eyes sting. Flakes of grey settle in my hair, and my vision of the world wavers and clouds.

Only the spirit, whispers the still small voice, as the air clears once more. In the beginning was the word, and the word is spirit.

In the beginning was the word, sang the voice, and the word was made flesh for a while. Sing only of the spirit.

Light fades from the sky, and the smoke darkens. In the distance I can see other fires burning: a flicker of flame, smoke rising, and figures moving in the deepening dusk. Brightness falls from the air, murmurs the voice, as the summer shuffles off the last of its leafy splendour in a burning heap of damp and rust, not only queens have died young and fair, but the boy king too. And the fires that had burned at his accession were lit for his sister, but now it was more than just wood that burned.

There was stillness for a little while. Beyond the rising smoke I could see a faint star glimmer as the dusk gathered round the point of light.

Books burn, bodies burn, sings the voice in the flame through the damp wood hissing, the sudden cracking of living tissue. But the spirit refuses to die. I, Ann of the fire, bear witness.

They christened her Alice, Joan's firstborn, murmured the voice coming out of the flames, as the fire died a little, leaving a smouldering, glowing heap in the dusk. Poor Alice, what a time to be born. A sigh came up from the ground, followed by stillness. I cracked a few twigs and threw them into the flames, which revived and spurted. She was born in the same year as my mother, the Lady Elizabeth. Poor Alice, simple Alice, whispered the voice, tossed about like a shuttlecock in a game not of her own choosing. My mother too, come to that, for all her learning. The voice sank away for a moment, dying as the damp wood hissed and exploded. Then it continued.

Alice never understood any of it, which was hardly surprising, being born humble. To her dying day she could not write her name. All she could do was endure. But she was strong, blessed with rude health from birth, that I do remember. A dark, sturdy

64

woman, always working. She would lift and carry and scrub and bake and turn the churn and be on the go from early morning till nightfall without a word of complaint passing her lips, which was why the nuns took her, no doubt, and not for her lit candles or Paternosters.

Alice would never have made trouble, not in a thousand years. She was a simple girl, loyal, hardworking, and by the time she had scrubbed the pots and swept the hearth and fetched water and spread the washing out to dry and done the million and one things which made up an ordinary day for her she could not have told you, as her head hit the straw, the number of the sacraments, whether two or seven. For to tell the truth, she was often asleep before her feet were off the floor and her black hair touched the bolster, without so much as a Matthew Mark.

It was her brother Jack, apprenticed to a weaver, who heard of the new doctrine and began going to Bible readings. And being a high-spirited young man in a group of other young fellows, they rode, as young fellows will, cross country to the church one night, stole into the church with a mouse and fed it the holy bread to prove it was but mouldy bread and could not be the body of Christ. But being young men, and wanting to show the same to all and sundry, they shut the mouse in the pix above the altar, so when it jumped out during mass on the priest, those who saw it shrieked with fright, thinking the Devil had come among them, whilst those who had seen nothing thought their neighbours possessed by him.

And the evildoers were excommunicated by bell book and candle, with the priest clad all in white. Those who saw it say the candles on the crucifix flickered with the rage that shook him. Cursed be they, he chanted, his voice shaking with fury, he or she, in cities and towns, in fields, in ways, in paths, in houses, out of houses, and in all other places, standing, lying, rising or walking, running, waking or sleeping, eating and drinking, and whatsoever they do besides. We give them over utterly to the power of the fiend, and let us quench their souls, if they be dead, this night in the pains of hell-fire, as this candle is now quenched and put out (putting out one of the candles) and let us pray to God if they be alive, that their eyes may be put out as this candlelight is put out (as he snuffed out the second candle) and let us pray to God and to our

65

Lady, and to Saint Peter and Saint Paul and all holy saints, that all the senses of their bodies may fail them, and that they may have no feeling, as now the light of this candle is gone (taking a deep breath to blow out the third candle) and as this holy cross staff now falleth down, so may they, except they repent and show themselves. And he crashed the staff on the stone steps to the altar, after the cross had been taken off it.

After the hushed silence, so they say, several began to weep and cry with terror, and fell on their knees to confess that they thought it unnecessary to bear palms on Palm Sunday, or that it would be better to give alms to the poor and help fatherless children than to go on pilgrimages and light penny candles to a block of painted wood. Several were made to wear painted faggots on their sleeves as a result, but Jack and those with him were neither named nor caught. But in the winter that followed five men rode to a church not twenty miles from here where a miraculous statue kept the church door open night and day, for it would not shut. And so they took it out into the snow, and set fire to it with a flintstone, till it burned brightly enough to light them half their way home through the night, throwing long shadows before them on the dark road. And five men were hanged for felony, though nobody could be sure if it were the right five, or if Jack should have been amongst them, since he was not, being by now betrothed to the weaver's elder daughter and likely to take over the business in due course.

A gust of wind scattered some of the dry leaves I had swept in a heap for burning. But somehow, whispered the voice of the flames, things could never be undisturbed again. It was nothing to do with my mother's books really, or that was only a part of it. Travelling tinkers brought hidden scrolls, and passed on stories from mouth to mouth, how the dead went right off to hell or heaven and there was no such place as purgatory, and how there was more virtue in any common herb of the fields than in holy statues, which could neither heal the sick nor mend broken bones, so that giving candles was a waste of poor men's pence. And the women in the village started to quarrel among themselves, because Margaret Weaver accused Agnes Fletcher of saying, when both were attending the labour of Joan Forester, that crying upon the help of the Virgin would do no good, frightening the poor girl even more than she

66

was frightened already, so she began to weep between each Mother of God, and after the two women had almost come to blows, with several trying to restrain them, Margaret Weaver left the house and told the priest, who said tut tut, all this pother because the king wanted a divorce so he could have a boy for his heir and no woman, and surely she could not wish poor Goody Fletcher to burn for a heretic? And so the matter was left to lie, since no visitation had been made in living memory either by the bishop or his summoner. But after the lying-in of Joan Forester there were those who would not attend a birth if Agnes Fletcher was known to be going, whilst others stayed away if Margaret Weaver so much as showed her face in the door.

There was a lull as the leaves smouldered. The black shadows of bats flitted across the deepening sky. Such foolishness sang the voice, as the green wood hissed and whispered in the smoking heap. So the king with his mortgaged kingdom took a new wife in the hope of having a son for successor, and was given a daughter. And poor Alice came home one day, with her hair cropped and a few rags on her back, knowing nothing of this, knowing only that the bell had stopped ringing for prime and tierce and compline, and that within days objects of beauty and value had begun to vanish, candlesticks from the altar, a crucifix of silver and ivory, the gilt chalices which had once been part of the Lady Blanche's dowry, and the precious things brought long ago when the Lady Aethelfrida came to be with her daughter Hilda, bringing wood and pasture, and in search of peace.

And suddenly she was not required to polish the worn flag-stones or serve at the long refectory table and the lectern itself had gone, and when the rain began to drip through the roof long before the last of the confused women, some of whom had been there since childhood and were now on the verge of dotage, were forced out into a strange world they had not known for a lifetime, and which did not know them, long before that tragic farce, when they were pushed out of the door and even their habits were denied them, so they felt as strange in their unaccustomed garments as they did under a secular sky in a material world of earth and fields and water without walls or rules or silence, without the sound of the matin bell or nones or tierce or compline or the reading voice at refectory, moving in a world that did not know them and had no charity, long before that final leavetaking it was obvious that the steward had foreseen the dissolution and taken the lead from the roof with him, which was why rain dripped on to the flagstones in bad weather.

But poor Alice knew nothing of this, knowing nothing of the great world and its ways, how even kings have debts and those given to godliness can forestall asset-stripping by doing a brisk trade in embroidered altar cloths and church brasses. So she arrived back at her mother's house on foot, with the dust of the road on her threadbare cloak, having eaten nothing but roots and leaves for three days, and drunk only spring water. Her shoes were worn through and tied with rags, and the growing stubble of her shorn hair stuck out in an ugly black mass when her hood fell back, and she stood like a lost animal, mute and tired and confused, with a question lurking in her wide eyes that nobody could have been found to answer.

And it was as though she had never been away, except that she had grown so tall that no clothes in the coffer would fit her, and boys in the village would laugh at her cropped head if they got near enough to pull off her cap. They would surround her at dusk at the bend in the lane, pull at her clothes, and jeer, making loud quips about the bride of Christ being sent home because she was not good-looking enough for him, and since the king himself could put aside an ugly wife why should the King of Heaven make do with the likes of her?

Alice bore it all with a kind of dumb fortitude for a time. It was her mother who scolded when she came home with her clothes torn and a stubborn look in her grey eyes, since the pitcher was broken and the cow should have been milked an hour ago, and she had been fussed enough at an extra body to sleep and feed when Alice could have been wedded or put out to service years ago, but who would look at her now when the Lord himself had turned her away? And all this because the priest had picked her out for her humble piety, she thought ruefully, when Alice took to carrying a kitchen knife under her cloak and lashed out at the lads lying in wait for her at the crossroads, so that Will Mason ended up with a vicious cut across his left cheek, and was lucky not to lose the sight

68

of one eye. For which the priest had no choice but to make her do penance, seven days on bread and water, though by this time there were many who held that doing penance set by the priest did no good, all that counted was feeling sorrow and contrition in your heart, and I doubt that Alice felt an inkling of remorse. Bread and water was no hardship for her, and she had begun to walk home unmolested at long last. Will Mason's scar saw to that, and by now her cropped hair had begun to grow.

Poor Alice, whispered the voice from the centre of the smouldering heap. Just a victim of history. Twigs snapped, autumn leaves glowed for a moment, turning black in an instant. A flotsam of circumstance. I threw on another handful of leaves, but they were too damp, and the tongues of flame subsided. What could she know of the Word, when she still marked her dough with a cross to make sure the bread would rise, and signed her name with a cross too. I went indoors to fetch one of the old discarded textbooks which my daughter had scoffed at only a few hours earlier. I tore out a couple of pages, crumpled them, and tucked them under the heap of smouldering twigs. Sudden tongues of orange flame leapt skyward. No, said the voice from the fire, it was my mother, the Lady Elizabeth, who began to read books secretly. Part of an underground brotherhood, long before I was born. There was Maud Feathergood, who travelled with rolled scriptures hidden in her sleeve, and could recite the entire gospel of Saint Matthew behind locked doors with the windows shuttered. There were travelling tinkers whose goods were not what they seemed, and the locked coffer in my mother's chamber held more than gowns and linen. So much I know. But Alice did not know, though she had been told by the priest that it was wrong to use the holy bread to rid her cabbages of caterpillars, as all the old women in the neighbourhood were wont to do, hiding it under their tongues for the purpose, instead of swallowing it.

And Alice could not know, what my mother might perhaps have known, that money had to be found to pay for the endless wars, and that the gifts of land, pasture and forest rich in venison brought by the Lady Aethelfrida seeking a refuge from killing and a life of peace, made rich pickings for a bankrupt king seeking not only a son but an unmortgaged kingdom to make him heir to, and so by a sleight of hand he was able to clear his conscience and his debts at one and the same time. Something my lady mother must have known, since the castle had long since fallen into disrepair from a fall in the family fortunes brought about by wild expenditure on the crusades, and the French wars, and though an attempt was made to find part of the ransom demanded for Lord Robert by marrying off his son for a handsome dowry, the money was never paid, and it was too late to return the bride, being five months pregnant.

The fire seemed to die a little, flickered and glowed. A few sparks flew to the darkening sky as I threw on a handful of dead leaves, and the voice murmured of birds nesting in the great hall, and stone falling from stone, till the moat was no more than a tangle of weeds growing in mud and the drawbridge had rusted. A new moon, sharp as a sickle, had begun to rise above the trees and into the darkening sky, still empty but for the lone star glimmering. And so it was, snapped the voice as more green twigs exploded in the simmering heat, that the sole suitor for the Lady Elizabeth, living in a dank and draughty corner of the once splendid castle, was an up and coming wool merchant, son of a mere yeoman, without so much as gules to his name but with profits enough to buy up the land lying round about, the fields, pastures and forests given long ago to the holy order by the Lady Aethelfrida in search of peace in perpetuity, and now sold off to help pay for a century of war and replenish the king's coffers.

And so he became a gentleman, with a coat of arms to his name and a wife whose ancestry was rooted deep as a noble oak and higher than the most ancient tree in the neighbourhood he had chosen to make his own. And he built a house of the finest stone and timber, with large mullioned windows overlooking the deer park, and gravel paths and a maze of high-cut green hedges, and a terraced walk running the length of the house from which one could see far over the countryside, and the gleaming river beyond. And within the house there were comforts such as the Lady Elizabeth and her nurse had not seen or dreamt of in the grim draughts of the old castle, with its damp and rats and foul straw. No, here there were cosy rooms with dark wainscoting, and when the mullioned windows were closed and the hangings drawn it was snug to sit by the fire in the large hearth. And instead of suits of armour and weaponry hanging on grim stone walls there was a picture gallery, and a minstrel gallery above the great hall, and a library, which her husband called his study, and large fireplaces even in the bedrooms, so that when one drew the curtains of the great fourposter it was snug, and not a bit like the old days up at the castle, as her nurse was never tired of pointing out. And each time she came up the long broad avenue of oaks which her husband had planted as a statement of his ownership the Lady Elizabeth could not but see how the tall high chimneys above the roof proclaimed her bodily comfort.

But not the ease of her mind. For strange as it might seem she could not sleep in the great fourposter with its embroidered hangings, though the mullioned windows were curtained off against the prying white face of the moon and the door with its coat of arms freshly carved in the lintel was heavy enough to cut out draughts and footsteps, and the comings and goings of servants.

Now whether she missed the sound of the wind whistling round the old castle keep, or whether the high fourposter with its rich hangings was too soft with its bolsters of duckdown and goose-feathers, I do not know. Perhaps the room with its fire in the hearth and its windows tightly shut behind the curtains of figured damask was too stuffy, so she felt she could not breathe as she tossed and turned through the hours of darkness. Her old nurse swore it was them dratted peacocks screeching on the lawns all night, and wanted them put down, the nasty noisy things, but my mother would have no such thing, for during her daylight walks she delighted both in them and the fallow deer which graced the wide prospect.

No, she told me afterwards, when I was old enough to understand her meaning, it was the spirit calling. For my father was often absent for weeks at a time, and she spent those long hours by candlelight, reading books kept secretly in her coffer, under the linen and velvet gowns, and she wore the key at her girdle. And who brought the books I cannot be sure to this day, though I heard rumours of a visiting traveller whom my mother received behind closed doors, and some say my father, far from being deceived, had dealings not of a merely mercantile kind while he stayed in the city, and brought back more than household provisions when he returned. But whoever brought them secretly to her chamber, in the long nights before my birth she devoured them hungrily, as the flame devours the candle, from *The Right Pathway unto Prayer*, and *The Spiritual Nosegay*, to *News Out of Heaven* and *The Lantern of Light*.

And she told me afterwards, as I lisped through the scriptures in the English tongue, by which time the old king was dead, how her heart had wellnigh stopped with terror in her breast when the order was made that all such books should be burned, and handed over to the chief constable within forty days. How I prayed, my dear child, she went on to tell me, her finger still on the line of scripture we had been perusing, knowing how the fire could burn, if not books, then this body, but my child's immortal soul was far more precious to me, so they stayed in the house under lock and key.

A kind of hush fell over the landscape. Not a leaf stirred. The clear sky, darkening now, seemed to rise and rise to a blue infinity. The voice in the flames was still too, but I felt its presence more palpably than ever in the breathing depth of the smouldering heap, that glowed and grew dim and then glowed afresh. For the first time I was aware of myself standing there, expectant, a stout elderly woman wearing an old jacket with a garden rake in one hand and a bundle of dry twigs in the other, but I was thinking of myself eight months pregnant oh so long ago watching the first light coming through the gap in the curtains with my head full of plans for her, it, us, childish really in the long run, but oh so good that I felt myself suddenly growing, a swelling inside, I could have hugged my daughter, myself as I was once, the young woman minding her child's immortal soul as she understood it.

I sing, said the fire, of the spirit.

My birth was a difficult business, though I was born without visible blemish after many hours. I was swaddled and decked in lace for my baptism, and my father had twelve silver gilt apostle spoons especially made, and a cup with my name engraved on it as a gift. But my mother seemed not to regain her strength, for months afterwards a mysterious malady left her weak and ailing, so that each time she tried to rise from her bed and resume her duties about the house she would fall back dizzy and gasping, with the sweat breaking on her forehead. She did not like to speak of it, but instead sent her young maid Peggy, who was little more than a child at the time, to bring back a healing potion from old Joan, still living in the same cottage with Alice back from the convent, and grumbling mightily about it. And each day my mother, the Lady Elizabeth, would put aside her book of devotion, *The Golden Book of Christian Matrimony* or *An Invective against the Most Wicked Vice of Swearing*, and bravely swallow the bitter brew with only a slight grimace of her pale features.

Till one day the lord and master, who was much away on business, returned to the house rather sooner than expected, and, what is more, instead of shutting himself up in his library to savour an undisturbed cup of claret, clattered straight up the stairs in his riding boots and burst into my mother's chamber in a mood of unwonted tenderness. But when he saw his lady wife bent over a pewter bowl with the sweat standing out on her forehead and her fair hair damp and streaky, heaving Joan's vile green brew into it between gasps for breath, his mood changed rapidly.

What is the meaning of this, goddamme? He roared in a voice of thunder, and the terrified serving wench scuttled out of the room with the bowl of noisome vomit as fast as her legs could carry her. Have I earned enough wealth from my labour to buy up half the neighbourhood, that my ailing wife should still be drinking some filthy potion concocted by ignorant peasant women? Streuth, what's in it, for heaven's sake – frog spawn? Toads' livers? Newts' eyes and lizards' legs, with a few roasted snails thrown in for good measure? He paced about the room, whilst my mother watched him, eyes wide with alarm in her ashen face, leaning back on the pillow and too spent to utter a word. By Jesus, he went on, standing with his arms akimbo at the foot of the carved four-poster, I'll send for a doctor of divinity, a physician from the university, and no cost shall be spared. Shall it be said of me that I spend less on my dear wife than I do on my horses and dogs? That I tend the trees in my orchard and my box hedges but allow my own bedfellow to wither away for want of a little physic?

And he strode out of the room in a fury, so that young Peggy, who had been hiding all this while behind the arras, shook with the terror of it, as though it had been a draught from the slam of the heavy oak door as they heard his spurs clatter down the wide oak stairs and his voice bellowing orders to servants below.

Henry Dinsdale, learned doctor of divinity, had not left his chambers at the university for several years. Here he was in the habit of examining urine specimens brought to him in a glass vial by special messenger, and sent back a written report by the same messenger, who was asked to wait in an antechamber while he examined the liquid in a good north light. His prescriptions invariably included pepper for a urine unnaturally dark in hue, and parsley or celery if it was clouded in appearance, preceded by a purgative of rhubarb and black hellebore in all cases. If enough foresight had been shown to send an astrological chart with the urine specimen he would also prescribe a course of radical bleeding before returning gratefully to his study and the laborious translation of a medieval Latin commentary on the gospel of St. John, on which he had been engaged for many years. It was, on the whole, an agreeable way of life, since he was spared the sufferings of the sickroom and only rarely heard the outcome of his ministrations. If the patient recovered, he heard nothing, and if the sufferer died he could always imply that his instructions had not been properly carried out or, worse still, that someone in the household must have been practising witchcraft. He knew this to be the quickest way to kill criticism.

So what induced him to leave the stuffy sanctity of his books in my mother's case? Certainly it had nothing to do with her person, since he managed to spend six weeks in my father's spacious house without once coming into her chamber. Perhaps he was lured by the agreeable prospect of country air, and my father's broad parklands with their herds of fallow deer had by now become famous. So too had his cellar, with its choice wines from Burgundy, and the doctor was known to enjoy a good tipple and, once in his cups, liked to expatiate on the colour, body and aroma of certain wines in a thoroughly academic fashion. So much so, that some of his fellows at the university put it about that if he was really gone in his cups he would not know if he was testing wine or urine, and could be made to hold either up to the light and call it clouded, or limpid, or full of foreign bodies, and had even been known to drink it. But young men always delight to make fun of their elders in such places of learning, so I have heard.

On his arrival, with the dust of the journey still on him, Dr. Dinsdale was ushered into my father's inner sanctum, the study, where he showed a considerable interest in his collection of books, and seemed inclined to embark on a lengthy discourse on Origen, would no doubt have done so, had not an offer of refreshment to wash the dust of the journey from his throat cut him short. After the third glass my father ventured to steer the conversation from the art of cellarage to the topic at that moment uppermost in his own thoughts, the continuing ill health of his wife. Ah yes, declared the worthy doctor, pushing his empty glass forward, I have been giving this matter some thought, and I have come to the conclusion that the most likely cause of her failure to respond to treatment was in the astrological chart made preparatory to radical bleeding. He was convinced, without, you understand, ascribing any blame to any person or persons unknown, since such errors could easily occur, that he had not been given the precise time and date of birth of the lady concerned when he drew up his chart. He had been told, weighing each word for emphasis, that her ladyship had been born just before midnight when the moon was in the third quarter, and he had, in good faith, advised on a course of bleeding accordingly. Now, if she had been born shortly after midnight, and in view of the fact that Venus and Saturn were presently in a most unfavourable conjunction, the prescribed bleeding, far from doing her good, might be positively harmful.

My father, whose knowledge of astrology was as scanty as his acquaintance with Origen, said nothing, but looked decidedly gloomy. Henry Dinsdale, however, carried away by his own eloquence and his host's excellent spiced wine, was nothing if not optimistic. All that is really required is accurate information on the precise circumstances of your wife's birth. Surely there must be, in your household, some servant, an old nurse, whom I could question? Her ladyship's lady mother perhaps?

The Lady Isabella died in giving birth to my wife, my father told him. He sent for the old nurse, by now quite toothless and considered to be not quite in her right mind, who stood on the threshold of the master's sanctum as though dangerous animals might be lurking under the furniture and mumbled how the babe had been born to her poor dear ladyship who was killed of the draughts in that terrible old castle just before the clock struck midnight with a cord round her neck and it was only old Joan in the village who saved it, though she was not so old then, and kept all the nostrums handed down from her grandmother, the seventh child of a seventh child, and if he didn't believe her he could send down to the village to ask her, for though she was old she was not in her dotage. Which my father was unwilling to do, since it was his wife's taking her ridiculous folk remedies that had made him consult the worthy doctor in the first place.

But in the presence of Dr. Dinsdale my father had no alternative but to send down to old Joan for precise details of his wife's birth, whilst the doctor explained to him the methods whereby he fashioned the kind of sigil which his dear lady was at present wearing round her neck for the furtherance of her health, and hinted that it might be necessary to make one of a slightly different design if, as he suspected, he had been misinformed as to the time of her birth. These sigils, he explained, as he followed his host in to dinner, had to be cast at a propitious time, when the planet corresponding to the metal used was ascendant in the heavenly house that influenced diseases. And no doubt in the case of her ladyship, he smiled, giving a sideways glance at my father, nothing but gold would do. Furthermore, he added, surveying the richly decorated board with its glowing candelabra, the sigil would have to be hung round the patient's neck at a time which was also astrologically propitious. All of which, he added, giving an appreciative look at the richly laden sideboard, might take weeks rather than days.

Meanwhile, he suggested, as he allowed a slice of roast beef to be put on his plate, it was advisable to keep the sick person on a very light diet.

For himself, Henry Dinsdale did not favour a light diet, but, like many a university man, he believed that the true salt of any feast was conversation, or, in this case, since his host had come up through trade and was therefore not really qualified to take part in such a twosome, in discourse. Picking at a pheasant bone with his teeth, he explained to my father that his wife's *pneuma zoticon*, that is to say her vital spirits, which mingles with blood in the heart, might be affected, which would account for a certain lassitude. He drank more wine and helped himself to a brace of stuffed quails while he went on at some length on the movement of the blood which, in its ebb and flow, conveys the vital spirits to the rest of the body. As for the *pneuma psychicon*, or animal spirit, which has its seat in the brain, allowing his goblet to be replenished, this was naturally somewhat unstable in women, on account of the mother, as had been observed since ancient times, and it was the *pneuma physicon*, or natural spirit which would really hold the key to her recovery, coming as it does from the liver. The liver, he opined, sucking a shred of gooseflesh from between his teeth to make way for the syllabub, being the centre of nutrition, is always severely affected in times of sickness, when the body takes in less food, so it follows that the natural spirit is subdued.

It was whilst the worthy doctor was taking a postprandial stroll with his host down the long gallery, admiring the many portraits spaced along its walls and occasionally gazing upwards at the carved and gilded ceiling with its endless repetition of the newly purchased coat of arms, that a serving woman came to report that her mistress had been able to take a little chicken broth but was now flushed with fever. Henry Dinsdale stopped in his tracks, contemplated the tips of his boots for a long moment and re-marked: Ah, but what kind of fever? Whereupon he stared at the serving wench, who blushed dark as a beetroot and had not a word to say for herself. It is no use your telling me of a fever, unless you can also tell me whether it is ephemeral, which is in the spirits, putrid, coming from the humours, or hectic, which has its source in the solids. Moreover, if the fever is continuous we may safely assume it is in the blood, whilst tertian fevers have their source in the yellow bile, quartan fevers emanate from the black bile, and quotidian fevers are caused by the phlegm. Having come to the end of his disquisition, the doctor looked first at his host and then at the bewildered serving maid, during a moment of awed silence.

She just feels a bit hot, stammered the girl, and her face is all flushed. I've noticed it before, of an evening.

During the days and weeks that followed, Dr. Dinsdale consumed a vast quantity of game, sweetmeats, and my father's finest Burgundy. He also spent many hours in the library, working his way through my father's modest but, he said, interesting collection, and it was in the library that he prepared a more definitive astrological chart based, it must be admitted, largely on hearsay and the evidence of old women, for a course of bleeding to be carried out by a local surgeon. He left precise instructions on the amount of blood to be drawn and the placement of leeches before allowing himself to be persuaded to ride to hounds through his host's pleasant and spacious parklands, though his horsemanship was slow and cumbersome, owing to his physique.

But my poor mother did not improve. Indeed when, after regular bleeding for over a month she showed no sign of rallying and seemed, if anything, rather more poorly than before, Dr. Dinsdale, having made the most intimate inquiries of her serving women, lamented the total absence of laudable pus, which might by now have purified the system, and prescribed a strong purge of aloes, colocynth and black hellebore, known to the ancients, he informed my father, as *hiera logadii*, and much extolled by Ptolemy. This caused her violent stomach cramps, and that night the fever rose higher, so that she began to babble, which, being reported to the worthy doctor in the library, he opined that the fever's heat was burning the humours, and that fumes of melancholy adust were rising from the crucible of the spleen to her brain.

But my father was by now too anxious to be reassured by this theory. He rushed up to his wife's bedchamber, where young Peggy, without instructions from anybody, was bathing her mistress's face in cold water, and then her hands, murmuring words as though to a baby and wringing the cloth out in a bowl to cool it, and rushed back to the library to confront Dinsdale. I know nothing of theory, he shouted, of melancholy adust or humours or anything else, but I do know that if something is not done soon, and quickly, my wife will die.

It was now that Henry Dinsdale rose from his chair and

consented to accompany his host to her ladyship's bedchamber. Not, he hastened to point out as they mounted the broad oak staircase, as a doctor of medicine, but in his function as doctor of divinity. We are all, he added solemnly, entering the bedchamber for the first time with a measured tread that struck terror into little Peggy, who spilled her bowl of water before scuttling out of the room as fast as her little feet could carry her: we are all in the hands of His Mercy. He looked down at the flushed face of my mother, at the scarlet cheeks and the lips murmuring inaudible words as her head tossed first this way, then that, as though trying to escape some invisible bondage. Lord, I beseech Thee, he prayed, touching her racing pulse with his fingers, that the corruption of Satan come out of this woman, that doth so trouble her that she cannot serve Thee. And he made the sign of the cross before drawing my father to the window embrasure, where he told him that he proposed to prescribe a purge consisting of rhubarb, senna and myrobalans known as *confectio hamech*, and much used by the Arabs, he added, as though this should still any lingering doubt in my father's mind.

The following day my mother had six stools in as many hours and lost consciousness for a while. When she regained her senses she said she would have no more of the doctor's purges. He will be the death of me, she declared, and if it is meant that I should die I would rather do so in the way my Maker shall decree, than by his ministrations.

Dr. Dinsdale rode back to the university and his translation of the medieval commentary on the gospel of St. John, convinced in his own mind that the fuming melancholy from her spleen had turned the poor lady's wits, but he kept his thoughts to himself. He had enjoyed a most agreeable vacation from his academic labours in some comfort, with the benefit of fresh air and a pleasing countryside. And both his paunch and his purse were a good deal heavier as he rode away.

The sky was darkening from purest azure to a darker hue, ink blue, royal blue. My mind was fumbling for words to fit something quite stupendous. The bonfire sank, smoking, having no more natural leaves to consume. I wanted to see it go on burning, so I went indoors and fetched some more of my old nursing textbooks, the ones Kate and I had been arguing about a few hours earlier. They were well made, those old books, and it took all my strength to rip the pages from their stitching and out of the stiff covers.

Oh dear, I said aloud, as the first flames leapt upward and the paper curled, turning black. Such sad mistakes, after a lifetime of trying.

Worse, said the voice from the fire. If that were all.

It was, to say the least, unusual for my father to relinquish his authority enough to give in to my mother's wishes, and sending Dr. Dinsdale away was one of those rare occasions when he did so, if only because he thought she was dying. But she lived, and for a while that was enough for both of them. She continued to wear the sigil round her neck, but the leeches had to find other prey. She began to read again, and I was brought to her chamber for a few hours a day, for she was determined that the first words I uttered should come from her lips. But she was not strong enough to leave her room.

For a while my father bore it patiently, and if he knew of the secret comings and goings between the house and old Joan's hovel, with young Peggy mostly the guilty messenger, he turned a blind eye and said nothing, heard nothing, and smelt nothing, in spite of the fumes of rosemary and feverfew, and the hot baths of rose leaves, orris root and juniper berries.

But after a time he tired of dining alone, sitting alone and, for that matter, sleeping alone. Besides, he wanted a son and heir, and the Lady Elizabeth was in no fit condition to give him one, or even a second daughter. He began to make inquiries amongst his numerous acquaintances, both in the neighbourhood and during his frequent visits to the city, where there was one name which seemed to be on everyone's lips.

Dr. Robert Pendlebury did not belong to the orthodox school, he was no Henry Dinsdale, and this was enough to recommend him to many clients, who had suffered enough in the hands of approved medical men. Indeed, it could be said that his chief claim to fame was his open attacks on the followers of Galen, and it was rumoured that this flirting with danger, this glamour that surrounded his name and person, was not confined to theory. It was whispered that he meddled seriously in alchemy, and that powerful men occasionally consulted him to influence the future. And because he had travelled much abroad, did not keep a wife and had a somewhat saturnine complexion, it had even been suggested that he was a foreigner.

This man, who regularly mixed with the great and powerful, could not easily be induced to attend on anyone, and could certainly not have been tempted by a mere fee. If he did my mother the signal honour of concerning himself with her case, it was theory rather than practice that interested him. The very fact that Henry Dinsdale had failed so conspicuously to find a remedy was reason enough for him to take up the challenge. Dinsdale is an ass, he told my father, stroking the black beard streaked with grey which, with his conspicuously black eyes, did a good deal to enhance his somewhat *risqué* reputation. He told all his clients that their regular practitioner was an ass or a fool, something which inspired immediate confidence in them, since they had already been driven to the brink of despair, and hence to his door. But Robert Pendlebury was a remarkable man, he believed in himself, and his theory. Not content with calling Dinsdale an ass, he intended to prove him one. And for the purpose of showing him up he was prepared to undertake any journey, however incommodious. He came to my mother's bedchamber.

His arrival caused something of a stir. Hearing the sound of horses on the gravel below, my mother told me to make haste and put the forbidden books back in the coffer, under the bottom layer of linen, for our lesson for the day was ended. She bade me sit quietly in the window embrasure, and closed her eyes wearily on the pillow, with a resigned, exhausted look I already knew well. Down below I could see a couple of stable boys holding the horses for my father, and the strange man, who made an instant impression on me, as he did on everybody, being clad from head to foot in black velvet, with black satin trimmings. Afterwards I heard the servants whisper that he must be the Devil himself, and I saw that they took to crossing themselves surreptitiously if they happened to pass him on the staircase, and complained of feeling the shivers for hours after if his unusually black eyes looked in their direction. It was a time of great unease, much uncertainty, and nothing in the house was ever quite the same from the moment he arrived, or so it seemed to me at the time.

Why should this be, I ask. Asks the voice from the fire. But memory plays strange tricks, especially in childhood. Was it really the very same day that Robert Pendlebury came into the house with his knowing black eyes and his odd black beard streaked with grey that the church bells began to ring, singing that the old king was finally dead and the young king would reign from now on, that the bells went on ringing and ringing, and the bonfires were lit at dusk from hillside to hillside, not for the burning of books but for freedom, since my father, coming into the room, with the weird-looking doctor behind him, laughed at my guilty looks and said something about no need to go on hiding them now, and kicked at the coffer in a fit of high spirits. Or was the unease, the uncertainty, the feeling of things changing to do with the words used by the strange doctor, with the large ruby ring flashing on the middle finger of his left hand? For he spoke of a *mysterium magnum* as he lightly touched my mother's pale forehead with his fingertips, and glanced round the room as though looking for the *astra* of which he was speaking in the corners of the ceiling or up among the hangings of the fourposter, so that I expected to see I know not what hovering among the beams and plaster.

Nothing is quite what it seems, he said, and the room was suddenly full of shadows. The *astra* are not really the stars, but influence their development. Each disease has its *astrum*, and we must find the corresponding *arcanum*, which, though they may be herbs and metals, are not really herbs and metals but signs for the *arcana*. What should act on the brain will be directed by Luna, what on the spleen by Saturn, the kidneys by Venus, and so on and so forth. Through the leaded window I saw a dark cloud pass from the sun and the room was suddenly filled with lozenges of bright light scattered across the floor, the hangings, the dark panelled walls. When wood burns, he said, pointing at the logs crackling in the stone hearth, it is not the wood itself that burns, but a sulphur; the smoke is mercury, and the ash that remains is salt. Conversely, whatever burns is sulphur; whatever is spiritous or vaporous is mercury, and that which is solid and indestructible by fire is solid, and salt. He looked thoughtfully at my father, stroked his beard with his white jewelled hand, and began to unroll an astrological chart tied with a scarlet ribbon.

What has all this to do with my wife, murmured my father, diffident and confused.

Salt, sulphur and mercury, he said, his voice never changing in tone, as unnerving in its steadiness as his dark eyes, make up all living matter, and man is formed of the same materials as the rest of the earth, and subject to the same laws. Thus excess salt will cause skin ulcers if the astral equilibrium of the body is disturbed, or the *archaeus* of the stomach fails to separate pure from impure substances, causing tartaric diseases which obstruct the system. We must discover the correspondence between the star which caused the disease, and the star which heals through its specific drug or *arcanum*. He rolled up the astrological chart and gazed thoughtfully at my mother's pale face on the pillow. Her eyes seemed to have grown larger and darker as he talked, with something unusual flickering in their brown depths, like fish at the bottom of a pond. Was it anxiety, or wonder? I could not know, being a mere child, but she had never once stopped watching him as he talked.

However, he continued, and her eyes followed him round the room, while he tapped the rolled-up chart for emphasis, there are five possible causes, or *entia*, for diseases. Besides the stars, we must consider the body's natural proneness to disease, the mind, divine purpose, and, pausing for emphasis, foods and poisons, which in this case seems the most likely.

In the silence that followed one could have heard a pin drop. But in fact the sound was much louder, as young Peggy dropped the water jug, and began to snivel. My father sent her out of the room for a dishclout to mop up the mess.

Normally, continued Robert Pendlebury, who seemed not to have noticed the interruption, one would suspect some village woman in the case, some ignorant old hag brewing herbal stews without rhyme or reason, knowing nothing of theory, of the *astra*, or the *archaeus*, and who thinks salt is simply something you put on meat or fish to stop it going foul.

The spilled water was running in rivulets across the wood floor. I saw it reach a long lozenge of light and begin to gleam. It shone, and vanished into the light. Looking up, I saw that my mother was frowning slightly, her eyes flickering nervously round the room. My father, on the other hand, looked embarrassed about something, almost ashamed. When Peggy came back into the room to mop up the water he made a great to do about telling her to hurry, clumsy child, and then hustled her through the door.

Watching from the window embrasure, I know that the strange doctor saw nothing of this. He did not hear the jug fall, or notice my mother give Peggy a warning look, or, for that matter, see Peggy coming or going. Vaguely conscious of an interruption, he waited for the door to shut, for his words to fall on stillness.

However, and I saw how a glint of light caught his large ruby ring as he lifted his hand before another cloud passing over the sun made the pattern of light on the floor fade away, since Henry Dinsdale has been involved in the case I think we need look no further for a possible poison. For the first time he smiled, or rather sneered, showing his teeth behind the smoothly trimmed beard. My father tried to smile, knowing it was expected of him, but his heart was not in it. He sat down suddenly, on the coffer where the books were hidden, that now could be read openly, and dropped his head in his palms.

Pendlebury put his hand reassuringly on my father's shoulder.

But there is a solution. Like drives out like. Just as salt will cure diseases caused by salt, poison cures diseases caused by poison. The Galenic principle of opposites is quite false, which is why Dinsdale and his cronies effect so few cures with their hot for cold and wet for dry. So, I propose to begin by giving your wife a compound of antimony to purge her of such poisons. Failing which, we can try other methods.

I saw my mother blench. She gave a little cry, and looked imploringly at her lord and master, who was hardly master of himself at this moment, and would not look at her. Instead she asked for time to herself so she might pray, and my father took me out of the room with him, and the doctor vanished to his own quarters, where, as I heard the servants whisper, he had set up a den of Satan, with vials and alembics, since all physic had to be

84

made volatile, removing the dross from the spirit, to be effective. As for my mother, the compound of antimony drove her clean out of her mind for the best part of a fortnight. Stark staring mad, she saw devils lurk in the corners of the room, and told of black cats with burning eyes who clambered on the bedhangings, as she sat up white with terror, staring with hollow eyes and her lips blue, and her maids trying to restrain her in the bed. I was kept out of the room, and saw her but once, yet for days I could hear her scream and sob from the hallway, the landings and stairs, as the sounds came through the door of her bedchamber.

It was a confused time, an uneasy time, said the voice from the fire, and a gust of wind sent flaming sparks whirling into the darkening firmament. A constant coming and going in the house, and the servants at odds with each other, some of them crossing themselves and praying, and saying within my hearing that her ladyship's sickness was nothing but a judgement on her, and the Devil was in her too. And my father at his wits' end, hearing nothing and nobody, though the church bells seemed to be constantly ringing, day in, day out, during the time my mother was out of her mind and after, and I hung about the house and garden, unattended, for there was no one to hear my lessons now, or mind what I was doing, so I watched the strange doctor in his black clothes, and thought about the *mysterium magnum*, and listened to the whisper and gossip of servants, and heard how there was to be no more creeping to the Cross on Good Friday, or ashes on Ash Wednesday, and how the fingerbones of St. Hilda had been thrown out for superstitious idolatry, and three of her shin bones over the hill, and how the village priest had proposed marriage to Alice turned out of the convent, now that her shorn hair had grown thick and strong, and been accepted.

Dr. Robert Pendlebury said that my mother's condition was due to fumes of mercury rising to the brain, and that the next course of treatment should take place during the time of the full moon, since Luna controls that organ. During this time he had been seen very little, keeping mostly to his quarters, where he supposedly conducted his experiments. He was abstemious in his habits, ate and drank very little, and rarely if ever went out of doors, either to stroll in the formal gardens or hunt in the deer park. Apart from my mother's bedchamber, he would only visit the library occasionally.

And it was in the library, where I would sometimes hide myself to continue the reading interrupted by this new and disturbing phase in my mother's illness, that I overheard the argument that ensued between Dr. Pendlebury and my father when a further course of treatment was proposed. Half concealed behind the vast English Bible, now no longer hidden in the coffer upstairs but kept in the library with other books, I saw over its rim how the terror of the past few days had left a lasting impression on my father's distraught face, still haunted by the sight of my mother sitting bolt upright in bed with eyes staring and mouth foaming, pointing at unseen devils and hobgoblins in the room.

Spirit of quicksilver, taken at the full moon, said the doctor. Of course, if the original poisoning was arsenical, then arsenic should be tried. But once antimony has failed to purge what remains of the poison, and since all vaporous fumes are mercury, it is mercury we should try first.

My father frowned in disbelief. You would think so much spewing, such sweats, would have been enough to cure her, he said.

Pendlebury shook his head. Merely side effects of the physic, my dear fellow. That is where the Galenicals are so in error, in considering that an end in itself.

My father sat brooding. He looked at his hands, he regarded his feet, and shifted his weight about in his seat. Not once did he look directly at the commanding figure in black velvet, with his olive skin and those knowing black eyes which seemed to take in everything and give nothing back, smooth, alert, unblinking. Instead he was frowning, something stubborn in his look.

I want a second opinion, he said at last.

The fire had almost died. I poked at it with my garden rake, then threw on it a few more crumpled pages of textbook. Bright tongues of flame flared up suddenly, making me step back.

It was a time for second opinions, said the voice in the fire. There were so many opinions that fighting would break out in the

86

church, about anything and everything – candles, the new prayer book, the altar which was taken out and the table put in its place. Arguments would start round the new Bible, now that those who could read were able to, and those who could not would listen, and afterwards add their voice on communion under both kinds, and statues being taken out, and whether the table should stand east to west and the priest leave off his vestments and say 'in remembrance' in giving out the host.

It was the time of the new learning, said the voice. We were all learning, now that the gospel was in the English tongue, and nobody was forbidden to read it, neither women, nor apprentices, nor serving men under the degree of yeoman, as formerly.

By all means, said Dr. Pendlebury.

If my father expected him to object, he did not fully appreciate the doctor's temperament. Pendlebury was a theorist, and he delighted in the possibility of putting his theories to the test, of proving himself right and the other fellow wrong. Unlike Henry Dinsdale, who thought that any body which failed to conform to the descriptions laid down by Galen must be a malformation of nature, an aberration, a vile deformity, Robert Pendlebury was inclined to be discursive, speculative. Far from being offended, he positively welcomed a second opinion, since it allowed him to embark on an argument he felt confident of winning.

Let's have old Dinsdale back, if you have any doubts.

The disputation began in my mother's chamber, with the two men confronting each other across the bed. Robert Pendlebury was touching my mother's right wrist with his white hand on which the ruby glowed, whilst Henry Dinsdale was trying to find my mother's pulse with his stubby fingers fumbling on her emaciated left wrist.

The pulse is erratic, said Dr. Dinsdale.

Dr. Pendlebury merely nodded.

A mild fever, commented Dr. Dinsdale, putting his hand to my mother's hot forehead.

A mild fever, agreed Dr. Pendlebury, hardly hiding the contempt in his voice.

Not enough phlegm, opined Dr. Dinsdale.

Too much sulphur, argued Dr. Pendlebury.

The vital spirits are affected, continued Henry Dinsdale, now going rather red in the face, but trying to keep his temper.

The quintessence has been subdued, sneered Robert Pendlebury, cool contempt in his voice. Dead matter has overcome the spirit.

A putrid fever, on account of the humours, declared Dinsdale, raising his voice somewhat for the benefit of the onlookers.

My mother had closed her eyes in sheer weariness as their voices rose. Now both men moved away from the bed to get closer to each other.

Fiddlesticks! shouted Pendlebury. I defy you to show me your ridiculous humours. The universe is made up of inorganic materials. Man is in the universe. Ergo, man is made up of inorganic materials.

I deny your argument, spluttered Dinsdale. Man is made in the image of God. God is not made up of inorganic materials. Ergo, man is not made up of inorganic materials either.

I deny your argument, retorted Pendlebury. I suppose you would say – and his voice was mocking – that since man is made in the image of God then God too must be subject to the four humours, and likewise has meseraic veins bringing blood and chyle from the liver.

Dr. Dinsdale began to sweat and his face went a deeper shade of red. You blaspheme, sir! You know I mean no such thing. I mean only that the dead matter which is our flesh is made holy by the mystery of God, just as the bread is made into the body of our Lord by his Grace, which is likewise a mystery.

The bread remains only bread, answered Pendlebury with scorn.

Heretic! screamed Dinsdale, now quite beside himself with moral outrage. By this time half the household had found their way into my mother's bedchamber, attracted by the noise, and were listening intently. Dinsdale wiped his face, took a deep breath, and glared at the cool Pendlebury: Prove your argument.

Dr. Pendlebury stroked his forehead thoughtfully and looked round at the eager faces watching from the panelled corners of the room. There was just the hint of a smile on his lips, a touch of conscious superiority rather than a desire to play to the gallery.

The analogy and resemblance between the sacrament and the thing signified must be kept in all sacraments. In the sacrament of the Lord's body this analogy cannot be kept, if bread be transubstantiated. Ergo, the bread must remain bread.

A murmur of approval rustled through the room.

I would myself argue, continued Pendlebury, that since bread conforms to all matter in being made up of salt, sulphur and mercury, it could only be transubstantiated either by burning, or by being submitted to the *archaeus* of the stomach – in other words, by being eaten. Which, indeed, it is.

Loud laughter rocked the room. The door opened, with difficulty, as curious faces peered in and found themselves a place by squeezing up against the walls.

St. Augustine, declared Pendlebury, flashing his ruby ring in a gesture of triumph, says that the sacraments must bear a similitude to those things whereof they are sacraments, and without the substance of bread and wine there is no similitude.

Henry Dinsdale now found his voice. Christ said this is my body. He did not say this bread is my body.

Meaning this bread signifieth my body.

I deny your argument, thundered Dinsdale, banging his fist on the bedpost, so that the canopy shook. He looked round at the watching ring of faces, which now included not just the household, but a number of neighbouring clerics, who had heard that something was afoot. He raised his voice:

The same body is in the sacrament, which was given for us on the Cross. But bread was not given for us on the Cross. Ergo, bread is not given in the sacrament.

A murmur went round the room, which was now getting very hot and airless. There was an overpowering smell of sweaty bodies, of stale linen and boot leather. I could not see my mother's face, surrounded as she was by a crowd of people come to hear the disputation, but not a word or a sigh had been heard from her since it began. Several people were standing on the coffer for a better view of the two learned men, and one small boy had even clambered up the bed-hanging.

89

Pendlebury's mocking smile grew more obvious as he heard the last argument.

The body of Christ he said slowly, as though addressing himself to someone slow-witted, was broken on the Cross as a full satisfaction for the sins of the world. But the sacrament is not satisfaction for the sins of the whole world. Ergo, the sacrament is not the body of Christ. Moreover, whatsoever entereth in by the mouth goeth into the privy. Christ's body goeth not into the privy. Ergo, the sacrament is not the body of Christ.

Dinsdale shook his head. By this sentence is not meant all kinds of meat. For instance, not that which Christ ate after his resurrection.

Pendlebury laughed.

Since Christ sitteth on the right hand of God the Father, he cannot also be present in the bread of the sacrament.

Applause greeted this last rebuttal. During the noise that followed nobody but I heard my mother's serving wench, young Peggy, let out a cry.

My mistress has fainted, she squeaked. Some air!

She tried to force her way to the window, but the crush was too dense, and several people were perched on the window seats for a better view, blocking both light and air. Meanwhile the two doctors had moved very close to each other, oblivious of the bystanders, intent only on each other, heads lowered, glaring, like two rams about to engage horns. I doubt whether either had any recollection of why they had come here, or the origin of their dispute.

Then Dinsdale, his jaw set rigid with rage, spat out: Christ sitteth at the right hand of God the Father. But God the Father hath no right hand. Ergo, where is Christ now?

I could see young Peggy struggling to get to the window, but nobody heard her crying Help, my mistress has fainted above the din, half laughter, half jeering, as though the crowd no longer knew which side it was on. Only I saw her lips moving and read the message.

Burn a feather under her nose, I yelled, but I doubt whether she heard me.

Burn all heretics, growled Dinsdale, and began quoting St.

Cyprian, followed by the holy Chrysostom. I think he thought himself back at the university, for his tone changed, and he lapsed into long Latin quotations. I tried to push my way to the window, pleading for air, for someone to make way, but nobody heard me.

Christ, I heard Pendlebury booming behind me, never devoured himself. Christ did eat the sacrament with his apostles. Ergo, the sacrament is not Christ himself.

I do not know how long this disputation might have continued, or how my poor mother would have fared. I was still trying to push my way to the window whilst an argument had begun as to whether St. Ambrose had indeed written *De Sacramentis*, since St. Augustine's doubts on the matter were expressed in a text which had itself gone missing, when the bedchamber door opened and a great cry went up:

'The king is dead!'

The hubbub suddenly died away, and within a few moments the room was empty. A hush of fear seemed to come down suddenly, and I heard Pendlebury tell my father he would take ship abroad the very same night if he could. By the time I reached the window to give my mother some air I could see the first fires lit on a distant hillside.

It was dark now. Through the valley, between the trees, I could see bonfires flickering, dark figures moving across the flames. How quickly night comes now the summer is ended, falling so fast, it startles me. How quickly the summer has ended.

Dark times, hissed the fire, and it was not just books that burned. There was an end to childhood games, too, when Alice's husband was deprived of his benefice for falsely marrying a nun, though they had six children by now, and no way of providing for them. By this time the poor old man was half out of his wits and quite befuddled with not knowing what was required of him from this day to that, which book or which tongue, whether kneeling or standing, and some wanting one thing and some communion of another sort, so that when he was told that his wife was not his wife, and never had been, though she had nurtured him for six years and borne him as many children, he knew that his wits were turned and that he was not long for this world. After which he wandered off into the countryside, no one quite knew where.

And the games grew ugly too, with half the parish absenting themselves from mass, and afterwards a cat was found hanging from the lychgate with its paws tied together and a round paper like a wafer of holy bread stuck between them, and the fur of its head had been shaved off. And the village boys took to fighting each other and threw Sarah's idiot boy into the pond and wellnigh drowned him for not knowing the answer to the riddle of the mouse that ate the singing bread and whether the mouse was Christ or no. And some say that the new parson could not sleep at nights, for fear of those who hated his coming, knowing that a group of women had made a solemn vow not to receive the sacrament, and held to it, having also given food and clothing to Alice's children when they could. And on Easter Day somebody removed the crucifix and pix out of the sepulchre, so that when the priest put in his hand and said devoutly *Surrexit; non est hic*, it was so indeed, for the space was empty. And even those who had come to mass could not hold back from mocking laughter, and if anyone knew the culprit they chose to keep silent, in spite of the new priest's curse, and threats of excommunication.

Foolish pranks, said the voice from the fire, as a sudden gust of wind sent the flames wavering, and I shivered as a chill went through me. Smoke billowed, making my eyes smart. But God is a spirit, to be worshipped in spirit and truth.

There was silence for a while. All over the valley bonfires glimmered, glowing red in the dark.

And the spirit wins, sang the voice from the flame. I thought about going indoors to fetch a coat because I was cold to the bone, but nothing would have induced me to stir from the spot at that moment in time. The sky was quite dark now, with a cold sprinkling of stars.

I gazed into the heart of the flames.

They took me, whispered the voice, and asked me too many questions. I am the Way, the Truth and the Light, I said. Knowing that nobody can kill the spirit. This my mother taught me, after the books were taken off to be burned, and before. So when I was

92

taken out of the dungeon and asked whether the bread in the box were God or no, I told them simply: God is a Spirit, to be worshipped in spirit and truth.

Of course it was not my soul they wanted, I knew that. They wanted names, of those I served, they wanted proof of conspiracy, since great ladies had been known to bring food and wine to my prison, and some of those were known to serve, not the queen, but her sistersistersister sighed the voice from the fire. But I did want my soul, so I stood firm.

And when they asked me, if the host should fall, and a mouse eat it, whether the beast received God or no, I told my Lord Chancellor to answer the question himself, since he had taken the pains to ask it. Whereupon he said it was against the order of schools that he who asked the question should answer it. So I told him that I, being but a mere woman, knew nothing of schools.

And the Chancellor rebuked me for uttering the scriptures. St. Paul, he said, forbade women to talk of the word of God. So I told him St. Paul spoke only of teaching: how many women, I asked him, had he seen go into the pulpit and preach? So then, when I kept silent for several days, and they rebuked me for it, I told them that Solomon saith: A woman of few words is the gift of God.

There was laughter in the fire, it sang and spluttered. Bright sparks twirled in the smoke as the flame danced, and flew up into the dark sky, dimming the stars.

So they told me: I would burn burn burn.

And you said? I whispered in awe.

If it be so I will burn burn burn. Though I have searched all the scriptures and could not find that either Christ or his apostles put any creature to death.

I would burn burn burn, they told me, bishop, archdeacon, Lord Chancellor. For saying that a piece of mouldy bread was not the flesh and blood and bone of Christ. And I told them, if it be so, I will burn burn burn, though this is indeed my very flesh and blood and bone, for God is a Spirit, to be worshipped in spirit and truth, and the spirit you cannot touch, or kill.

It was very quiet, suddenly, in the surrounding dark. Not a breath of wind in the trees, no night birds calling, no dog barking far off in the valley. I threw a piece of wood on the fire. Tried to

93

think. Tried not to think. A twig cracked in the heat, and I heard bone bursting, flesh and bone being consumed with the spirit burning within. Willingly? Could this be done willingly? A spark touched my hand and I screamed. Though nobody heard me, I heard it.

But first they cracked my bones on the rack, whispered the voice. In the name of truth. It was only a broken body they brought to the stake, an aching burden I was glad to put down. I had to be carried, since I could not walk, but the spirit, the spirit was strong.

The wood was singing now, red-hot at the core. Stop stop, I wanted to cry, feeling my face beginning to burn, let me hear no more. But the fire roared and the singing voice within told how the flesh burned and the wheel of iron turned and when she lost consciousness they asked if she carried an unborn child within her, for then they might have spared her the rack. And the voice began to laugh, laugh in spite of the scorching flame, thinking of the mind of this man who would spare the unborn but not her, and pity her immortal soul, which had no need of it, rather than her poor aching body, which did. And all for their mouldy bit of bread. In the name of truth.

Ashes glimmered and turned white at the heart of the blaze. Dark shapes of trees wavered through flame and smoke.

The lords temporal and spiritual had all come to watch me burn, said the voice. They brought me in a chair to the market place, since I could not go on my feet, and put down gunpowder to make the end quick. But my Lord Chancellor was nervous of the gunpowder and had the seats of their lordships moved back from the pyre.

There was silence for a while, only a gentle hissing of embers.

Green wood is the worst punishment, said the voice. It burns too slowly.

And then: I would not give up my faith. It was all I had.

I know, I said. I can see that.

My eyes were smarting from smoke and heat.

But what about living?

Silence. The embers glowed.

I would like a happy ending, I admitted. Just now and then.

I know, said the voice, softly, almost mockingly. Think of Alice.

She got her husband back, old and confused as he was, and he got his living again, when the queen died without issue and her sister came to the throne. And though he had no notion of the correct order of service, when to stand and when to kneel, and whether the bread was a symbol or the thing itself, and sometimes he would lapse into Latin by mistake or forget to give the chalice to his parishioners, they stood by him loyally because he was old, and had suffered, and had a good wife, who was known for healing the sick, and would take no reward.

The night was very dark. I felt stiff and cold, and tired. No, not so much tired, as old. The fire was almost dead now. I poked about in the white ash, stirring a few last remnants of fire, a red glow which throbbed like a dying star.

No need to mourn, said the fire, though I was crying.

I found the crumpled page of a book which had somehow escaped burning. The edges were scorched, but I could still make out black letters printed on white.

No need to mourn, said the fire. I, Ann-of-the-fire, died to tell you this. The word feeds the spirit, and the spirit lives. This is the age of the word.

Four

It has just begun to snow. A slow, desultory fall of white flakes beyond the window from an opaque grey sky. For the past few weeks I have watched the year ageing bit by bit, from green to brown, from brown to grey, until trees turned to a skeleton and the bare fields were exposed as a dull patchwork, a chequerboard of furrowed earth and rough grassland between thin lines of hedgerow. Now only the evergreens are left, the hollybush dark, spiked and glossy, small bright berries, red as blood, spattering its density, and the snarled thorny tangle of hedges along the road. It draws the eye, this landscape, as the lush comfort of summer never did, and the mind follows, noting the muted shades and the logic of root and branch. Large birds scavenge the empty furrows, and the cry of the rooks is hoarse in the high treetops. And now it has begun to snow, slowly, large drifting flakes come down at intervals through the grey light from the heavy overloaded sky.

The chessboard stands on the coffee table between the two armchairs under the window, almost empty except for the few pieces needed to corner me. The old retired colonel from down the lane was in earlier and had little difficulty in finishing me off, though I gave him a run for his money first, and took several of his pawns and both bishops before I had to go on the defensive. He clearly enjoyed having someone, anyone, to play against, though I could tell he did not expect much of a game from a woman. So when I managed to avoid fool's mate and even had him on the defensive for a few moves he was pleased, told me how I had gone wrong, and suggested a return match next week.

He is interested in historic battles, strategy, that sort of thing, and when he is not reading about them likes to reconstruct what is supposed to have happened on his living room floor, using model soldiers and miniature cannon. He told me a little bit about this hobby over coffee. As a military man he is interested in the logic of armed combat, on which the course of history depends. He laughed somewhat ruefully, said he did not expect me to understand: nor did his wife, who grew roses. She regarded his reconstructions as a nuisance that cluttered her carpet, and said it was time he grew out of boys' games. And then he said, did I know that there had been several skirmishes in this area during the Civil War, and that the local manor house had been under siege for months? Since he retired from the army he had done a fair amount of reading, and even visited the local records office.

A far cry from the Normandy landings, he said. But it keeps my mind occupied.

So now we had come to it: the real topic. We skirted round it, tactfully, D-Day, the high point of his life, everything since a falling off, though the loss of life was dreadful. In three days he had lost his entire platoon. I mentioned my schooldays, how we had coloured in the map of France day by day, starting with a tiny red dot at Caen and following the daily advance with our crayons. I mentioned my father, away all during my childhood on active service, till I hardly knew what he looked like.

He will come by for a game of chess in a few days' time. Allow me my revenge, he said gallantly, and we both laughed. This is the first time he has been up to my house, though I first got talking to him over the garden fence in the summer, when I stopped to stare at their magnificent rose garden. His wife's roses, he told me.

It is dark now, but snowflakes are still falling: I can see their white ghostly shapes against the window. Before he left, the colonel advised me to lay in food. At least a fortnight's supply, he said. Tins, stuff for the freezer, a sack of potatoes. Once the snow starts in winter, you never know, he said.

I suppose he is right. Tomorrow I will drive into the village and get enough dry goods and tins to see me through a spell of bad weather.

I stared out of the darkened window, seeing my own reflection, dimly. Aunt Doris kept a supply of dry biscuits and chocolate in the cellar, in case of an air raid, but in all the months I stayed with them I never once heard an air raid siren. Ada and I would play games down there, using the 'secret' staircase hidden in the panelling, pretending to be Roundheads or Cavaliers hiding from the enemy as we munched biscuits and made cautious inroads on aunt Doris's tiny chocolate ration. Of course the secret staircase was really only the servants' back stairs, I know that now, and the cellar had always been used for storing things, but Ada and I thought the house was built for hiding people, and plots, because it was large, and rambling, and dark after nightfall, since it had no electricity. Only flickering candles, and the shadowy glow of an oil lamp pushing the darkness back into the corners of the room.

We could stay down here for weeks, said Ada, huddled in a cardigan too large for her, and nobody would find us. Imagine the enemy riding to the door, their horses' hooves clattering in the courtyard, and mum with her hands tied behind her back, and the officer in charge saying When did you last see your daughter? And I'd ride away in men's clothing, with spurs and a sword, and when it was safe I'd find the prince in the hollow oak where he was hiding and bring him back here.

Ada had an immense capacity for fantasy when it came to swashbuckling adventures. She wanted to dress up as a man, complete with big hat and curling feather, and ride off into the night. If I would be a maiden in distress, or captured by highwaymen, she would rescue me. Sometimes she would tie me up with a skipping rope and leave me alone in the dark, so she could come down and free me from dragons, or enemy soldiers or whatever, and I would stand in the dark, listening, hearing voices far off or, worse still, hearing nothing but my own breathing, my own heart beating, while I waited for her to find me. She took her time, I seemed to stand like that for ages, my heart beating faster with fright. Once I screamed out loud when I heard rustling, scrabbling sounds, and thought a rat was near me in the dark. Once she simply forgot to come back, or chose not to. Aunt Doris found me, coming down with a flashlight to fetch some stored potatoes. What on earth are you doing here, child? And she led me up the wooden steps, shivering, stumbling as bright daylight struck my face. But I refused to say anything, she thought I must be sickening of something, and afterwards, in bed, I cried for the first time, so homesick, I thought my heart would break. When did I last see my father? Months ago, for a few hours, looking like somebody else in his uniform, with his heavy boots and the rough khaki cloth that scratched my skin when he put his arms round me. And I had not seen my mother since she came down for the weekend and the train, she said, took hours.

I stared at the dim reflection outlined against the darkening window. I look now, I thought, as aunt Doris once did. Stocky, middle-aged. Ada, hearing me sob in the dark, though I tried to muffle the sound in my pillow, asked: what's the matter? And when she got no answer, said she was sorry, she quite forgot, she'd been sent on an errand and quite forgot. I'll make it up to you, she said. You can have my new brooch, the one with the scottie dog. And when I still did not speak: Cry baby, she said scornfully, and threw a pillow at me.

This morning there is a light dusting of snow over the entire landscape. Trees and hedgerows show up stark black or dark brown, and the sullen grey sky is full of more snow to come. I took the colonel's advice and drove into the village for supplies. As it was I had trouble starting the car, and the shop had already run out of candles and was hoping for a delivery some time next week. I bought a sack of potatoes and stacks of tins, baked beans mostly, but also some soups and a couple of cans of corned beef. Also enough flour to bake my own bread if it comes to it. During the drive back I had trouble getting up the hill: my back wheel started to spin and I had to wedge it with a stone before I could get going.

Once back indoors with the car unloaded I turned on the radio for the one o'clock news. Disruption on the railways from next week. Power cuts now a distinct possibility. Hospitals taking emergency cases only. And more snow forecast.

I made myself a cup of tea and stared out at the barren landscape with its thin covering of snow under a heavy grey sky. A sense of foreboding, of waiting, knowing such a dense sky could not hold off much longer, so that everything was unnaturally still: nothing moving, no birds singing. The pieces on the chessboard still stood with my black king cornered by two pawns and a knight, whilst, at the other end of the board, my two castles sat in the corners, having never been used at all. I thought about this for a while, then

100

arranged all the pieces, black and white, on opposite sides of the board, as if for a new game. Then studied the layout again. It was a long time since I had played with anyone, and if I was going to tackle the colonel again I needed to familiarise myself with the more obvious moves and pitfalls.

The telephone rings. Kate. Thank goodness something is still working, she says drily. She is in a thoroughly bad mood, since conditions at the hospital are getting intolerable.

We have to run the gauntlet of the picket line to get in. What's worse, so do the patients. Yesterday one of mine was in the second stage. Sheer luck she didn't give birth in the ambulance. All routine operations cancelled, meaning a lot of poor old women stuck in high-rise flats won't get their hip replacements. What, I ask myself, is it all for?

Those cleaners and people are very badly paid.

Kate was scornful. And d'you think they'll be any better off when this is over? My houseman works an eighty-hour week, and he's not on strike.

But then he's —

And I've had a row with Sally.

There was a short pause. So this was what it was all about: confession time. Ever since she was eight years old Kate had felt responsible for her sister, and would own up to me when they argued. I sighed.

What about?

This bloody dispute, of course. She thinks doctors and nurses should show solidarity for the low-paid ancillary workers currently on strike.

Well, she has a point.

Including strike action.

Oh dear. Surely not.

Through the window I saw a blackbird hop and stop, hop and stop on the thin layer of snow. Time, I thought, to start putting out crumbs and bacon rind. Kate's voice was still coming through the crackling line. As always, when she knew herself to be in the right, she became aggressively self-righteous. It was the price I paid, that we both paid, I suppose, for the fact that I relied on her so heavily

101

to keep the household going whilst I went back to work. It was Sally this, and Sally that, when all I wanted to do was shut my ears, have a hot bath, and sleep.

Of course you're right, I said wearily. But I'm sure Sally didn't mean it quite like that.

The blackbird outside had found a snail shell and was busily trying to crack it on a stone. To and fro it went with its beak, to and fro. How else did she mean it? Kate was storming down the line. I suppose she wants me to down tools and let people die? Can't these people see that they're only harming themselves, every time, that it's their own kind who suffer?

No, I don't suppose they can, I said sadly.

The blackbird had not succeeded in cracking the snail shell. Now my cat had come on the prowl, and the bird fluttered up into the nearest branch, just in time.

Make it up with your sister, I said.

She's a fool, stormed Kate. She's really upset me.

I can see that, I said. But you must remember, she's an idealist.

Meaning I'm not? Are you taking sides?

I laughed. The old sibling rivalry. My kids.

No, of course not. You're practical, the realist in the family. Where would any of us be without you? But Sally's your sister –

The times you've told me that. I could hear the tension in her voice going, and something like a dry laugh.

I know. But it's precisely because she's the idealist, with deeply-held principles and political convictions, that you should make allowances.

Meaning what?

Meaning, I said, that ideals are peculiarly vulnerable.

Kate laughed, heartily this time, her rage totally dissipated.

You're not half bad as mums go, she said, and hung up.

Sisters, I thought, remembering the arguments over territory, a corner of the bedroom for instance, the banging of doors and shouting, and how they would instantly close ranks and defend each other if I so much as scolded.

It had begun to snow again, slow thick flakes falling out of the upper density, drifting under their own lack of weight. I looked at the chessboard, the lines of pawns neatly drawn up, black and white, the two queens facing each other. So it must have been with those other sisters, Lady Lucy, Lady Sarah, with their husbands belonging to opposing factions when the fighting started. And another pair, Alice's granddaughters, with Jane still practising as midwife and healer as her mother before her with Emma's caul hung up in the chimney corner, and sister Susan up at the big house, cut off from the countryside for months as they prepared for siege. And who had the worst of it, when all was said and done? Neither would ever know, though they might argue about it afterwards, when the stories were told and retold.

The only thing no one could be quite sure about was how it had all started, though money came into it, and so did God. And the question was, somehow or other, that if God was on your side you were entitled to collect taxes, meaning money from the poor, and if God was not, then it was despotism. And so they fought to prove that God was indeed on their side, and not the other, since the Almighty never backs a loser. Something along those lines. The ordinary people, who had to pay the taxes, were never quite sure about the whole thing, and the only result they knew about was having to pay taxes to both sides while the fighting was going on.

So it was largely a fight between tax collectors, levying troops, or trying to, from the poor folk who had to pay, one way or the other, and usually in more ways than one. The bishops had a say in it, and the knights, as the king, the touchpiece, was shunted round the board, hiding in his castles, or those friendly to him, in a purely defensive position.

But the outbreak of scrofula, that they did remember, how no one had ever seen so many swollen lips and gummy eyes, such sores and blisters and swellings on the neck, and the despondency that struck the whole parish when the money was found to send the sufferers to London to be healed by the King, but the King had fled north, and could not be reached. And Lady Lucy's husband, Colonel Francis, away at the Parliament in London, sent back a message that it was all blind superstition, and that the King could not heal, since God was not on his side, and that they should trust in physic, and the new tobacco in particular, which his wife would dispense freely to those in need.

103

And the deaths were dreadful that winter, Jane reminded her sister, rubbing her hands by the fire.

She did what she could, sighed Susan, who had good cause to remember. She had helped Lady Lucy to prepare many a cordial, and distilled eye water in the big kitchen, and stirred orampotabile dissolved in cordus water, and boiled barley with liquorice, and hung a bezoar stone round a swollen neck as a special favour, though the sufferer was unmindful enough of the rarity of the gift to complain that it could not do the work of the King's gold coin hung round his neck as a talisman. And since he died two months later, he might have been right.

So Colonel Francis rode about the countryside, levying troops, and somehow all the villages round about had nothing but babes and old women in them, and young women who could not for the life of them say when they had last seen their husbands. Gone off to market, they said, or broke his back in a fall two summers since, God rest his soul, and he rode back to London with no more than a handful of fools and idlers, or those not quite right in the head, and that was the last time he was seen in the neighbourhood till it was all but over, though he was sheriff hereabouts, and owned most of the land, so the rent was due to him.

It was Lady Lucy who, for a while, saw to it that the rents were collected, while the Colonel, so folks say, was away in London, debating the issue in Parliament, and did not come home for months while the menfolk there were arguing in the longest debate that ever took place. But her ladyship was strict about rents and would allow no dues to fall behind, not for herself, but for the troop of horse of which he had taken charge. Three of her own horses had been sent up, together with a stableboy who would not come back, though he did not know it, since she gave him a note for her lord saying 'I do not trust this man. Use him there as you will, or he will surely serve the other side'. And since he could not read he did not think to break the wafer and read how he would surely become the King's man, but delivered the horses safely, and himself, and the letter, and served the Colonel with dumb devotion throughout the turmoils that followed, sleeping with his horse and caring for his mounts with a single-minded devotion it was hard to fathom, and the only time the Colonel ever heard him speak of the King was to say he had heard he rode the finest chestnut in Christendom, and he would give his right arm to see it, and he had told her ladyship as much, when she talked with him about taking horses down to London for her husband's troop.

But it was not only horses Lady Lucy had to send, with the odd man or two in search of adventure at a time when every man was needed to defend the house. Little by little she had to send her dowry of silver gilt plate, platters and goblets and a finely-wrought salt cellar, and though she spoke of wifely obedience and the will of God as Susan helped her to pack it up for the carrier, Susan could see how it troubled her, and that she did not obey lightly. She saw how she sighed as she fingered the pretty salt cellar for the last time before wrapping it in an old rag. Oh Susan, she said. And: I do not know how we will pay for this war once the rents no longer come in. And who is to collect them? And who will pay? And somehow Susan persuaded her to hide part of the household treasure, the rest of the plate and the finest dishes of all, those which had belonged to the Lady Elizabeth and were so rare and fine as to be used only for weddings and christenings, and the two women buried them in the cellar, wrapped in an old gown and two petticoats.

Outside the landscape looks like an empty chequerboard, white fields fringed with black hedgerows and stunted trees. No movement. Not an animal to be seen.

Lady Lucy would have had to begin laying in provisions at the big house, and prepare defences for a state of siege. She did so reluctantly at first, fearful not only for her own safety, being seven months gone with child, but anxious for the welfare of her younger children, Robin and Tom and Isabel, who were in the house with her. She wrote, more than once, while the Colonel was debating the issue, and the storm clouds gathered, that she might join him with the family, and come to London, for only there could she feel safe, but Colonel Francis invariably reminded her of her duty, which was to defend the house in his absence and send rents and provisions for the conduct of the war. Men too, insofar as they could be spared and were willing to serve their country.

105

And so she sent sides of venison and new shirts, puddings and fresh fruit, as well as horses and some of the best silver, and when he returned the carrier brought muskets, powder and shot. And once the storerooms were full to bursting with flour and bacon, salt butter and fish, enough provisions to last out a year's siege at least, the long avenue of oaks planted during the time of the Lady Elizabeth had to be felled in order to build a stockade. Trees that might provide cover for an enemy were cut down, and hedges torn up too, and a few high fences. Earthworks and trenches were dug round the palisade, and the only large firing piece, an antiquated drake, was put on a platform erected above the stockade. It was quite useless, since it could not be fired, but was placed in position to deter the enemy.

And all this time Lady Lucy continued to be fearful. Not a day passed which did not bring news of a servant stopped, of cattle stolen, or the park plundered of venison. Coded messages were intercepted, and the few rents that were still willingly paid were collected at the risk of life and limb. Worse still, she did not know whom she could trust, either inside the growing household, with its armed men, or beyond. And, though her husband wrote constantly that God was working His Will through their army and she had always shared his faith, both in principle and in her prayers, her waking moments were full of dread that someone might set fire to the barns, or steal the colts from the paddock, or, worst of all, that a single servant, whether man or maid, would turn spy for the enemy and creep through the defences during the night.

That was how Susan remembered it, under siege in the big house. She remembered Lady Lucy brought to bed at eight months, and the child dying after three days, and all the time her ladyship, sick and feverish, babbled of her firstborn, Master Edward, who had left his tutor at Oxford to become a captain of horse, and how this news had first brought on the pains, for no mother ever doted so much on a son, and she would send him apples from the orchard, and pigeon pies, and angelica root and liquorice for colds or sudden ague, and eye-water against too much study by candle-light, and bade him be sure to take enough exercise, and not eat too much fish, of which he was inordinately fond, and be sure to remember to pray for the good of his soul.

And all the time the pains were coming on she cried out for Edward, how he had left his tutor and his books to join in the war at the head of a troop of horse, on his father's side, on God's side, and yet she would have him by her side now, by his mother's side, she murmured, where a boy belongs, forgetting that he was a boy no longer, except in her fevered mind. And the maids bathed her privy parts in a decoction of chervil, boiled in water with honey and roses, and kept her in a darkened room for three days, to spare her weak eyes, and boiled plantain leaves for the fever, and so she should hear no noise they took the crying infant, a feeble girl, to another part of the house, and though they paced up and down the floor with it, night and day, and shushed it and rocked it, and though they gave it seven drops of blood from the navel after birth because it was weak, it would not cease its crying till the third day, when it had a sort of fit and died.

But Jane, midwife living on the other side of the palisade, and not called in for this particular delivery, remembered other things. Men hiding in the woods when the press gangs rode through. And rode out again, taking our best heads of cattle. Levies and free quarter for both sides, first one, and then the other. Roofs leaking, nettles running wild in uncut corn, and a few men drifting back at harvest time, having deserted. Others came back more slowly, minus an eye or a limb, who would never be fit for hard work again. I remember horses taken away, and widow Carpenter rocking herself by an empty hearth, year in, year out, after both her sons were taken, and did not come back. I hid flitches of bacon under the straw, and buried our grandmother's gold ring under the cabbage patch. And if her ladyship's steward got thrown in a ditch whilst trying to collect her rents, can you blame us, sister? For though Colonel Francis might say it was the Lord's work afoot, when he took the men off in his trained bands, and though the minister said we must rejoice that the Lord has showed himself so mightily to his people, so he told us on Easter Sunday, and on Easter Monday he kicked the constable into a ditch and dislodged two of his teeth for daring to ask for money to help the King, the truth was we were having to fund both sides in a war that was none of our doing, a quarrel not of our making, as the troops marched and counter-marched, raising levies at pistol-point, demanding free quarter, and taking our livestock with them, and fodder, and such dry goods as they could find. And our able menfolk, of course, those fittest to pull the plough when the horses were taken.

Sometimes, said Susan, stirring the embers of memory, messengers brought news of troop movements, or a carrier had been told of a posse comitatus no more than five miles off, and then for a while the house would come alive as men went for their muskets, and clambered up to the leads to keep watch, and scouts saddled their horses. And her ladyship would make sure the children were safe indoors, and had us prepare plasters and bandages for the wounded, and called us all in for a special prayer, till the rumours were proved to be false, or, more likely, the troops had simply moved off in another direction, since there was neither rhyme nor reason in their marching, and news never travelled fast enough, but it was old before it was heard, and not to be relied upon.

But most of the time it was stitching, shirts and more shirts, and scrubbing and baking and no chance for a little mirth, while Lady Lucy taught the children their alphabet, and saw to the stores, and gave physic to those that needed it. It was the menfolk who found the hours tedious, cooped up for too long in barns and outhouses, with nothing to do but wait. Quarrels broke out, and sometimes a brawl in the courtyard, and one man was shot in the arm and had his wound dressed by her ladyship, who asked the minister to preach a sermon on patience and brotherly love, and who halved the ration of ale thereafter.

The whole land a chequerboard. Marching and counter-marching, covering the same ground, once, twice, any number of times, from black to white, and back to black once more. A never-ending stalemate, after the opening moves, which are: knights prancing about on their horses, this way and that, from shire to shire; bishops coming out early in defence of the King but soon taken out of account by a couple of determined pawns; the Queen going abroad for assistance while the King castles himself into a

108

defensive position. Then what?

The old colonel, when not up on the stockade with the drake that nobody could fire, was teaching young Robin the rudiments of chess. It helped to pass the hours, and kept the boy, who was far too eager to join the men with a musket for his mother's peace of mind, out of mischief.

You have lost a pawn, he said reprovingly, when the boy moved forward rashly.

It's only a pawn, laughed Robin.

The colonel shook his head, but said nothing, and the excited boy brought out first one bishop, then the second, to cover the board from the sidelines.

A small audience had gathered by now. The minister, watching over the child's shoulder, shook his head. No bishops, he murmured, and laughed, as the colonel trapped and took them.

God, it seems, is not on their side, he growled. Always mind the pawns, my boy.

Flushed, slightly tearful, young Robin surveyed the board.

I've still got my queen, he argued. She's so powerful, she can go anywhere.

To France, I suppose, laughed the minister, catching the colonel's eye.

But the colonel did not laugh. Take care, he said kindly, noting that the boy was far from calm, his face a mixture of anxiety, excitement, and trembling eagerness as he fingered the queen. You may lose more than a pawn in defending her.

He showed the boy how to castle, to avoid an immediate check to his king, and the boy obeyed reluctantly, not wishing to go on the defensive. His knights leapt about the board to avoid capture, and one even took a castle, getting itself hemmed in quite uselessly as a result.

Meanwhile the colonel had been moving a single pawn forward step by quiet step, and Robin thought himself mighty thoughtful in keeping out of its way, so that nothing was captured, not even one of his own pawns, at risk at one point. And he captured a knight with his castle.

The colonel moved his pawn one more time and announced: This is now a queen.

109

But it can't be, protested Robin. How can a common pawn become the most powerful piece on the board?

Ah, but it can, if you don't stop it. And the colonel explained the rule.

Robin was nonplussed. Does that mean your pawn can take my king?

The colonel shook his head. It means checkmate. It means your king can't move, so you have lost. But nobody is allowed to take a king.

Why not? asked Robin. For a moment there was an uneasy silence. The colonel glanced at the minister, then cleared his throat.

Because the king is still the king, and must not be touched, he explained. It's the rule.

But that's silly, said Robin. If he's really lost. If it were my pawn, I'd take him.

Out of the mouths of babes, muttered the minister, as the disgruntled colonel swept the pieces off the board, and Robin felt the tears prick his eyes as his mother remarked: For shame on you, child, to talk so. And gave him a smart cuff on the ear from behind.

Later, he was to remember that blow on the ear. It was to be confused in his mind with other things, particularly his father's return from the war, though this must have occurred months afterwards.

Tonight we had out first power cut, which lasted four hours. I lit candles and sat staring out into the darkness. The candle flames, reflected in the darkened window, shone back at me, like ghosts from the past. Aunt Doris lighting a candle to make sure no German airman was hiding in the barn after we heard the radio. My mother putting a match to the ring of blue gas after the all clear sounded to make tea. Ada sitting cross-legged in the cellar, trying to see how long she could keep her gas-mask on, and knocking the candle over in its saucer when she attempted to walk about wearing it.

The darkness must always have held special fears. The men took

110

turns watching from the roof, but it was hard going, looking and listening into the dark. Sights and sounds could be deceptive, even a glow-worm could start the heart pumping and the crack of a twig, a rustling in the undergrowth might be anything, or nothing. Once, before the first siege began, when Robin had somehow persuaded Lady Lucy to let him stay up with the men on guard, they saw rows of lights begin to flicker in the glimmer of dusk, like will o' the wisps, and fired all night long without once hearing a return shot. And in the morning they found that the enemy had hung lengths of tow on the hedges, and lit them, before riding off into the night. And so we wasted much shot, said Susan.

And then, when the first siege began, it was really not what anyone of us in the house had expected, Susan went on. Days went by without a shot being fired. Messages were sent in every fourth day, with polite offers of credit and quarter if her ladyship surrendered the house, and were refused just as formally. But no horseman was allowed to come further than the first barricade, in case his mission was to spy out our forces.

One of our maids, young Rachel, offered to try and escape, so as to get a message through to the garrison in the nearby town, but was caught scrambling under a hedge and taken off to jail. And when a local man was sent to bribe the guard, they pretended to take the money but told her ladyship, so that night when the posse rode through the gate the shots rang out and two men were killed before the rest turned their horses and fled.

They hung the man for a traitor, after the war was won, added her sister bitterly. Poor fool. And all for the promise of seven years' free tenure of land, if the land should be theirs to give.

And then, quite suddenly, and without warning, they simply rode off one morning. We thought it was a trap for a while, and waited, but they really had gone. Some said they had ridden off to engage with the enemy marching in from the west, whilst others thought they were running from them, since no battle occurred, but the likelihood of troop meeting troop was always slim, communications being what they were. By the time anyone heard that a troop was on the way from the north-east and men were sent out to meet it, the likelihood was they had veered off to meet or avoid another troop, which might also have changed course.

It could have gone on for years.

It did go on for years.

It's a wonder it had an end.

We thought at first it would have no end.

Everyone got tired of it, the comings and goings. Men were enlisted, and re-enlisted for the other side, several times over.

The second siege was much like the first, except that the church was fired.

We could hear the horses screaming in the flames. They must have known it was used for stabling.

The women had a song that year, trying to get the harvest in without their menfolk. You could hear them in the fields, the humming sound spreading with the swish of the sickle, bent backs with babies strapped to them now and then, but faces hidden:

> *Poppies flow in the standing corn*
> *They took my man when the babe was born*
> *Now winter is come and the land is shorn*
> *Which is the rose, and which the thorn?*

Nobody knew how the song started, but it spread through the ripening barley like wind stirring the high dry stalks, whispering through the brittle ears which swayed and rippled in the breeze.

And then my lady's sister, the Lady Sarah, whose husband had supported the King and was now fled to France, came to stay, since her house had been taken by our troops and all their land sequestrated. And she was big with child when she came, with only the clothes she stood up in, and a maid who frighted us all by her tale of plunder and burning when the army arrived, how they had ripped out hangings and carvings, and taken pictures from the walls, and flung platters and candlesticks into a sack before every manjack and maid was driven out of doors in the night to watch the fine old house razed to the ground by fire.

And some in the house thought the Lady Sarah was not quite right in her wits, for she would laugh rather than weep at her misfortune, a dry hard cackle that came out of the back of her throat as she paced the rooms with her swollen belly, and would turn her mind neither to prayers nor sewing, nor teaching young

Isabel her stitches, and when young Robin set up the chessboard she laughed at him, and would not play, though she knew the moves as well as any man in the house. And though Lady Lucy felt pity for her plight she found it hard to bear her nervous, restless presence, the way she would pace up and down, up and down for what seemed like hours at a time, rubbing her swollen belly and murmuring 'Sister, sister, what folly' and mock the minister to his face when he spoke of providence and the arm of God wielding his sword; and when the message came through that her brother-in-law Colonel Francis had been purged from the House and imprisoned by his own side, by the army, since the army was now in control and the Generalissimo's word was law, her laughter became loud and fierce, so the minister thought her hysterical on account of her condition.

What of the arm of God now, she gasped. Has he not shown his power?

And she laughed so hard and long, holding her sides with the pain of the stitch in them, that Lady Lucy, in spite of her own distress at the news of her husband's arrest, was anxious for her sister, fearing she might bring on the birth too soon, and begged her to go to her chamber and lie down, and she would bring her a few drops of laudanum.

Lady Sarah shook her head, wiped the tears of mirth from her eyes, and tried to catch her breath.

Sister, sister, I truly am sorry, she gasped, and offered to join her in prayer. But even as she spoke the titters broke out of her like a demon who would not be still.

And there's no doubt in my mind, added Susan, that if it had been one of us and not her ladyship's sister that the Devil would have been in her, and no mistake. But her ladyship did not believe in such stuff, saying it was all nonsense, and that witch-hunters like Matthew Hopkins should be hanged for persecuting poor harmless women.

And when Colonel Francis rode home at last he was like a ghost of his former self, with his hair quite white and the bones sticking out of him, and his eyes so deep and dark in their hollow sockets as could frighten the soul out of your body, and young Isabel began to cry when she saw him, for she had not the least notion who he

113

was, her being so young and him away so long, and his hands shook as though with the ague as he reached out for her, so she shrieked with terror, and hid her face in my lap, and would not be calm for all my shushing.

And I saw the tears run down his face, and when her ladyship tried to make the child come to him he said nay, nay, leave her be, and sighed, and listened while Lady Sarah tried to divert him with the fable of the lion and the ass, how the ass asked the lion to win him a bigger share of the oats, and how the lion took the lion's share at last, including the ass too, for his dinner. And she laughed, and the children laughed with her, having heard her tell the tale before, and Robin, who laughed loudest, and stood near his mother during the telling, got a blow round the ear for his pains, without knowing the why or the wherefore.

But Colonel Francis drew the boy to him, and young Tom too, and reproved her ladyship for being harsh with the boy. For he is not to blame if he has an ass for a father. And your sister has not lost her wits, though she has lost all else in this war, for which I am truly sorry.

And he told how he had tried to stop the sequestration of her husband's lands, and her house being burned down and its valuables sold.

But, he said, now that the usurper, the Antichrist, that foul idolator, has absolute power, reason and justice have flown out of the window.

Is it the King you speak of? asked Robin.

And got a third cuff on the ear from his mother.

Sisters, said Susan. That night I heard them argue, Lady Lucy and Lady Sarah, for the first time ever in all the months they were cooped up in the same house together, and I think Lady Lucy could not forgive her sister for her husband's white hair and hollow eyes and his look of an old man, no, for looking like the ghost of an old man. And I could hear her shrill voice berating her for having told such a fable of the lion and the ass, knowing as she did how it would be heard, so she had struck her own child and won the reproof of her husband when she would have wept for pity at the sight of him and could scarcely bear the pain within her. And the two voices rose and fell, carried down the stairwell, echoed in the rafters, one high, one low, rising and falling in counterpoint, until a stillness suddenly descended on the house and the minister, knocking on the chamber door, entered to find them weeping with their arms round each other.

More snow. Even before I drew the curtains this morning I was aware of a subtle change in the light. And in the quality of the silence. Telephone lines seem to be down, and are unlikely to get repaired unless the union decides to make a special exception for elderly women in remote country areas. The railways are also not running, I hear on my battery-operated radio.

It was a bad harvest, with a worse winter to come, Jane reminded her sister. Those men who did come home limped on crutches, crippled, weary or blind. And Jake Fletcher turned coat three times to get himself back for the reaping. Old man's beard hung on the hedgerows, and the barns were half empty. Children were born weakling, and took sick easy. Women picked ivy berries for fear of another mouth to feed, or boiled fresh roots of rue and drank and drank until the cramps and vomiting started. Annie Taylor, with a sick cow and four mouths to feed, and her man taken off to fight, died of the savin.

Men came to the house, recalled Susan, demanding money which my ladyship had already paid. And Colonel Francis would have run them through with his sword if Lady Lucy and her sister and the minister had not held his arms between them, for he was in a towering rage at their insolence, but my ladyship said she would not have men killed in her presence, and with her sister in her condition, and the men took themselves off. And Colonel Francis slept neither day nor night, but rode round the defences, and mustered more men from the neighbourhood to defend the house, not, he said, against one army, but against both, and on those terms he found men willing enough, for indeed, of the men still able-bodied in the neighbourhood, most had already armed themselves against all comers, and would allow no troops to come through, refused pay of any kind, and beat up stragglers from either side if they were foolish enough to ride through the lanes.

And then, said Jane and Susan with one voice, it began to snow.

Small flakes tumbled out of a grey sky, blinding the men on watch as they stood on the leads.

Large flakes drifted to earth, blocking the mouth of the drake which would not fire, and filling the trenches.

It snowed until the palisade became invisible and the stockade was buried in deep drifts, useless, unnecessary.

Snow caught in the rough texture of bark, snared in fences and brickwork, covered the windows.

It snowed until the old man's beard was thick with it, and the hedgerows half buried.

Until only bright holly berries were visible.

And squirrels scampering on garden walls.

Clawmarks, the footprints of wild animals imprinted on smooth white each morning.

And silence. No sound but the weight of it sliding from the roof.

And Lady Sarah's time had come.

There was a pause.

We knew, said Susan, that her time was come, for it was nine months, almost to the day, since her lord had fled to France.

But the pains would not begin.

Sister, said Lucy, anxious at the small stubborn swelling, and made me serve her roasted apples with sugar to keep her body loose. And she herself boiled mallows with honey enough to sweeten it, and a spoonful of white salt for a glister, but the Lady Sarah shook her head, and smiled, and said the child would come in its own good time, and she could feel it kick well enough inside her, though it seemed so small.

And she began to laugh.

I see nothing to laugh at, sister, replied her ladyship, who knew enough of lying-in to know it a serious business, and sat her in a bath up to her navel with hollyhock leaves and roots, mugwort, marjoram, mint, camomile, linseed and parsley, and put a bag of herbs to her navel and a second for her to sit on, though she was laughing the while with her head wreathed in steam as though

116

fumes of opium had addled her wits, and when you anointed her privates with ointment made of hollyhock roots, fenugreek seeds, butter, quince kernels and gum tragacanth with hen's grease she began to laugh so loud that you thought her ticklish, for in all my born days I had never heard a woman laugh so when her time was near, nor Lady Lucy neither. Weep, yes, pray, often, but laugh?

And we continued the baths for two months, week in week out, and the anointing of her privates, and though the child leapt within her it seemed unwilling to take the last leap and come into the world, which Lady Lucy found wondrous strange, for neither garden tansy nor the eaglestone would draw it out, and yet, that it was living there could be no doubt, for she and you both had felt it quicken under your palms, and Lady Sarah, far from having slack breasts and a cold belly, was fit as a fiddle and full of some hidden mirth, and her breath not stinking, which is a sure sign of a dead child, but sweet as honeysuckle when the laughter broke out of her.

She laughed when she heard the eaglestone rattle, and said that from little eaglestones do mighty vultures grow, and sighed, and said: think on it, sister. And, when Lady Lucy brought her a cup of garden tansy ale and told her she would give birth to an heir yet, she laughed so loud that the men could hear her in the stableyard and the maids in the kitchen, and Lady Lucy, thinking of the house burnt to the ground and the very lead from the roof sold off and her lands all taken, could have bit her tongue off for having spoken thus, and said so, but her sister just smiled and shook her head, and said:

No matter, no matter.

Besides, she added, it might be a girl. For in all the bathing and anointing that had gone on for the past six weeks no one could say for sure whether it lay on the right side of the womb, signifying a boy, or on the left, for sometimes it would lie on one side, and at times on the other, and mostly it was plumb down the middle. And as you know, sister, what are girls heir to but sorrow and pain?

And all this time the snow had been falling, softly and silently, both day and night. It covered the tracks of the battleground, and buried the graves of the men who had fought and died.

It muffled the countryside in silence, and made all movement impossible. Carts stopped in their tracks, messengers rode into deep drifts, burying their horses utterly. Markets, already disrupted, were cancelled, and troop movement stopped. A hush fell over the land, so profound, that men heard their thoughts for the first time in the stillness, clear as the call of a far-off bird or the cry of a child in the night.

And the light changed too. Walls appeared to become transparent, so thin in the bluish light that they seemed to float. The windows were covered each morning in a crystal lacework of fern fronds which glittered in a pale sun when it stopped snowing for a time. And the long icicles would drip and gleam and lengthen, only to freeze harder than before. And our faces, too, seemed to become more translucent, as though you could see our souls through the flesh.

Lady Sarah held her hands to the light and saw her thin bones through the skin.

Aaah she cried, as she felt the first spasm, and her pale hands clutched at her sides.

Her cry shattered the ice in the washtub, and set the icicles tinkling. A mirror cracked in her chamber, and Lady Sarah looked, startled, into her sister's face and saw herself reflected there, in the pale skin stretched over skull and cheekbones, in the wide eyes now full of alarm, ice blue in the snowy light.

Sister, she said: I think it is beginning.

And I saw Lady Lucy, pale as death, help her to loosen her clothes with her hands trembling, and lead her towards the bed, and sure enough, on the spot where she had stood when she held her hands to the light, was a wet pool on the waxed floorboards, showing the waters had broken.

And, sister, when I knelt on the floor to mop it up I came over queer, for in that cloudy pool I saw a white face with a black hole for a mouth and two black holes where the eyes should be and nearly cried out in fear, till I saw it was only me in the murky fluid, and that was but little comfort.

And when you came into the chamber you said this is no ordinary child, meaning it had taken wellnigh a twelvemonth, but still it was living, for you could feel it stirring when you wet your hand in warm water and rubbed it on her belly, no larger now than if it had been a seven-month child, and the blue veins stood out on her white skin as you stroked her belly to bring the child downward, and spoke cheering words to her, for her eyes were dark as death with the fear in them, and her lips trembling and white as the sheets on which she lay, or the snow beyond the window.

And we put pillows to her back and head, a larger pillow to her buttocks, and splayed her legs with the knees wide and both feet pressed to a board across the bed. And two of us lifted the swathe band under her thighs when the throes came, while two more held her down by the shoulders to help her push. And the sweat stood out on her forehead and ran into the roots of her hair, and she begged for us to open the window wide and bring her a handful of snow to cool her, and though you refused her in the first instance, and the second time too, saying what harm it could do, when you saw her turn her head away from the bowl of chicken broth, and begin to puke at the sight of the poached egg, and refuse even to sip the wine that kept all our spirits up through the day and following night, then you told me to open the casement and do as she bid us, for there was no gainsaying a woman's whims in such extremity, for mother and child were like to die if it came not soon, so if its eyes and hair were white and its body cold as ice, what matter?

And so I went to the window, which I opened wide, and a gust of cold air blew into the room, and sent the hangings flying. And I saw a new sickle moon in the sky, hanging up there in the inky blue for some frosty harvest, and a scattering of icy stars in the dark, shining hard and clear as diamonds, and beneath the dark sky, in the sharp light of the new moon, a frozen world with fields of snow and white hedgerows and stark branches of trees all glittering like cold crystal. And I took a handful of snow from the sill, and felt how it burned my palms and left them stinging, but she took it in both her hands with a gasp, which might have been pain or pleasure, I know not which, and opened her mouth to suck on it, and rubbed her face and neck and breasts with it, and her lips that were pale before turned blue, and though her white fingertips began to shrink and shrivel, and the cold wet soaked into her shift so her nipples showed stiff and purple through it, and she began to

119

shiver and thrust, thrust and shiver, so fast that we could not hold her, and her hands like ice though you tried to rub life back into them, and bade me shut the window and stoke up the fire no matter what she might say, for she was out of her wits for sure, as she turned up her head, gasping, and I saw the whites of her eyes as though she had entered some dark world of her own, and could hear nothing that was said to her, but only her own screams coming from far off, and obey no will but her own, the will of her body shivering and thrusting, and then, suddenly, before you had time to apply oil of lilies, the child's head appeared in a forest of dark hair, and the small body slithered out, and its first cry was heard in the sudden stillness.

Five

It has begun to thaw. Slowly, day by day, the snowline in the garden recedes, turns from soft limpid crystals to water as the ground re-emerges. How dark it looks, how sombre, with the covering of snow diminishing, dirty now with smut and twigs and unidentified motes, the surface pockmarked with water dripping. Sometimes the surface freezes overnight, to shine like a glassy crust in the morning sunlight, and then it turns soft and mushy once more, and withdraws a little further, leaving the ground exposed and dishevelled, quite unprepared for a new day and another season.

Water drips from the branches of trees, and snow slides noisily from the roof. A damp patch has appeared on my bedroom ceiling, and the bathroom window is jammed. I went up into the roof space with a torch and found water dripping steadily into a pile of old sacking, already soaked through, and under it a heap of old papers, also damp. A plastic bucket and an old zinc tub left behind by the previous owner took care of the leaking roof. I threw away the sacking and spread the papers out on the living room floor to dry.

The telephone rings. The lines are working again for the first time in weeks. Kate.

Are you all right?

Yes, fine. But the house is not so good. The roof is leaking, amongst other things.

Talking of houses, I think I've found something. It's quite large, four floors, and it's a bit dilapidated. But I think I can get a grant, and I could rent off the basement as a self-contained flat, that would help pay off the mortgage. The area's a bit seedy, but it's going up in the world, and it's very convenient for the hospital.

Sounds like a good idea.

It is. But it will need a lot doing to it. Rewiring, damp course, new floorboards. And central heating, of course. I'll have to convince the bank manager.

I had been thinking while she spoke.

What about the basement . . .

What about it?

Would it do for Sally?

There was a long silence.

You know she has to get out of that dreadful place she's in anyhow. It's due for demolition.

Another long pause. I took a sudden decision.

I can let you have some capital to do up the house, if you let Sally and the kids have the basement.

As a loan, you mean?

As a gift. I've been wondering for a long time how I could help her. The thought of those kids growing up in that dreadful slum of a house gives me nightmares. I'm not saying give her the flat, of course, just let her have security of tenure at a rent she can afford.

All right. I'll think about it. Sounds like a sensible idea. You'll have to convince Sally, of course.

I'll talk to her.

I felt pleased with myself. Finding a way of helping her that I could afford had kept me awake at nights. At times I scare myself silly with visions of Emily catching pneumonia in that damp bedroom, or little Adam falling through rotten floorboards, tumbling down the area steps where the iron railing is missing, or falling down those dreadful stairs.

Meanwhile, my own little house would need money spending on it. I climbed up into the roof space with a dry bucket. It made me think of my mother during the war, bombed out twice while I was down here with aunt Doris, finishing up in that dreadful little house where the roof never stopped leaking and the pipes burst every winter, so when I went home I was always picking my way through an array of buckets and enamel basins and the odd saucepan laid out at strategic intervals on the floor.

122

Outside, the countryside is transformed. Fields of snow have turned into fields of mud, and marshy bogs are everywhere. As the snow melts, the river rises, and many fields are lying under water. I managed to get the car down to the village for the first time, to buy in some supplies, and heard of trees washed away by the roots, and several low-lying houses flooded. As for the bundle of papers I found in the attic, they have begun to dry out. The ink is quite brown, and only a shade darker than the paper, but the hand-writing seems legible enough, though I do not know if they are supposed to come in any sort of order. I had to peel the pages apart in order to dry them out, and they are not numbered. I picked up a page and began to read at random:

After the great snow, she told us, came the great thaw, and that was the time when everything began to change in these parts. It was just after Lady Sarah gave birth to a girl, whom they named Charlotte Maria, that the snow started melting, and though we was glad of it at first, as icicles dripped away in the warm sun, and the road to market was open at long last, we had to wade ankle-deep in our pattens across the courtyard to get to the cows, and we was always wringing our skirts out and trying to dry them in front of the fire. But then the lower pastures got flooded, and the river kept on rising, and flooded the houses, and sitting on high ground, safe and sound, we saw how it turned into a torrent, till it swept away age-old furniture that had stood in them houses as long as anyone could remember, trivets and bolsters and old oak chests, along with pewter mugs and platters and iron pots.

I had heard tell of the great flood from Jack's mother, who sure knows how to tell a good tale, and she could remember when the mere beyond the wood was full of fish which would keep poor folk alive in a bad year, roach and dace and silver-coloured eels, and my own mother too remembered how they used to collect free peat from the bog in boats till the mere was drained and fenced off and the peat sold at eight pennies the yard and carted away on a stone causeway. And how when the woods were cut down they lost their free feeding of hogs, and then part of the common too, and how hard it got, not just to collect firewood, but the herbs they used for their remedies.

My Jack has a lease on that land now, I told her, and he pays good money for it. And then the poor soul begins to cry, and her daughter unable to comfort her. I never thought I'd come back here to die, she sobs, and I gave her some hot broth to comfort her, the poor old soul, and tucked the shawl I had brought from the house round her thin shoulders that shivered and shook, though whether from cold or sorrow it was hard to know.

My man be a good man, I told her, but he don't like beggars, so I'll have to come by and bring you things when he don't know nothing about it. And she began to sob again something terrible, so it broke my heart to hear her, and Abby was fair shook up too, I could tell, for the sloppy girl was snuffling like anything.

But she be a good girl, hiding my writing for me in her room so Jack will know nothing of it, and she never so much as batted an eyelid when I told him the dog got the ham we gave to those poor vagrants.

The telephone rang. It was Sally, to thank me. She and Kate have been talking about my offer, and have decided to come to some sort of arrangement, provided I really mean it.

Of course I mean it. I only wish I could afford to do more.

Don't be silly. Sally's voice sounds tearful. You've done everything. Where would either of us be without you? I just hope I can do as well for my two. I can hear her sniffing quite loudly now.

Of course you will.

And to change the subject I told her about my leaking roof, and the flooding down in the valley.

I put down the receiver, thinking how, ever since childhood, Sally had been the one to turn on the waterworks. Kate so controlled, perhaps too much so, and Sally vacillating between rage and tears. She manages well with the kids, all things considered, but I sometimes wonder how far I am to blame for the way things have turned out. Would she have married Geoffrey, or someone like him, and would it have made any difference if she had? I put a kettle on and stared out at the brown barren landscape, thinking thoughts I had gone through many times before, and for the hundredth time came to the same conclusion. I doubt it. And in any case, I am not to blame for her childhood, the lack of a father, the lack of economic support, my having to work full-time. If that was her lesson in life, so be it. And Kate is its product too, in her different way.

I took my cup of tea into the living room and got down on the floor to have another look at the papers spread out on it. I picked up a sheet stained brown with water:

> To cure a calf of fever: a spoonful of crushed pansy seeds, one of parsley chopped fine, two eggs and a measure of cream, all beaten up with hot water and a glass of brandy.

And further down the page, after a few lines made illegible by water:

> Abby and me know how to get round my Jack, and humour him. And nothing do put him in such a good frame of mind as some of my lemon pudding and a glass or two of my homemade wine, and I have a good store from last year of dandelion and fuzzy wine. And now that the spring is here Abby and me will go to the woods to pick primmy roses for wine-making, which I makes with lemon and ginger, six sticks of cinnamon, and eight pounds of white sugar. You need two bags of primmy roses, a quarter of brandy, and then keep it in a cask for a year with two clean eggshells.

I was not sure whether I was dealing with a recipe book, a journal, or some attempt at story-telling. I picked up another sheet, brown, brittle, but untouched by water:

> They do say it was Lady Lucy's youngest son, Tom, who made his fortune in sugar. The stories they did tell about him, how he was always the wild one, and fathered a child in the village when he was scarcely fifteen. By the time he was eighteen the boast was he could drink any man under the table and still go hunting next day. Some say it was his gambling habits that forced his brother to enclose the last bit of common, which he was able to do with no trouble, him being the sitting Member of Parliament for the borough, but there be them who say he would have done

125

it anyhow. But it was after he killed a man in a duel that he got shipped out to the colonies, to come back a rich man. So rich that when he married his cousin, Charlotte Maria, he brought back a little black boy to wait on her, all dressed up in blue satin, with a turban of yellow silk on his head, and he walked behind her to church, and carried her prayer book with his hands in white gloves.

There be no black boy up at the big house now, but I once saw a black man at the market fair, who juggled and swallowed fire. And a Performing Dog that could spell any word from letters laid out in front of him. I never saw the Learned Pig that came round after, which some say was better than the dog, being big with child at the time, and Jack thought I was not fit to travel all that way in the cart. But now we have our own chaise, and I sit as fine as any lady, in my pink silk with the parasol, and last Michaelmas we saw the Female Automaton, the like of which I never saw before, the strangest sight of all surely, with her wax bosom going up and down as though she truly was breathing, under a blue canopy with yellow stars on it. And when the man spoke to her she opened her eyes, and sort of sighed, and real tears ran down her painted cheeks.

Nobody knew then, or knows to this day, why Master Tom should have come back so rich and married his cousin, unless it was that she happened to be around at the time and still unspoken for. For they do say she was no beauty, on account of her nose, but for all that she was tall and graceful and had read all the books in her father's library, which frightened the men off, for she made no secret of it. But she could ride to hounds better than any man in the neighbourhood, leaving them miles behind in some ditch, and Tom I reckon, having been such a harumscarum from a boy, must have liked that. And at night, when the candles were lit, she could make everyone laugh with her witty tongue, and when they were tired of laughing she would make them smile with the songs she had learned to sing at her spinet, so nobody minded that she always won at whist, or the odd shape of her nose. And some do say it was forceps at birth that did it, but I know for a fact that be a lie, for it was my very own aunt Jane that helped bring her into the world, and no

126

woman was allowed to handle them devilish things, as she called them, unless they smuggled some man-midwife into the room in the half-dark with his head and arms under a sheet, to fool her, and spare her modesty, which they did sometimes, but not if my aunt Jane could help it.

After he married his cousin, what with all his money, there were big changes at the house. Some I saw for myself as a child, and what I did not see with my own eyes I heard tell in the village, for everyone was agog with it. Floors inlaid with black and white marble, in a fancy pattern, all regular, and walls hung with dark red silk in some rooms, blue or pale green in others, and huge mirrors above marble fireplaces that reflected the light of gilded and crystal chandeliers so it dazzled your eyes. They took out the old casement windows and put in new sash ones, and the old oak furniture was chopped up for firewood or put up in the attics for the servants to use, and they sat on chairs covered with damask with thin spindly legs and put their fine china cups on tables inlaid with rosewood and cherry so delicate that a man could no more put a tankard of ale on it than piss in the church pew, as my Jack said when I did up the front room in like fashion.

And after they had done up the inside of the house, they had to be doing fancy things to the outside, so they clad it all over in white brick, and put up a portico with big columns. And they even turned the gamekeeper's cottage into a temple, which some say made him go funny in the head, so he thought himself God Almighty and killed two poachers with his blunderbuss, including my uncle's cousin who had come back from the wars with little to show for it but a blind eye and two fingers missing. And afterwards he was found in the woods with a knife in his back and his eyes wide open, and nobody hanged for him, since nothing had been seen or heard, not a sign, not a whisper. There was a lot of grumbling, though, in them days, and I remember some of it from my childhood, how some folks with so much money to spend were not satisfied with the land as the good Lord had made, but must needs improve that too, for once the house was as grand as could be his lordship decides that the land itself must be changed, and turned into a landscape, not for use,

127

but to be a vista from the house, and it was like the great thaw all over again, with pastures flooded to be a lake, and earth moved, whole slopes carted about to flatten one place and make a hill in another, and the place where the old stockade had been during the siege became a ha-ha, the oddest name I ever did hear, and I was told as a child that it was because of the Lady Sarah, who could not stop laughing, and small wonder, knowing it was all for nothing, and now they have more than ever they did in the old days. And though the men were happy enough to be paid sixpence a day to dig drains in place of the old ditches, and put up fences by Act of Parliament, and cart earth about for what seemed no more than a whim, and build a road for her ladyship's fine new coach, I know, for my mam told me, that the womenfolk grumbled from the start, for where shall we get our simples they said, as the fences went up and the old hedgerows came down. For with them went bramble and honeysuckle, dog rose and scabious, raspberry and hawthorn, the hips and haws and cures that we know about. And the grumble grew to downright anger when the entire village was moved, for with the old trees down and the new ha-ha the master could see the houses from his new sash windows and found them not to his liking, and though he built two rows of new houses half a mile to the left where he could not see them the womenfolk had nothing good to say of their new houses, all neat as a new pin and set in a row, for the chimneys smoked and the windows rattled. There was trouble with the water too, it tasted salty and ran dry in the summer, and some of the children took sick and died. Everyone was sure the water was to blame, for the best and purest water had all gone into his lordship's fine new lake, which was not for use but only for looking at from the house, where it mirrored a fine stand of oak and ash newly planted, but was out of bounds for the likes of us.

And then the work ran out for those as had done the heavy work, digging and carting, though there was still money to be made by those that knew about planting trees and building waterfalls, though most of them came from other parts, and the menfolk found, what they should have known from the start, that with the land enclosed and no call for their labour, that nothing now was to be had for free, neither grazing, nor wood for the fire, nor fish from the stream, not even so much as a rabbit for the stewpot. And it was then that the great exodus began, with men taking to the roads with naught but a few coins sewn into their jackets to look for work and wages, and it was mostly the womenfolk who got left behind, to mind the babes and grow such food as they were able, and eke out a living in the winter months with spinning and stocking-making.

I unpeeled two pages which had stuck together with damp and read:

Mistress Clary did show me how to make tuckers out of old-fashioned ruffles. We did cut the lambs' tails today, and I made pies the way my mother used to, stewed very slow and then baked with layers of sliced apples and parsley.

I was interrupted by two men come to inspect the roof. The damage not as bad as I might have expected, just a few tiles. Then Kate telephoned. She is putting in two bathrooms, new wiring and central heating, but the old fireplaces are to stay.

I'm having an open-plan kitchen on the ground floor, she said, then paused. I've had an argument with Sally.

Oh dear.

She was over here so we could go through the plans together, and she started asking me about who had lived here before, and so I told her about old Mr. Hobbs being a tenant, and how he had been put into a home. And the next thing I knew she was accusing me of exploiting the system, meaning, I suppose, the improvement grant, and making some poor old boy homeless. Mother, he was ninety-four!

Kate sounded aggrieved. I heard the echo of old quarrels in her voice, the nights when I came home late and had to arbitrate about some minor dispute over who had or had not done what they ought to have done, usually the washing up or tidying the bedroom.

Oh dear, I said. And added: Never mind. You know Sally.

Kate sighed. I'm not sure this is going to work.

Of course it's going to work, I said briskly. It's got to.

*

Took my first walk today, in rubber boots. Everything very muddy, and the lower fields still waterlogged. The earth looks dark, heavy, incapable of growth. And yet I saw one or two celandines, pale stars of yellow, showing up under the blackened hedgerows.

After some tea I went back to reading the loose sheets of paper from the loft. It got dark beyond the uncurtained windows as I held them under the soft ring of light from the lamp.

Jack being gone to market, Abby and me took some pies to them poor women hiding out in old Nat's house. And I told them how we had thought there was ghosts in the place, seeing how old Nat had been dead less than a year, and him known for being a cross old stick who swore something terrible. And it's lucky for you in a way, I says, for the whole neighbourhood thinks the house be haunted, and if you lie low in the daytime, no one will turn you away.

So the old one says bitterly: My name be in the parish register, how can they send me away? And I thought she was a bit turned in her wits, poor thing, so just to warn her I says: Oh can't they just, and told her how last year they moved a poor woman already far gone in labour so her child should not fall a burden on the parish, and looks at her daughter who be seven months gone for certain sure, and the girl looks frightened enough as I told her, and, I added, even if it be true, they'd be asking who your man was, and where he come from, and what sort of work, any old thing so the babe won't fall to the parish. And we'll manage as best we can, I added, looking at the girl's swollen belly.

And then the old one tells me how her mother had been a midwife, and her mother before that, and that for as long back as anyone could remember there had always been healers known for their skill in the family, and though they would gladly do it for free it kept them from going hungry in a bad year, for one would bring eggs or a basket of vegetables, and always a few coins at a christening, and more than a few if it was up at the big house. But now folks had more money to spend, and took all manner of strange concoctions which came from no

130

meadow, James's Powder and Goulard's Pomatum and Daffy's Elixir which are sold in the market towns, and no man knows what is in them. And I said how there was nothing so good as old-fashioned home remedies, and how I makes my Jack swallow some peppercorns and then drink the juice of a lemon with a pinch of ginger when he be liverish, and she says to me: Since when do them grow in our hedgerows? So then there was silence for a bit, till we started talking about how fine folk now turns up their noses at midwives, and how, when Lady Charlotte Maria was brought to bed, his lordship wanted the best that money could buy, and a girl who worked up at the house told how the curtains were pulled across the windows and he worked with a bedsheet round his neck, and all that flummery of darkness and screens as much to protect his forceps from prying eyes, them being a closely guarded secret in his family for nigh on a hundred years, as to spare her blushes at being attended by a man with his instrument. Though she would know soon enough, I added, when she saw her child's head, and the state it was in.

It's done away with our livelihood, said the beggar woman. For how else could a poor widow, and them that was worse than widowed, ever keep body and soul together?

And I could not but think how lucky I am, with a good man for my husband, and him with a lease on land which gives good crops most years, and me with my own china cabinet just like the quality, and a spinet which Mistress Clary has taught me to play, though I can only pick out a tune with one hand, and being able to read and write in my own book, though Jack must know nothing of this, which is why Abby hides it under her mattress in the attic. And she be a good girl, and I know will tell no one, least of all my Jack.

My name be in the parish register, the old woman says again, bitter like, with a hard edge to her voice. The least they could do is let me die here, and bury me decently in the churchyard.

That shook me up for a minute, for the poor creature did look stricken, and I had seen a pair of pigeons billing and cooing by the chimney stack with my own eyes, which is supposed to be a sign, and I did not say a word to Abby, who helped me bring

131

food and blankets out of the house so that Jack would know nothing about it, for though he be a good man he do not like to see things go for anything but profit, unless it be by his say-so, and when sheep-stealers were caught in the neighbourhood and almost hung two years back, he said it was no more than they deserved, though I was sorry for their poor families, and right glad when the sheep were found trapped in some gorse bushes. He be not a hard man, not really, though he whipped young Ben within an inch of his life for stealing a meat pie from our pantry, and I know for a fact that he and his father have given shelter to them as were wanted by the law, who would have been hanged else. But I suppose it's another thing when it's your own meat pie that goes missing.

Let's not talk of dying, I said. I'll see you be looked after. The land, I told her, has never been so rich, thinking of our fields of corn glowing in the summer sun, and the hay-making, and how we had more lambs last year than ever before, and how we sat down twenty at table for harvest supper, with our best glasses and silverware just like the quality, and how I bought a new straw bonnet with my egg money only last week.

Aye, she said, that's true, but it's leasehold, with the common land all gone, so some of us have had to move into the city to eat. And it be true that some folks be mighty hard on them, calling them no better than gipsies if they come to the door to beg for a day's work or cast-off clothing, and I remember Jack telling me how they pulled down shacks and old cottages so the riffraff would have to move on. And it's no wonder that many a farmer don't sleep easy in his bed, and talks in favour of hanging, when barns are set alight of a night, and horses go missing, and there even be tales of children vanishing.

But these two women be harmless enough, God knows, and Abby and me have arranged between us to put some things aside which will never be missed, eggs and butter and the like, and at bread-making today we baked some extra loaves. And Jack knows nothing about it, nor the parish officers, for they would surely move them on, even if the old one has a right to stay, and be buried here, which won't take long, from the looks of her, poor thing, for she be hollow-eyed as a skeleton.

I be worried though, about the girl, who is near her time, for how can we get the midwife to her and the whole neighbourhood not be knowing? I said as much to the mother. It had been better for your Rose if you had stayed in the city, I said, but the tears began to roll down her thin cheeks and she shook her head and said it was because of her they had come back, and she would rather her Rose took her chances here, on the clean earth, like an animal, than die in a hospital as she had seen others die. For, she said, as soon as a man touched them they were as good as dead, the doctor's curse they called it, for though the child might be born with no trouble, within two days they were babbling in a fever, with a dry skin and moaning of pains in the belly, and then they went cold as death, which soon followed after.

Interruptions. Miss Balfour, organising spirit of the women's institute, and something of an authority on local history, dropped in for a cup of coffee. There is to be a special open day at the big house, with a garden fête in the grounds, a flower show, and an auction of antique and second-hand furniture, the aim being to raise funds for major repairs to the structure. The regular open days do not attract enough visitors, and hardly pay for themselves, when you consider that extra staff have to be employed, the wear and tear on carpets, and so on.

Do come in, I said politely, and remembered too late about the brown, water-stained papers spread all over my limited floor space. But you'll have to mind your step, I added, before going into the kitchen to put the kettle on.

She had brought me a slim pamphlet, privately printed: her history of the big house and its family, which she wrote some years ago. Also an auction catalogue. I could see her eyeing the papers as we talked, but she was much too polite to ask about them, and I said nothing, beyond apologising for the disorder as I came in with the cups.

I flicked through the auction catalogue, and my eyebrows went up. It occurred to me that Miss Balfour might also have had something to do with its preparation, judging by the rather colourful descriptions. *Item 32: A brace of pistols, inlaid with ivory, said to have been used by Thomas in a dispute over the honour of his sister Isabel, as a result of which he was forced to make a rapid departure for the West Indies.*

What happened to Isabel? I asked.

Miss Balfour settled herself more comfortably in her chair before getting into her stride. She cleared her throat, smoothed down her tweed skirt, and spoke with the authority of one used to the local lecture circuit.

The story goes that she was induced to elope with a young ne'er-do-well, hoping to make a good match and come into a fortune – she was very young at the time, you understand – but that her family was tipped off by a serving maid. Thomas gave chase and, being famous as a daredevil rider, caught the couple halfway to London. A duel was arranged, and they say he shot the man clean through the forehead at forty paces, and was then smuggled off to the nearest port under cover of darkness.

And Isabel, I asked, does anyone know what happened to her?

Miss Balfour shook her grey head and allowed me to refill her coffee cup. There's very little information about her. Except that she never did marry, apparently. Tradition has it that she was a bit odd, not quite right in the head. The treatment for lunacy was rather bizarre in those days, you know. They used to plunge them in cold baths. I suppose the shock was meant to bring them round.

Like electro-convulsive therapy nowadays, I suggested.

Miss Balfour stared at me with her rather bulbous grey eyes.

What they call ECT, I added, thinking she had not quite understood.

She was still looking oddly at me, as though she had lost the thread of her narrative.

Do go on, I prompted. About Isabel.

Miss Balfour blinked, took a deep breath, and seemed to pull herself together before going on.

There is also a tradition that she did all those samplers which hang in the house. There must be at least a dozen, and not one of them is signed or dated which, as you know, is most odd. They are also very plain, which is also unusual, no colour, very little ornament. Just a series of mottoes – Patience is a Virtue – that sort of thing. Rather dull really. To be frank, I have no idea whether she

134

stitched them or not, and I suspect nobody else does either. But somebody must have done them, and if she was not quite right in the head, that would explain them. I mean, a whole series, all sewn in black. Well, you'll see for yourself.

I'd like to, I said, flicking through the auction catalogue. *Item 25* I read, *Card table, folding, stand inlaid with rosewood. It was perhaps at this very table that an entire sugar plantation was lost in a single night, gambling being a favourite pastime of the period.*

Well, I must be going.

Miss Balfour cleared her throat, smoothed down her tweed skirt, and did her best to read one of the papers lying near her foot, without seeming to do so. Her head turned awkwardly, but she kept her neck rigid, like some curious bird. After an awkward little silence she finally got up.

I'll be glad to come along, I said, and got up too, to see her to the door. Miss Balfour made one last attempt.

Family archives? she asked, as we picked our way across the strewn floor.

Sort of, I mumbled.

How interesting. Standing on the doorstep before turning to go she threw a last lingering glance over my shoulder.

Today me and Abby did pick a whole bag of violets in the copse to make violet pudding, which be just the thing for putting husbands in a good humour. And Abby did flatter Jack at supper, saying what a good master he was, and how she would never be wanting to leave for no other place, not even to get married, however much the Weaver boy be asking her. This pleased Jack mightily, and what with the violet pudding and a glass or two of my gooseberry wine that I made last year, he said we could take the horse and cart for the day, and he and the man would manage so long as we were back before nightfall. He thinks we be going to visit Abby's mother with some things, but of course we be taking some bedding and the cradle my mother left me to the poor women in old Nat's house.

Most of the pages are just about legible, now that they have dried out, but they are not numbered, and some are merely household accounts. There are also quite a lot of cooking recipes, for pies, cakes, different kinds of wine, and homemade remedies for both the farm animals and the human household.

Today I was lured out of doors by pale sunshine running fitfully over the bare fields, chasing cloud shadows. The lanes are now somewhat drier, and the air feels soft on my face. There are primroses out by the garden gate, and a few more clumps flowering along the roadside. The fields down by the river are still waterlogged, but ploughing has begun on higher ground, and flocks of birds follow the wake of the newly turned earth.

Mistress Clary did admire my tulips, which she said be very pretty. She said at the big house they be planting all sorts of strange foreign plants, including something they be calling a tulip tree but be no tulip at all, but pink and white and branched like a fine candelabra all lit up for a dance. And that the quality be planting them huge bushes called rhododendrons with purple flowers, which come from the same parts of the world as our tea, but that she, for her part, likes nothing better than a camellia, for so many flowers, she says, you never saw in your born days, so heavy they be dropping off their stems as quick as my man can sweep them up. But the tulip tree I should wish to see, for it must be the strangest thing since they had a hermit's cave with a real man inside it, and a beard growing down to his chest.

Jack back from the market and grumbling that the heifers fetched only a poor price and we should all end in the workhouse. So I looks at Abby and she looks at me, and we try hard not to laugh since we hear the same story most market days. And then he tells how Farmer Barnes do say that their maid Sukey be five months gone and had told the justice that the Weaver boy be the father, and a warrant for him had been issued, and they was to be married by parson on Sunday with the overseer looking on, since the lad did not have a penny to bless himself with, let alone indemnify the parish. And Abby suddenly goes white as a sheet and drops one of my new china plates with the roses on so it breaks clean in two, and sits down sudden saying she feels queer, and Jack makes her drink a glass of my gooseberry wine saying he hopes she be not coming down with the spring fever, but I have my own thoughts on what be wrong with her, the silly goose, and takes her up to her room and shuts the door, so that Jack will not hear her sniffling. And I think she be well rid of the rascal, and tells her so, and that it be Sukey Fletcher she should be crying for, married by order of the parish to save the cost of keeping her and the child, and that no marriage could start worse, and she would rue the day she had named him under oath. Whereupon Abby quietens down a bit, and dries her eyes, and says she be sorry about my plate, and not to say nothing to the master.

Kate telephoned with a progress report on the house. Things are moving slowly, and there is still quite a bit of work to be done. And she would need to buy more furniture.

Perhaps, I said, half jokingly, you'd better come down for this auction. And I told her about Miss Balfour's visit.

Any chance of a dining table? And I'll need some chairs.

Let's have a look. And I started flipping through the catalogue with the receiver jammed between my ear and a hunched shoulder. Tables . . . card table, folding, a loo table, at which an entire estate is said to have changed hands. You have to take a certain amount of local colour with the goods. No other tables. Two chairs with seats said to have been embroidered by the Lady Isabel after her confinement for mental instability.

Who the heck was Lady Isabel?

According to Miss Balfour she tried to elope, but her brother shot the man in a duel. She then went slightly dotty.

I don't blame her.

Apparently you should. According to Miss Balfour, who is a great authority on local history, the man was only a fortune hunter, after her money.

And her brother wasn't, I suppose. Kate sounded scornful.

Miss Balfour doesn't see it quite like that. She will talk about the family honour, and keeping things in the family.

The question is, whose family. Poor Lady Isabel. What day is the sale? I might come down, if I can fit it in. You know how I love auctions.

I thought the girl was beginning her pains yesterday, but

137

nothing come of it, so I sat with them both for a bit, and made some tea that I brought with the hot water, and the old one tells me she was not going to have her Rose delivered in one of them hospitals, and how they had walked for more than a month, mostly at dawn and dusk so as not to be seen, and she tells me in confidence, I not liking to ask, that the child's father had been press-ganged to fight the French and was far away on the other side of the world, off some colony or other, though whether it be for tea or sugar she had no notion, and either way it could make no difference now for the parish overseer, since there was no going back to where he had come from. But I know where I come from, she added, clenching her fist and banging it hard on her knee, and my name be in the church register to prove it, along with my mother, Jane, who worked as a midwife in these parts –

Whereupon I gives a great cry and tells her that I be Nancy, Susan's daughter, and how I thought all along she be reminding me mighty powerful of my aunt Jane, and we fell into each other's arms with so much laughing and crying it must have been a sight to see, and the girl sitting there with her eyes agape and mouth wide open, and I says, now there be no more hiding from the overseer of this parish, nor from my man Jack neither, for nothing in the world is going to stop me helping my own kith and kin, and I tells her how he be a good man, but a bit close when it comes to profit, and him always thinking we be going to the workhouse after one poor harvest, which we haven't had yet, but that he be always good to his own family, and mine too, come to that.

And then my cousin, for that she be, and not much older than me really, only hard times have made her look so, tells me about my poor aunt, and how she had died in the city hospital. For they went off years ago, when the quality stopped using her, and wanted only doctors with their instruments and gold-topped canes to attend their wives at lying-in, and the poor who still used her not able to pay for her services, except now and then some eggs or a pudding or two. And how she had great hopes of doing better in the city, and maybe getting a licence from one of the new lying-in hospitals, which was giving instruction for a fee of twenty guineas, though what she didn't know by that time was not worth knowing, adds my cousin, her having brought half the neighbourhood into the world. But how to find those guineas without help from the parish, nor the parson neither, she might as well be crying for the moon, and her a widow with more than one mouth to feed, and the little money they had going out faster than it could ever come in, since poor folk in the city have even less to give, if there are no coins in the pot.

My poor cousin begins to cry as she tells me how she took sick, and they put her in the hospital. If only I could have cared for her, she says, but how could I, with taking in washing to keep us all in bread, and her too weak to stand or lift a spoon to her mouth. But if I'd known what they was like I'd have done anything, even steal, for the stink in the place was so dreadful you see the people that work there walking about with a sponge of vinegar under their noses. I tell you, she says, it was all I could do to keep from heaving, the air was so foul, and the windows all tight shut, and the walls running alive with creatures, and not a bed in the rooms that had less than three poor sick bodies in it, and in some beds there was four.

And, she says, the stories I could tell you while my mother was in that bed, though luckily her wits were gone half the time, so she could not see what I could. There was a young girl, no older than my Rose, who got her living by sewing, and after she drove a needle through her thumb it turned bad, and though the stump be healing nicely where they took off her hand, which be rare enough, they tell me, the girl was glum as glum could be, for how could she earn her living, she says, with her hand gone, and though I tried to comfort her, and brought her little titbits when I come in, she was saying no more than the truth. And when she was gone from the bed she drowned herself in the river, so I heard, and the surgeon cut her up a second time.

They put girls who be just starting their pains in with the old and dying, for the comfort of both, they say, since there be not enough room in the lying-in ward, and while my mother was mumbling and wandering in her wits with the fever, she was talking across the feet of the sempstress, for they was lying head to foot, to some poor girl who had just been brought in with her first pangs, frightened almost out of her wits and maybe calling for her mother, and praying God to save her, for she had heard such stories of these places, and my mother, out of habit I suppose, would mumble now now my girl, no need for such a carry on, and ask me to heat up some chicken broth with an egg in it, and burn shavings of hartshorn under her nose. And I would say yes mother, and stroke her poor thin hand, and thank God she was not in her right mind, for many's the girl I saw in that bed and dead of the fever three days after, though the doctors tried to keep it a secret for fear of women in labour having hysterics, and crying and screaming to be let out, as many a one did.

My cousin shook her head and wiped her eyes when she came to this bit of her story. And then, one day, she said, they put in her bed a pale young woman with long fair hair, though it was all streaked with sweat, and her blue eyes staring with great dark shadows under them, and my mother suddenly lifts her head as though the fever be quite gone and cries: Isabel, my poor child, what have they done to you? And the poor girl begins to weep, with the tears running down her pale cheeks, and for a while she was quite mute, but for the crying, after which she says something like: I have been a foolish girl, and love has undone me, and now I must be punished for it, and die. And my mother says hush hush child, you must not be talking like that, and begins to croon as though to a child in a cradle and not a grown woman with death coming on, and new life leaping inside her. And the girl becomes quite calm after, crying out only when the pains took her, and talks of trysts on a dark night, and how she had been deceived, deceived. She kept murmuring the word, and my mother said: hush child, it's all one in the end, and you must have some barley water. And the girl said, lifting her head: I was never a bad girl, but I loved him, with such pleading in her eyes as would have turned a heart of stone, and my mother answers: I know that, Isabel, seeing I brought you into the world, and you so like your mother, for a finer woman never walked this earth.

They took her away when the pains grew stronger, but my mam kept on as though she was still with her, telling her not to mind the pains, but to drink her rhubarb and senna for an easy birth, and all the time her poor old fingers were rubbing the coverlet as though it was a woman's swollen belly and she helping to ease the child's passage, and she kept murmuring hush Isabel, hold your breath now, that's a good girl, grip tight, and aah she cried, and then louder, aaah, with her poor old head going from side to side and her eyes tight shut as though it was her giving birth, and the Peruvian bark could not save her, nor salt of wormwood to make her sweat, nor bleeding every two days which, as the doctor told me himself, was more to make her feel she was not left unattended than because he had any hope. And he said that the girl Isabel had given birth to a living child but was sick of the childbed fever, and he said it low so my mam would not hear, though she was too far gone to hear anything now, for which I was right thankful, for it would have broke her heart. And the girl must have died, I'm thinking, at the same moment as she took her last breath, for the last words she ever did say was: I'm coming, my girl, and I heard so after when we come for the body.

At this point I was overcome by a sense of immense depression, wondering whether, with hindsight, some of our own so-called expertise would be recognised as doing more harm than good. It is something I have often discussed with Kate, who is fighting a losing battle at her own hospital against increased intervention in the delivery room. It started with induced deliveries for the convenience of nine-to-five doctors, she says, and a lot of high technology which frightens the women quite unnecessarily, and it has now got to the point where we are doing far too many caesarean sections. If they weren't necessary twenty years ago, why now? It seems light years away from my own training, listening to the baby's heartbeat with a metal ear trumpet, which we had to rub first so it would not feel cold on the mother's skin. Of course we are a long way from spreading puerperal fever from the autopsy room, but that is hardly the point. Those very same doctors were always going on about filthy old women without a proper knowledge of anatomy who practised midwifery, and were puzzled that some women should prefer to be delivered at home, and by them. That sounds familiar.

I had almost come to the end of the manuscript. There was a recipe for cough mixture made with honey, a few sheets of accounts, and one last paragraph:

Rose gave birth last night, a fine girl, and mother and baby are both well. We was all with her, Abby seeing to the hot water and broth, and me and her mother walking her up and down, and talking to her when the pains come on. Rose is to call the child Nancy, after me, seeing how I've been so kind (she says) and I'm to stand godmother too. So I am to give her a little silver cup for her very own, and Jack is to pay the midwife out of his own pocket, which be mighty good of him, I reckon. But then he says, since they be our own flesh and blood, and nearly related, it be no more than proper.

Six

An uneasy beginning to summer, with a lot of cloud and rain. Not a bit, of course, like the childhood summers I remember. I suppose it must have rained then, but my memory only holds endless days of clear blue sky, a long hot glow which made the fields and meadows sing, fading slowly into red-gold evening light. Red as fire, as embers, like Ada's hair as she tucked her cotton frock into her knickers and did cartwheels, which I could never do, arms and legs spinning through the air, or sat with her legs crossed, chewing grass, as we argued about the future and played cat's cradle, pulling the same patterns over and over with the same surprise. It was as though the day could never end, should never end, and sometimes, when we heard aunt Doris calling our names, Ada would say shush, and we would hide for a bit in the cowshed, or lie flat on the ground behind the cabbage patch, and afterwards, if we got told off, she would pretend we had not heard her, had no idea how late it was. And grin at me behind her back.

I used to hope those days would never end, and then, with the war, and the bombing, it suddenly seemed that they really might go on indefinitely. I could hardly contain my joy when mother decided to leave me with aunt Doris on the farm, and I tried not to show her how happy I was, and felt bad when she cried a bit at the station. I suppose that must have been the first protracted guilt of my life, feeling vaguely that it was wrong to be glad not to be at home with her, especially as she was in danger with the bombing, and dad was away in the army, and she must be missing him, and me. But I was glad all the same, and hoped the war and the bombing might go on for ages, so long as nobody got hurt.

Funny thing: how we never thought much about people getting

killed. We knew it happened, but only in the abstract. Why was that? Of course, adults must have played down the truth, since we were children, and the news on the wireless never said much about people dying, just how many enemy planes had been shot down. But there is more to it. The fact is that children, knowing nothing of it, have no fear of death. Which is why they do such daft things now and then.

I was much more aware, at first, of death on the farm. Chickens killed in the yard, the pig squealing shrilly as my uncle and his man tried to get it into the truck for market. That was the first lesson I had when I came down here, but so much more was to follow. Sometimes it seems to me that everything I learnt for life, everything that has made me what I have become since, was picked up in these surroundings, almost casually, and that normal life afterwards, back home, the years of formal schooling and the training that followed, simply built on it, and somehow confirmed it. Which is why I had this strong urge to come back, quite suddenly, having not thought about the past for years.

I suppose this is the beginning of old age, when the past has such a hold on us. And there is no future to speak of. But I also know that the war had this kind of effect on many people of my age, a disruption, an exposure to unaccustomed sights and sounds, both good and bad, which either changed them, or went underground, to haunt their dreams and give shape to unfulfilled longings.

It changed me, what happened here. The sights and sounds of that unending summer. Hiding in the hayloft with Ada at bedtime, the dust tickling our noses, and aunt Doris's voice ringing through the dusk, so clearly, from so far off, as she called our names. The bomb crater in the orchard, since the farm was only a few miles from the airfield, and the new cowshed, so aunt Doris surmised, must look like a hangar from above. And my uncle jokingly saying how maybe we should paint the word COWS in huge letters on the roof, and Ada adding that he would have to do it in German. Ada always had the last word, managed to go one better. She even found out that the German for 'cow' was 'die Kuh', from a Jewish boy billeted at the vicarage, who was in her class.

And Granny Martin telling us stories when she gave us high tea, or when we knocked on her door in the hours between supper and bed, ignoring my aunt's warning, not too long mind, as we hurtled out of the back door. My grandmother knew more of the world than anybody, having been in it so long, and what she knew was infinitely worth knowing. Ada and I sensed that, even if we did not always fully understand what she was saying, or misunderstood. For she had done things with her life, and was known to be clever.

Who knows, if it had not been for my grandmother I might have chosen a completely different career. I can see her now, standing with a teapot in one hand and a biscuit tin in the other, with the red glow of sunset coming through the window, and the long shadows, the light falling on the wax cloth and setting fire to Ada's hair as she lolled, head on arms, and asked her to bring out the box of photographs. And when the tea was cleared away my grand-mother would get out the old shoebox and either tip them out on the wax cloth for us to look at, or methodically pick them out one by one, explaining who everybody was.

I never seemed to tire of looking at them, those images of faded sepia. Women in long black dresses with stiff bonnets on their heads, men with large whiskers and watch chains strung across waistcoats, sitting, whip in hand, on the front seat of a gig. Rows of children in identical pinafores squatting cross-legged on the lawn of the big house or standing outside the old schoolhouse. I could not begin to imagine what it must have been like to wear those laced boots, or ride in a dog cart. I could not imagine this world ever existed, or those people, if it were not for the fact that I recognised the backdrop on some of the pictures, the church and the lychgate, for instance, the schoolhouse before it became a community centre, and the stone bridge fording the river.

Ada was inclined to laugh at many of the photographs, to make fun of the peculiar clothes and the rigid expressions they seemed to adopt for the camera. Look at this, she would shout, waving something in the air, till granny told her to calm down and mind how she picked them up, for she did not want buttery fingermarks all over them. But I found them eerie, somehow, all those dead people standing there in funny clothes as though there was nothing wrong with them, each tiny little detail so clear you had to believe in them, and I could see they believed in themselves. The men looked rather stern, almost fierce, with their whiskers and sideburns and spreading beards, and the women a bit glum, as though their clothes were rather too much for them. Only the children smiled, rows and rows of them, in boots and pinafores.

The school treat, said my grandmother, and pointed to a child in the second row, little more than a tiny white dot. We had to be on our best behaviour, I can tell you. Any child who didn't arrive in a clean pinafore was sent home.

That was to impress the gentry, who patronised the school. Most of our special days, fêtes, bazaars, that sort of thing, seemed to take place in the grounds of the big house. I can remember Miss Cora bringing presents and a Christmas tree to the schoolhouse. She was a great one for organising bazaars for missionaries out saving the souls of little black babies, and then we were all busy for weeks making pincushions and pen-wipers in school time. Handicrafts, they called it. I can remember wondering, in my first year, why little black babies should want pincushions and pen-wipers when the teacher had said the poor things went about naked and could neither read nor write.

Granny Martin laughed, and shook her head. The hours I spent cutting up my mother's old red flannel petticoat. And my hands were so small I could hardly hold the scissors. Still, I suppose we were lucky. My mother kept telling me, she never had my chances of an education, so you keep at it, my girl. As for her mother, Nancy, no messing with reading and writing for her. She was in service by the time she was ten.

Beyond the small window with its china ornaments and potted geraniums the slanting sunlight sent a final dazzle through the lower branches of trees, throwing moving black leaf shadows. The light in the room was half dark, half bright. It shone in my grandmother's face and lit up her eyes, so she had to shield them with her hand, and shift her chair back as she spoke.

What do you mean, in service? asked Ada, giving a yawn and leaning her head on her arm, so that the fire went out of her hair.

She worked at the big house, said my grandmother, getting up at five in the morning to polish rows of boots. Cleaning out the grates and setting a fire in the breakfast room, and carrying hot water up to the bedrooms, and their slops out after, and helping to make the beds, and dust and polish, and generally be invisible if a lady or gentleman passed by, so they could think themselves private and it was all done of its own accord, unless the bell rang and there were errands to be run, or something was not quite right, not quite as it should be, and somebody had to be called to account, for an unpolished fender or a dusty mantelpiece. That's what I mean, my girl.

Sounds awful, said Ada, with another yawn. I wouldn't do it, would you? And she glanced at me with her sleepy eyes.

No fear, I said stoutly.

You won't have to, said my grandmother. Though it's taken two world wars to stop it. There was a time when you'd have had no choice.

Granny Martin shuffled the old photographs about, looking for one picture in particular.

My grandmother Nancy worked for The Matriarch, up at the big house. Let's see – and she picked out a photograph of a stout old lady dressed from head to foot in black silk, with wide skirts and a black bonnet tied under her chin. She was short, almost as wide as she was high, with all those clothes on her, and she was posed in the middle of rows of children, the boys in sailor suits, the girls in pinafores over their dresses.

That's how I remember her, she said, pointing out the tiny blob, her white face, glum and rather stern, under the huge bonnet. But when Nancy started work up at the big house she was only a young woman, and looked nothing like that. But it was more than looks. I never knew a woman to change so much, she'd say, years afterwards, and there were others in the village who thought the same.

I could never be sure afterwards how much she told me about the early history of The Matriarch during those afternoons with Ada, and how much I picked up later, when I went to see her after the war. Once I was older, a student nurse training for midwifery, she would tell me a lot about her early experiences, and especially her work with Dora as a pioneer in family planning. Because what she might have said then could only be an adult rationalization of the stories she had already told us in some other form. If it had not been for those stories, told, no doubt, in a rather more fanciful form, or made more bizarre by our childish imagination, I would not have chosen nursing as a career.

The source, too, of this particular story is confused. Granny Martin claimed, when she told it to us as children, that most of it had come down to her through her grandmother, the girl Nancy who spent so many years in service at the big house. Servants know everything, she would say, in that forceful way of hers. They are not supposed to know anything, being invisible, and stupid. But when it comes to the secrets of the bedroom, there's nothing they don't know. Who changes the sheets, with their telltale signs? Who fills the bathtub and empties the chamber pot, wipes down the washstand and tidies the dressing table? How could they not know, even if they did not have ears to hear the whispers behind closed doors, the arguments, the fits of weeping and scolding? And if servants put their ear to the keyhole more often than most, it is not from curiosity, or a wish to spy on their betters, but because they know, in the manner that only servants can know, that to enter a room at the wrong moment, to become visible when they should be invisible, is to risk instant dismissal. So servants learn to listen before they knock, even when they have been sent for.

That's how it began, yes. With little Nancy staggering up and down the back stairs, carrying a slop pail almost as big as herself after she went into service. My grandmother would emphasise the hardships of such a life, knowing that Ada and I would identify with somebody of our own age. But Nancy was not the heroine of this story, but only an unwilling witness, the first source, though probably not the only one.

I always think of it as the story of Sophie and the doctor, which is how we referred to it then. Tell us the story of Sophie and the doctor, demanded Ada, that last summer, one eye on the kitchen clock. I think Ada was less interested in hearing the story repeated than in postponing the moment when we would be sent home to bed. I also think now, with hindsight, that my grandmother must have used this story, more than once, for proselytising purposes, and that she and Dora must have filled in a few missing bits between them, in order to get the message through.

Not that Ada and I were much interested in the medical details, which we found infinitely confusing. At least I did, and if I asked

Ada in bed about them, she would either make out she knew things but could not possibly tell me, or invent something to fill the gap. As for our grandmother, she probably did not realise that there were some facts we were not yet old enough to grasp. With true reforming zeal, she thought we could never be too young, and both of us loved her for it. Listening to her talk was like wandering through a mysterious forest, and we were as much enticed by the dark spaces as by the patches of sunlight.

I suppose for us the fascination of this particular story had to do with magical transformation, since Sophie was none other than The Matriarch of the photographs, or rather, had turned into her. That was a central mystery of my childhood, how the fat, glum old woman in her black clothes, known as something of a tyrant in her own household and in the village which she regarded as her back yard, could ever have been what my grandmother described: a slender, timid young girl, who kept her eyes down, and was rarely heard to speak, and then in a voice so low and soft that it was hard to make out what she was saying.

Sophie, it seems, had found herself sole heiress of the estate as a very young girl, but since she was not allowed to do anything with it, her life was very limited. Various elderly gentlemen, mostly distant relatives and solicitors in the city, were in charge of managing her affairs until her marriage, when her husband would assume this heavy responsibility. Even within her own household she could make no decisions, since a housekeeper, a rather forbidding woman of advanced years, had been appointed to keep a watch on her behaviour and, above all, her morals, once her education was completed at eighteen and the governess was dismissed.

At times Sophie felt like a prisoner in her own house. She had loved her governess, who had shared walks with her, and little amusements, as well as her rather patchy knowledge of French and geography. They had played duets on the pianoforte, and explored the library, sharing their haphazard finds and reading aloud to each other. The governess spoke of her past, of the impoverished rectory in which she had grown up, of the young and earnest curate who had proposed marriage before dying of consumption. Sophie spoke of the future, her future, and her voice would tremble a little: how could she possibly make a wise choice between those who would undoubtedly leave their visiting cards at the big house, when she was not permitted even a few minutes alone with them, and to give more than one dance to the same partner was considered compromising?

There were no answers to these questions. Perhaps there might have been hints, little tricks and subtleties to be learnt, if the governess, in many ways more like a fond mother or elder sister, had been allowed to remain in the house, but the elderly male guardians considered that their young lady was sufficiently accomplished, now that she could accompany herself at the piano, and embroider firescreens, and write little notelets in an elegantly flowing hand. Sophie's education was now complete, and the governess, who had been mother and friend and sister to the girl for half her life, left the house with a small portmanteau and a formal letter of reference to seek a living elsewhere. Sophie wept for a fortnight and would not eat. Mrs. Dobson, the housekeeper, would order trays to be left at her door, since she shut herself in her room for days on end, but Nancy, or one of the other servants, would find the food untouched hours later.

Mrs. Dobson threatened to send for a doctor and Sophie came out of her room, red-eyed, and agreed to take a little broth.

I used to feel sorry for her, said my grandmother, all by herself in that great big house. And to tell the truth, I think she was really lonely, in spite of the callers who left their cards, and the invitations which had to be answered in her best copperplate hand. For if she rang the bell for something, after I had stoked up the fire or run upstairs for her blue Indian shawl, she would keep me standing there, and ask about my family, how my mother was, and did I have any brothers and sisters, and was I happy here? And of course I said yes, and I would have been, only cook asked where had I been for such an age, and gave me a scolding for being gone so long. And once, when I brought fresh toast into the breakfast room, she not only kept me talking but led me out through the French window and asked, pointing at the huge expanse of green lawn all round the house: Don't you think it's dreadful, Nancy? It's like being shipwrecked on an island, in the middle of a green ocean.

Well, said my grandmother, I didn't really understand, being so young, and I thought she was a little bit touched, to tell the truth, but I said, remembering the cottage garden back home, that a few flowers would be nice, and she suddenly looks at me with a smile and starts laughing and says: You know, Nancy, I think you're quite right. A few flowers wouldn't come amiss.

And that's how I met your grandfather, for when the lawns were dug up for flower borders, all round the house, extra hands were wanted for the planting and potting that now went on all through the year, almost, and Jake was one of the lads taken on for the work. It was a fine to-do, I can tell you, with a new shrubbery by the east wing, and cartloads of plants always trundling up to the house, and a whole new rose garden laid out below the terrace. And Mrs. Dobson, the housekeeper, grumbled a good deal, and said the new shrubbery spoiled the view from her office, and muttered about absurd whims which she would soon have put a stop to, if she had any say in the matter. Which she did not, for her rule stopped with the running of the house, which she knew, as Sophie did too.

Nor could she say much when Sophie took to visiting the sick in the village, bringing gifts of calf's-foot jelly and firewood, or calling on the poorest cottages with baskets of fruit from the orchard, when she would stop long enough to play with the children or hear some poor widow describe her man's final illness down to the last horrid detail, for did not the church exhort us to charity? Mrs. Dobson was a dutiful churchgoer, and made it a point of principle that all her staff should go to church once on a Sunday, as part of their free time. But she had taken it upon herself to ask the mistress not to engage the servants in conversation of a personal nature. It gave them, she said, notions not suited to their station in life, and made them inclined to be slovenly.

Sophie was timid with Mrs. Dobson, and some of us thought she was downright terrified of her, for she never raised her voice above a whisper when she spoke to us, or rang for tea, or asked for the lamps to be brought in. And she ate what was put in front of her, without ever asking for something special, or sending for Mrs. Dobson to give her a menu, unless there was company coming, which was seldom enough.

151

Until The Master arrived. He seemed to take charge right away, being an older man and used to giving orders to his mill workers, up north, where he came from. In fact gossip in the kitchen had it that the very first time he called at the house and suggested taking tea outside, on the terrace, it being a fine sunny day, and Miss Sophie saying she was afraid Mrs. Dobson would not like it, he simply laughed and rang the bell for her, saying: My dear girl, Mrs. Dobson will do as she is told.

So it seems that Sophie made her choice, or had it made for her. She was certainly mightily relieved to find someone who knew how to give orders to Mrs. Dobson, and who always exerted his authority without thinking twice about it. And he, for his part, was touched by her timidity, and the delicacy of her physique, for the girls up north, he declared, were all great lumps, good for nothing but heaving coal, with their big bones and big feet, and clogs on them too. He had told Nancy as much, when he caught her in the passage one morning early, as she was bringing a pitcher of hot water to his room, making her blush to the roots of her hair.

Well, if he had a distaste for big bones and a hardy disposition in the fair sex, he certainly found his match in Miss Sophie, though whether her delicate constitution made her quite fitted for the rigours of married life is another matter. She made a charming bride, sure enough, in her white dress all covered with tiny seed pearls, and her tiny foot with its slim ankle on the sustaining pedal as she played the pianoforte would have turned any gentleman's head. As for her delicate wrists and slim white fingers, The Master would declare loudly to all and sundry, causing a rosy blush to rise to her pale cheeks, that the finest tea, which men had conquered half the world to find, would lose its savour if the hand that poured it were not just so soft and white.

But there is more to married life than pouring tea, said my grandmother, and her voice got serious. Dr. Forster had hinted as much, clearing his throat in some embarrassment, when he drove up to the house in a gig sporting one of the finest horses in the county to draw it, a mettlesome bay which would not have looked out of place in the field or on the race track. Miss Sophie had sent for him in some anxiety, since he had warned her on a previous visit that a delicate constitution in females made them unfit for marriage, without, however, suggesting any alternative mode of life. So she was greatly relieved when he told her that the most common cause of her complaint, namely, suppression of the profluvium, was damp feet, and warned her against walking in the grounds except on the very sunniest of summer days. However, four months of hot foot baths, carried up and down stairs by a perspiring Nancy each afternoon, produced nothing but chilblains and a bad back. Nancy's back. When her waist began to thicken it was obvious to the entire household that damp feet had nothing to do with her condition.

What condition? I asked, the first time I heard this story, having somehow got it into my head that a profluvium must be a runny nose.

She was having a baby, stupid, said Ada, and gave me a shove. Do shut up.

It was a boy, said my grandmother. Master Edward. Member of Parliament for forty years in this district, where he never opened his mouth, so they say, except once, when he wanted a window opened. But as a baby it was quite another matter, for his mouth was never shut, and he made enough noise to keep the entire household awake at nights.

The poor mistress had her nerves worn to a frazzle, for he would fall asleep at the breast and begin to cry as soon as he was put back in his cradle, and though she feared that the child was hungry, since she had not enough milk in her breasts, she was even more afraid to hire a wet nurse, for Dr. Forster had warned her of the danger to her life if she had a second child too soon, and assured her that suckling the baby was the only infallible safeguard.

So she wore herself to a shadow, with lack of sleep and trying to feed him, till the under-nurse took him out of her room one night and fed him some cow's milk on the sly, mixed with a spoonful or two of something stronger, as she told Nancy with a wink, for she had had just about as much as she could stand and poor madam, anyone could see, had had rather more, and was right at the end of her tether. And from that time on there was peace in the house, and though it was perhaps not the right thing to do, and Nancy, the only one in the know, being the under-nurse's particular friend, was sometimes scared of what she was doing, the child came to no harm, though they do say he had a great partiality for the bottle in later years.

I think poor Miss Sophie never had the least notion, for by that time she had other things on her mind. Dr. Forster was a frequent visitor, and assured her, his voice rising to an indiscreet pitch as she persisted in voicing her doubts, that her fears were quite unfounded, unless she had given up nursing. He called several times a week, each time taking half a pint from her arm, till the poor young madam was sick and faint, and Nancy, being required to hold the bowl, was not much better. A general fullness, he said, had brought on an inflammatory action in the uterine organs, which in turn prevented the occurrence of secretion and, in consequence, the depletion of the turgid vessels in the normal manner.

What does that mean? asked the under-housemaid when Nancy duly repeated what she had heard, after being revived with a strong cup of tea. I never could stand the sight of blood, she added.

It means, said cook bluntly, banging a frying pan with unusual vigour, that she's overdue. That's what it means. And if she was my girl I'd give her a good dose of pennyroyal, that's what I'd do. She put the kettle back on the hearth with an almighty thump after refilling the teapot.

She was right of course, said my grandmother, though Dr. Forster continued to pronounce her plethoric as late as the fourth month, and on one occasion even applied leeches to the inside of her thighs, a procedure of such painful indelicacy that even her personal maid was sent from the room, and the story might never have got below stairs if madam had not been found stretched out senseless on the floor shortly after his visit. A panicky parlour maid cried out for help, and in no time at all the entire household was round her, fanning and lifting and calling for smelling salts and urging the others to give her more air.

It was when she regained consciousness that Miss Sophie knew the truth, beyond a shadow of doubt. For she felt the child quicken inside her. The Master, on being told by the housekeeper of his wife's collapse, sent for Dr. Forster in something of a rage. The interview took place in the library, and was sufficiently heated to

154

be overheard in the hall, where young Jimmy the footman was minding the doctor's hat and cane and the second parlour maid was passing through with a message. The Master went so far as to mention the matter of fees, how he might be disinclined to pay for such services, but the doctor protested, loudly, that it was against all the known facts of lactation, and whilst he would be the last person to question the honour and probity of his lady wife, or doubt that she was being other than truthful, he had come across many young matrons who cared more for the shape of their breasts than for the welfare of their offspring, and were inclined to put their children out to nurse without confiding in their husbands or medical advisers.

This gave The Master something to think about, no doubt, for things quietened down behind the library door shortly after, and Jimmy the footman only just had time to jump to attention and tell the parlour maid to get moving when the bell summoned him to bring the sherry decanter and two glasses. For this was the time he was busily selling a portion of his wife's land to build a railway, and the doctor had expressed an interest in buying some shares in the company. As for the other little matter, he chose not to trouble his wife by discussing it, since she was often unwell during her pregnancy, and it would only upset her. But after the birth of Master Thomas he begged her, most earnestly, to persevere with nursing the child herself.

Miss Sophie sobbed a good deal after this interview, and continued tearful for a long time, and her maid, who considered herself something of an authority in these matters, declared in the servants' hall that she was as much upset at the sale of the lower meadows and the home farm, which had gone through without her knowing about it, The Master not wishing to disturb her with such things, as the low state of her physique following the birth. She had heard him call her a dear creature, with her love of beauty, but so sentimental, and how nobody could stand in the way of progress, which was good for everybody, though he did not expect the feminine mind to grasp this in quite the same way.

And it's true enough, added my grandmother. For if we hadn't had the railway we would never have heard about Annabel.

Annabel?

This was something new. Ada and I sat up, suddenly wide awake. Neither of us had ever heard her mentioned before.

Granny Martin smiled. Didn't I tell you about Annabel? No, I suppose not, since that's another story, in many ways. And then, to tell you the truth, it was never clear in my own mind, just what really happened, how much was fact, and how much was simply a sort of legend, nurtured on gossip and rumour in the neighbourhood. Those were troubled, uneasy times, when even working men were possessed and consumed by wild dreams and impossible notions. It began with the railway, and machines going faster and faster, and human beings, too, could feel the pulse inside them quicken, and their heartbeat racing ahead. Every tavern became a talking shop, where the world was turned upside down in the twinkling of an eye.

Annabel belonged to this world, stepped into it from a third class railway compartment, alighting suddenly and unannounced with nothing but a small portmanteau and a queer-looking man following on behind. The Angel and her Devil, they got to be called, for she was young and graceful, with fair hair and fairer skin and eyes that could turn from the colour of cornflower to violets when the sun went in behind a cloud, whilst her companion was black as sin, with the hint of a hunchback to his twisted spine, a black beard, sallow skin, and ugly crooked features.

Nobody knew where she came from, or where she went, for she would vanish as suddenly as she had come. But people came to expect her, like some rare phenomenon, knowing she would appear, but not precisely when, whilst rumour and hope and unbridled curiosity grew tall in a dark wilderness. How to weed out the small blue flower of truth from this tangle? According to one report, she was the illegitimate daughter of a duke, but others had heard she was a foundling educated in a charity school. It was even whispered that she had been rescued from a brothel at the age of twelve, but the most popular story, and the one that gained ground most rapidly, had her as the tragic outcome of an elopement, with the father killed in a duel, or forced to flee abroad, and her unhappy mother dying when she was born.

Oddly enough, her activities, when she did come to the neighbourhood for a brief visit, were also far from clear, and

156

seemed to vary according to who was telling the story. Some said one thing, some another. In particular, it was apparent that men told a different story from most of the women in the neighbourhood, and had heard quite a different message. That there was a message, everyone agreed, that people would gather under an oak tree to hear her speak, she standing on a cart so they could all see her, with her clear blue eyes and the fair hair piled under her straw bonnet, and hear her too, the clear tones of her voice ringing out, whilst the black man with the crooked spine was distributing printed handbills, and keeping a look out for trouble. He seemed to have a nose for it, large and hooked as it was, for he would have her off that cart and vanish in the wink of an eyelid long before the constabulary rode on the scene to break up the meeting and take her into custody. How he did it nobody quite knew. Some say she left on the milk train, dressed in men's clothing, with a cloth cap on her head, or was trundled out of the neighbourhood in a cart, hidden in a load of hay.

But the story that Nancy heard, as wild rumours flew down the back stairs, to be whispered in back passages and discussed in the privacy of the still-room, was that the lovely and mysterious Annabel carried with her a secret that could change women's lives, and that she was willing to share it with all and sundry at the risk of her own liberty. That there was some kind of secret formula was beyond dispute, everybody had been convinced of it for some time, and they were also sure that those who had it were unwilling to divulge it to the less privileged. For instance, it was rumoured that the doctor's lady was privy to it, since she had produced only two infants in ten years of marriage, but when poor Miss Sophie, by now a semi-invalid after the birth of her seventh child in as many years of matrimony, ventured to raise the possibility of some mechanical device, his moral and professional outrage knew no bounds, and the list of undoubted consequences which he bellowed out sounded like so many terrifying imprecations to the frightened lady. Acute metritis, he shouted, leucorrhea, ovaritis, he added, banging his fist on the mantelpiece, hyperaesthesia, hysteralgia, he went on, pacing between the window and the fireplace, mammary congestion, menorrhagia, haematocele – need I go on? No, murmured Miss Sophie, in a voice scarcely above a whisper, and buried her face in her hands.

This scene, overheard by an upstairs maid who was thoroughly alarmed at the doctor's tone of voice, was proof enough, if proof were needed, that no help, not a glimmer of hope, would come from him. But by that time the first faint rumours surrounding the delicate figure of Annabel like morning mist had gained substance, specificity, some sort of form. She carried something in her grey silk reticule, it was said, though accounts varied on precisely what that something was. It was variously described as a gold pin on the end of a silk tassel, a ring made of silver, or a cross of some other, as yet unknown, precious metal.

This was the time that my grandmother Nancy was first walking out with Jake, the young under-gardener I told you of, so she was curious enough to keep her eyes and ears open, both inside the house and out, and if it meant listening at a few keyholes and taking the risk of going to such unlawful meetings once Annabel was heard to be in the neighbourhood, it was worth doing, for how could she and Jake even think of getting wed if it meant having an extra mouth to feed every spring? And she told me herself how she saw her, standing on a cart under a spreading oak, with her blue eyes and the fair hair showing under her bonnet, and heard her speak, and took one of the handbills that the hunchback with the black features and crooked nose distributed, and hid it under her pillow when she got back that night, and the fright she got two days later when Mrs. Dobson, searching for a missing spoon, found it and took the scandalous sheet straight to the mistress of the house, as a matter which would probably call for instant dismissal.

To my surprise, said Nancy, she did not send me away, for I was terrified, I can tell you, and my legs shook so much I thought I would never get up the stairs when she sent for me to see her. But she was not angry, not a bit. Instead she asked me how I had come by it, and looked thoughtful, with the handbill lying in her lap, and when I told her about the meeting, thinking it best to come right out with it, she wanted to know more, about her, the Angel and her Devil, as they got to be called, what she had said, how she looked, how the news got around so we knew where to go, and when. And I told her, blushing – in fact, I don't know which of us

158

had the reddest face – that Jake and I were planning to get wed, thinking it would help. And she was very kind, and said she would talk to The Master about our moving into the lodge, and I saw her with my own eyes put the handbill into a drawer of her writing desk and turn the key.

And it was shortly after this that the dreadful scene with Dr. Forster was overheard, not just by the upstairs maid, but also by Nancy herself, coming in with the coal scuttle to replenish the bedroom fire. Hearing voices raised on the far side of the door, she did not like to knock, and feared it would not be noticed anyhow.

You must endeavour to methodise your conjugal relations, Dr. Forster was saying, by limiting them to the middle of the month. A woman will only conceive in the day or two before the profluvium is due.

And he went on to warn her that mechanical attempts to interfere with nature could lead to sterility, insanity and death, often by suicide.

Horse riding, my dear lady, he went on, just as Nancy crooked her forefinger to tap on the door, but desisted when she heard her mistress sobbing that she was far too unwell to think of riding, and anyhow, she had always been afraid of getting thrown.

Dr. Forster intervened to say that, though he was of course not recommending such a drastic course of action, he knew of several young ladies whose profluvium had been restored by a sudden fall from a horse.

She heard Miss Sophie murmur something about pennyroyal, and Dr. Forster got angry and excited again. Such popular nostrums, he shouted, the nonsense talked by foolish old women, as Nancy quietly put down the coal scuttle to take the weight off her arm, these emmenagogues recommended by old wives simply aggravate the plethoric inflammation they are intended to cure. And he began speaking of warm hip baths twice a day, which made poor Nancy sigh, since she knew who would be dragging the water up and down. She rapped on the door quite loudly, and glanced at her mistress's tear-stained face, where she lay on the day-bed, before kneeling down to bank up the fire.

Of course, the worthy doctor went on in a low tone, as Nancy stoked and poked to get the ash through the grating and rouse the flames into life, you might wish to try the latest method for restoring the menses – electricity. Several electric shocks passed daily through the pelvis, both from front to back and from side to side, the shock being increased as the patient is able to bear it.

It was just then, said my grandmother, that she heard a dull thud. Turning round, she found the mistress had slipped senseless to the floor.

It took them several hours to revive her, and the child, when it was born, was a weak and sickly thing. And for all his diatribes against mechanical devices, after this last birth the doctor fitted a box-wood thing inside her, or her poor tired womb would have dropped down between her legs. She could hardly walk for discomfort, and rarely left her room.

As for The Master, he was seldom at home, since his business took him up north to visit his factories, or into the capital for meetings of shareholders, and the like. Now that the railway had been built the need for such journeys seemed to increase, even though, or perhaps because, the time involved was so much less. Up in town he would stay at his club and he rarely came back empty-handed: there were small playthings for the children, and some kind of present for his wife. In the early days of their marriage it would be a new shawl, or a silk parasol, but as time went on and she was increasingly confined to the house, to her own room, he began to bring back bric-à-brac, china ornaments, small vases, glass lustres for the mantelpiece until, as one of the maids remarked to Nancy, you hardly knew where to put your feather duster without knocking something over and risking your position.

Even when he did stay at home The Master was never inside the house for long, since he was by now a justice of the peace and a magistrate, and sat on various committees, responsible for such things as the local prison, the workhouse, and an insane asylum. And it was about this time that he took to sleeping in a room at the far end of the corridor from his wife's, for the poor lady was far from well, and he did not wish to disturb her troubled nights.

Things went on in this way for some time, said my grandmother, and the mistress seemed to regain her strength after the birth of the last child, and the colour came back to her cheeks, and she took to coming downstairs, and even walked on the terrace a little, or went down to the rose garden. And she played with her children, and taught the younger ones to read, and smiled as she did in the old days, and laughed when the baby staggered towards her for the first time.

And then came the day of the big rumpus, the day when everything changed.

It was a fine summer day, I remember, with the weather so hot that all the windows stood wide open, which is how Jake came to overhear the start of the trouble, for he was bedding some new plants in the flower borders, and though he could hear the doctor's voice in conversation with Miss Sophie, he supposed it was only about one of the children, who had developed a tiresome cough, until, that is, he heard Dr. Forster saying loud and clear, overriding her murmured questioning:

My dear lady, please do not ask me. The cause of your complaint cannot be ascertained with any certainty, and far be it from me to wreck domestic happiness on mere suspicion or surmise.

At this point there was a terrible crashing sound, and Jake, thinking the mistress had fainted on account of the heat, a not uncommon occurrence in those days, when ladies wore so much clothing, and were laced into stays too tight for comfort, was about to drop his trowel and run for help when the first loud sound was followed by others, a crashing and a smashing which just went on and on. When the parlour maid was finally summoned by the distraught doctor she found the mistress shaking and white with rage, and the entire Turkey carpet littered with broken bibelots. Fragments of china, shards of splintered glass were strewn over the floor, and the shelves and little occasional tables, usually so cluttered with bric-à-brac, had been swept bare.

Get out, she screamed, staring at the doctor with a face chalk white, and swaying as she spoke, so the parlour maid said she was half scared out of her wits, and she held a Venetian vase in her hand, ready to throw it at the doctor if he tried to come near her.

My dear lady, the doctor kept murmuring, moving backwards to the door, please calm yourself. And once he had shut the door

161

behind him he said that she was suffering from a hysterical attack brought on by the heat and undue humidity, and must be put to bed at once with five drops of laudanum, and kept there with curtains drawn. Annie, the parlour maid, rushed off to find her personal maid, who was up in the sewing room and had heard nothing, and my legs were shaking I can tell you, she added, for I never saw the mistress look like that, and I thought she had gone clean out of her wits. Dr. Forster, meanwhile, was talking to the housekeeper in the hallway, as he waited for his horse and trap to be brought to the front door. Rest, rest and yet more rest, he told her, followed by a light diet and perhaps a steel tonic. But no stimulus of any kind, since exciting the nerves might prove fatal to someone in her condition.

I tried to get him to stay, Mrs. Dobson said later, when the events of that dreadful day were discussed, gone over and over. I told him The Master was expected back quite shortly, on the four-fifty to be precise, and that if he would care to take tea in the library meanwhile I was sure he would be anxious to learn of his wife's condition from his own lips, rather than at second-hand. But he seemed very nervy himself, and anxious to be off, muttered something about other patients to see, and his hand was shaking slightly as he pulled his gold watch out of his waistcoat pocket, and he would not be stopped from setting off even though the first rumble of thunder could just be heard over the hill as he took his hat and cane from Jimmy the footman and stood on the portico gazing up into a clear blue sky.

As blue as the forget-me-nots I was working on at the time, Jake would say afterwards. Though mind you, he would add, I thought the bay horse looked a bit nervy as the groom brought him round, and Mrs. Dobson also remarked on the fact that the animal began to twitch his ears and grow restive even before Dr. Forster had the reins and whip in his hands, and that he reared right up at the sound of distant thunder, so the groom could hardly hold him, and Jake came running up to lend a hand. All of which she put down at the time to it being a nervous, mettlesome horse more fit for the hunt than the humble work of pulling a gig, and that if the doctor had not been inclined to show off his good fortune by pretending to be what he was not, namely a gentleman born, and had been

162

content with an even-tempered old nag for his trap, the whole thing might never have happened.

So Mrs. Dobson watched him take the reins and heard the wheels rattle on the gravel as she turned to go back indoors, far too fast, I remember thinking, she claimed afterwards, but at the time her only anxiety had been to make sure every bit of broken glass and china had been swept from the Turkey carpet before The Master returned on the four-fifty. But though the room had been tidied and the mistress persuaded to lie down with the curtains drawn, and Rose kept coming in to ask what she should do about The Master's tea tray, there was still no sign of him, though Ben had taken the trap down to the station hours ago.

At first they thought he might have missed the train and would return on a later one, and when the sky suddenly grew dark and began to rumble, and they saw white flashes of lightning split it down the middle just before big fat drops of rain began to rattle in the leaves of the rose-bushes and run down the window panes, blurring the view, then it was assumed they had taken shelter while the storm lasted, as was only sensible. And it was only after it had blown over, and a blue sky rapidly coming in from the west, that the news began to come through, and then only little by little.

First thing was, a farmer's lad came running to the house for help, quite out of breath, panting that the doctor had been found in a ditch more dead than alive, and with every bone in his body broken, most likely, barely conscious, but murmuring to them that found him that his horse had gone wild when a sheet of forked lightning struck the trees over by Emmy's Barrow, and thrown him clear when it hurtled off out of control. And it was only after a cart had been sent off with blankets and bandages and a brandy flask that the rest of the news got through.

Of all the absurd things, it seems that the runaway horse and trap came to a stop on the railway line, either because the horse decided to graze in the lush grasses growing by the track or, more likely, because the wheels of the gig got jammed in the rails and sleepers. Even so, the driver swore he would have been able to stop, for he was slowing down anyhow for the station, and it would not have been the first time he had to be wary of a stray animal obstructing the line, and had said as much to the inspector, if a sudden flash of lightning had not blinded him as he came round the bend. As it was, only the first class carriage immediately behind the engine came off the rails, and the only passenger in it was The Master. They found him almost at once under a heap of splintered wood and broken glass, still clutching his newspaper, with a surprised look on his bearded face and scarcely a scratch on him.

Poor Sophie, I murmured.

Poor horse, said Ada, who did not believe in being sentimental about mere human beings.

Now that's the odd thing, Granny Martin told us. For the horse was quite unharmed, although the gig was smashed to a tinder. Apparently he was standing clear of the track, though how he failed to get dragged along by the harness and killed that way is a mystery. And the man who finally cut him free said he came away as calm and docile as you please, not lame, or anything.

Up at the house the shock of The Master's death had hardly sunk in. Nobody knew how to break it to the mistress, who was still in her room with the curtains drawn, and under the influence of laudanum. The housekeeper declined to disturb her, and told everyone to be quiet as mice while she sent for the vicar.

An eerie hush fell on the house, as the blinds were drawn and the mirrors covered. The older children had been told of their father's death and an uncanny stillness settled on the nursery after the lamps had been taken away and the door shut. The sound of the doorbell broke the silence, once when the vicar arrived, and a second time when the body was brought to the house, and both times it was Mrs. Dobson who went to the door and did what was necessary. The rest of us just sat round the big kitchen table, too shocked to know what to do with ourselves. We heard a murmur of low voices, a door opening and being shut, then nothing. Afterwards Mrs. Dobson came back with a tape measure to have us all put into mourning. It was when she told me to stand on a chair so she could get my skirt length that I began to snivel. I just couldn't help myself.

I got a right ticking off, I can tell you. Pull yourself together, Nancy, she said real sternly. Think of poor Miss Sophie. I'll have none of that. But I couldn't help myself, being very young at the time, and it had all happened so very sudden.

But the real shock was next morning, when Miss Sophie came down from her room in her black dress, with her face very stern and calm under her widow's cap. I never saw a woman so changed. Not a single tear did she shed, and her face was as if turned to stone. But there was something else, too, for she suddenly took to giving orders in a voice of quiet authority that threw the house-keeper all in a dither, since she had been used to making each and every decision that affected the household since before Miss Sophie left the schoolroom, and now here she was demanding to inspect the store-room and ordering food for the funeral reception and telling the upstairs maid that the first floor landing would have to be swept again, all in a low firm voice that there was no gainsaying.

But then Miss Sophie, as we had known her for so many years, had, in a manner of speaking, ceased to exist. From that day forward her heavy dresses were always black, and the widow's cap was never off her head, so nobody noticed much just when and how quickly her light brown hair turned grey, for it was all one really. From now on she was know as The Matriarch, and, whilst before she might have inspired a sort of patronising affection, from the time of her husband's death she provoked quite other emotions, a grudging respect quite devoid of love, but mingled with something very like awe and, at times, fear. Everyone felt it, her children, the servants, and those who lived in the village. In the early days nobody remarked on it much, thinking it only the result of her sudden tragic bereavement, the aura of her grief, so to speak, which would fade with time. But The Matriarch, with her black clothes and her stern face, had arrived for good.

Thirty carriages followed the hearse to the graveyard, and men standing along the route doffed their caps as the plumed horses passed. In the village every window had its blinds drawn, and the tavern stayed shut as a mark of respect. Later a horse trough was erected in the high street to commemorate his services to the county, but The Matriarch declined to attend the unveiling ceremony, pleading pressure of business.

And to tell the truth, this was no mere excuse, for, far from sitting indoors with the blinds drawn, declining invitations to fêtes and garden parties on writing paper edged with black, she was occupied in making grave and momentous decisions. Lawyers were sent for, deed boxes opened, ledgers scrutinised. Mrs. Dobson, who had had a severe shock to her system on the morning after the fatal accident, and half expected to be asked to relinquish her bunch of keys, was reassured to find that her services, far from being dispensed with, were called upon as never before. For, only ten days after the funeral, The Matriarch was seated in a first class railway compartment, on her way to take charge of her husband's business affairs. A week after that she travelled up north to inspect the clothing mill, and scarcely a day passed without her receiving a visit from someone connected with the business, textile designers or travelling salesmen, or a financial adviser from the bank.

They do say, added Nancy, that she trebled the family fortune in just a few years. And though folks were mighty afraid of her, and many's the time I've had to tell one of her own children, like Master Edward when he broke some glass in the conservatory, to speak up like a man and have no fear, yet she could also be kind, and did much good in the neighbourhood. The new schoolhouse was her doing, and the row of almshouses, along with the widows' fund, and each of us who was in her service got a tidy sum in a savings account. And though she never spoke of the old days, the time when I first started service as little more than a child, she would look at me sometimes, quite suddenly, with her grey eyes full of knowing as I came into the room or did my curtsey, as though we had shared something, when I was naught but a scared kid who felt faint at the sight of blood, and that something was between us still. And I was not as surprised as some folks that she should do so much for us when Jake and I were married, even to having the wedding breakfast in the house.

I remember it being almost dark in the room, long inky shadows, and beyond the window a sky glowing red and green and gold. The quiet ticking of the clock on the mantelpiece, and the little cakes she used to bake set out on the cooling rack. The smell of them filled the room.

I remember her telling us more and more, how quickly she could be induced to forget the time, and the long shadows swallowing the room. Ada swinging her legs under the table, picking crumbs off the wax cloth with a wet forefinger, her red hair blazing in the last of the slanting light. And afterwards too, when the room was no more than a dim pool filled by the incoming tide. It was always a flame.

Granny Martin would tell us about the time she worked in the clinic. That was before the war, she said, not this war, but the one before. We called it the Great War then, never thinking there could be another in our lifetime. But the clinic was my war, she would say, with a hint of pride in her voice, and it was no game, I can tell you. Men used to pelt us with bricks and verbal abuse, and our windows got broken more than once. One time our premises were set on fire, and nobody was ever charged. We took to opening up after dark because so many women were terrified of being seen coming to us, and several were beaten up by their husbands, when they found out, so we had to treat them for cuts and bruises as well.

I never would have thought to do anything of the sort, Granny Martin admitted, if it had not been for Miss Dora coming back to the big house when her grandmother died. And I'm mighty glad she did, for my life might have been uncommonly dull without her. She taught me that you don't have to put up with things, the way so many do, and how important it is to fight for what you believe in.

You remember that, girls, she added, and picked up the cat, which was purring round her legs. She smiled as she spoke, and it was difficult to think of her as anything but a soft pillow to hug, or perhaps cry into. Granny Martin chuckled.

You wouldn't think, to look at me, that I'd once been in prison, would you? Well, I have, and I'm proud of it. Dora and I were locked up together in a cell no bigger than this kitchen. The place was so cold at nights, and so filthy, the dark noisy with vermin, that neither of us could sleep much. We would talk to make the time pass, and give ourselves courage, for we were both scared of the cockroaches scrabbling in the dark. It was then that I got to know her, not simply as the woman I worked with, but as a person. She told me about herself, and for the first time I understood what had brought her to this place, exactly why she was locked up now with me.

The whole of my early life, said Dora, was full of illness. I can't remember a time when my mother was not either stretched out on the sofa with a rug over her feet, or in a darkened bedroom most of the day. As children we were always being told to hush, sit still and not run around, as the noise would disturb mama. My old nanny, who had been her nurse as a child, would tell us how, even as a young girl, she was prone to curious maladies. The flowers her mother was so fond of, even after her widowhood, gave her dizzy spells, especially blooms with a heavy scent. On more than one occasion she had to be helped out of church, and nanny would sit on the porch with her, and apply smelling salts. In fact, when her sister Connie was married and she, as chief bridesmaid, was required to hold the bridal bouquet, she caused a commotion by passing out completely, for which her sister could never quite forgive her.

And then there were those headaches. I cannot remember a time when she did not have headaches. It seemed as though the entire household was ruled by them: the slightest sound would shatter her nerves at such times, and a ray of bright sunlight from a window could produce agony. Servants, children, my father, all of us moved on tiptoe and spoke in whispers, while most of the house was shrouded in semi-darkness, with blinds down and curtains drawn. Doctors came and went, though with little effect, and her room had an odour of bitterness from the bottles gathered on the table by her bed. Nanny maintained that her hair had something to do with it, being thick and heavy and richly auburn in colour, since the headaches started about the time her hair was put up for the first time, and continued since, but nobody listened to her, except my sisters and me and perhaps our cook, who was old enough herself not to think her foolish and cracked with time. I did once ask papa, when I was still quite young, if it was possible that the weight of mama's beautiful hair might be too much for her, thus giving her a headache, but he simply laughed and told me not to believe some of nanny's foolish notions. Besides, he added, where would we all be without her crowning glory?

I took his word for it, because I trusted him completely. I adored my father. To me he was everything that could make my life worth living, and the hours I spent in his study were by far the most precious. He would teach me things, and lend me books from his library, and tell me something of the outside world. I think he was amused, more than anything, at my curiosity, my eagerness to learn anything he was able to teach me, and perhaps he might not have been so indulgent if he had had a son, or if my mother had not been shrouded in a sickroom so much. But he did give me time, and encourage me, within limits. He gave me hope for the future too, whilst the hours spent in my mother's room produced nothing but stifling depression.

So you can imagine how I felt when he was struck down quite suddenly, by illness. No, you can't begin to imagine. It was a stroke, you see, and suddenly this fine strong man, so capable, so wise and clever, as I had always thought him, was quite helpless. He had to be washed and fed like a baby. He soiled his sheets, and slobbered the mashed food we gave him by the spoonful, and wept like a baby. Perhaps worst of all, he lost the power of speech.

I looked after him for six months. I slept in his room, and though a nurse was hired it was I who tried to understand his wishes, who helped bathe him and change him and held the feeding cup to his lips and more than anything looked into his eyes, always his poor frantic eyes, for the tiny signs that might answer my questions: are you tired, shall I draw the curtains, would you like me to read to you, open the window, close it?

Dora's voice broke, and I heard her sob for a moment in the dark.

And then he died. It was as though the world had stopped turning. I felt as if I had been walking for a very long time and had suddenly come to the edge of a precipice. I looked down at space, nothing but empty space under my feet, and my head felt giddy. I thought I was falling, and to stop myself I froze and went quite rigid.

I could not move my arms or legs, and my neck was so stiff that I was unable to turn my head. There were pains, terrible pains, but if someone touched me I could feel nothing. They tried everything. One doctor, two, sometimes as many as three, came almost every day to visit me, trying to move my limbs, touching me here, there

169

and everywhere, massaging my arms, sending painful electric currents through my legs. I was immersed in hot water, cold water, and tubs of bran. Needles were stuck into me, mirrors were flashed in my eyes. Finally I was told to lie still and do nothing for at least six weeks.

Then strange things began to happen inside my head. It was very dark in there, and I could hear voices speaking to me in foreign languages, some of which I had never even learnt. The voices were telling me to do bad things, such as I would never have done in my normal state. One day I threw a cushion at the doctor as he came through the door. Another time I ripped all the buttons off my blouse as the nurse tried to dress me. I would not eat, and I knocked a bowl of soup to the floor on purpose. When members of my own family came to see me, I did not recognise them, and if the doctor spoke to me I would answer in a foreign language, and make him use it too. Otherwise, I said, I could hear nothing. And it was true: I would suddenly become quite deaf, with nothing but loud ringing sounds in my ears, and my eyesight also went peculiar, so that everything merged and wobbled and I was quite sure the walls were closing in on me.

Afterwards I would remember nothing. The attack over, I just felt tired, and sick, and anxious. I refused to eat, and the doctor came to the house twice a day to coax a few spoonfuls into my mouth. He would massage my arms and legs and my stiff neck for hours, and I liked that. It was somehow soothing, and made up for the dreadful pain of the high tension electric currents he passed through my thighs twice a week, which I dreaded.

It was a terrible time, and I look back on it with horror. The nights were worst of all. In the dark my loose hair would turn into writhing black snakes, and sometimes I woke the entire household with my screams. I saw spectres come out of the wardrobe, and dreamed that I was walking barefoot through a forest, where the pine needles underfoot turned into live leeches. At times I was in my own bed, with the doctor leaning over me, but there were bats flying out of his hair.

He had dark eyes, the doctor. Opaque as onyx and soft as dusk. He spoke to me softly too, after touching me with his soft white hands, with their manicured fingernails. Look into my eyes, he would say, his voice purring and soothing soft as the fur on the back of our grey cat: look into my eyes and tell me. I looked into them as he counted slowly and softly to five, and I could feel my body going heavy as lead, heavy and oddly light at the same time. I felt myself falling, falling into the cool dark pit of his eyes, their pupils growing larger as my body became smaller, till it was thin as a silver pin, light as a white feather, and I was no longer in it at all, but floating free as a feather, and falling light as a pin. And my voice seemed to come from far away, till I realised suddenly that it was not my voice at all, but my old nanny speaking to me as she brushed my hair by the nursery fire, and I knelt on the hearthrug staring into the smouldering depths of the burning coals with the hot tongues of fire consuming them and my face was burning even though I was shivering in my nightgown as the brush tugged at my tangled hair, and I screamed and held my scalp and begged her to stop hurting me. No comb, no comb, I yelled, but she went on tugging at the knots, saying you don't want it all cut off, do you, like they did to your poor mother when she was a girl, and she tugged and pulled with the comb saying my what a tomboy you are, miss, there's bits of grass and I don't know what in this here hair, and if I have to come with the scissors it won't do, you know, for a good girl to turn into a lady must have masses of long hair coiled up and pinned on her head to keep her down to earth so she don't float away like a flibbertigibbet, and if you don't keep still this minute I'll come with the scissors. And somehow, I don't know why, I was more terrified of the scissors flashing than anything, so I let her go on tugging and pulling at my hair, fixing my eyes on the coals smouldering in the grate, slowly turning to crumbling ash, and my face burned as she brushed, brushed, not just at the heat from the fire, but because of the words she used. For you know what they do with little girls, she whispered, and although I put my hands over my ears she pushed them away before tugging at my scalp with even more vigour: long before they come with the scissors for not being ladylike, the things they do to little girls who turn into tomboys and harumscarums, what they did to your mother when she was your age, as I saw with my own eyes, for I had to hold her down while they put leeches to the place, the naughty place, and she wriggled and screamed and swore for

171

nights after, so I got no sleep at all, that a leech had crawled right up inside her, and was hurting, though the doctor kept saying he had counted them very particular as they dropped off, and that it was perhaps too late to stop her going out of her mind entirely. And all the time nanny's voice was speaking, though it was my voice, I was counting, not from one to five but right up to a hundred, since I knew that only then would the brushing stop, it was the same every night, only then would the last of the tangled knots be tugged out of my mane. I began to pant, and gasp, twisting my head from side to side. No no, I shouted, pushing his hands away, as his soft voice told me to calm myself, to wake up at the count of three, and even though I was somewhere down in the dark pit I knew I was pushing with my frozen arm, which only an hour ago could not lift a teacup or stir a spoon, now it was flailing and punching in a wild fury, as though it could never be still, not ever again, even though I was still submerged in my dark pit with the voices, so many different voices, conflicting inside my head.

I think we are better now, I heard his voice coming through to me, soft and purring, it reached me even before I opened my eyes and looked into his. He was pleased with himself, I could see that, since he was smiling, and the smile reached his dusky irises. I could see myself, very tiny, in the shiny black of his pupils, and I thought that was the pit into which I had fallen so easily.

Good girl, he said to me, and stroked my arm, and my whole body seemed to be tingling with a curious sensation of well-being, so I knew I really was better, even though I could not account for it. But I decided to say nothing, and when he got up to go, saying he would be back tomorrow, I just lay still and looked up at him.

I wanted to please him. I wanted it to be a surprise. So when he came into the room next day I got up off the sofa and took a few steps towards him, a bit unsteadily, it is true, but I really was walking. He simply stood there, stock-still, as though shock had rooted him to the spot, and I was so pleased that I laughed and ran to him, throwing my arms round his neck, and kissed his cheeks with the tears running down my face. I was so happy, I was laughing and crying at the same time, and I wanted to share it with him. He was my friend, and it was his doing. I knew that, even if I was not sure how it had come about.

But to my confusion he did not seem as pleased as I had, in my naïvety, expected him to be. Quite the reverse. My arms round his neck seemed to alarm him, he kept trying to detach himself and push me away, so the absurd notion entered my head that I might have some contagious condition he had said nothing about, but I knew that could not be true, so I laughed and tried to reassure him, telling him I was well, well, with my flushed face against his, and it was all his doing. And I took his face in my hands so he really had to look me in the eyes and see for himself. But he suddenly grew quite frantic, and pushed me from him so roughly that I almost stumbled, and without so much as another word he simply ran out of the room.

That was the last I saw of him. No goodbye, not a single line of explanation, though I had come to expect explanations for every thing from him. Of what anyone might do. I had thought him so wise and good and kind.

It was silent for a bit, in the pitch dark of the cell, except for the rustle of cockroaches. Then I heard Dora chuckle, and it lifted my spirits. There had always been something very cheering about Dora's sense of humour, and it had seen us through worse crises than sitting in a prison cell for a few hours or days. Helping her to run the clinic had taught me to view our lives as a sort of battleground, and every day as a skirmish in an unending war. And it was Dora's cheerful bravado that got us through the worst patches, when some of the younger helpers were inclined to give up the struggle.

I think perhaps not all doctors want their patients to get well. After all, it's a living.

I spoke tentatively, as I always did with Dora, since she was so much older, and knew her own mind, and sometimes bullied young helpers like me without mercy. In fact it was very odd for me to be locked up with her like this. I felt I was really getting to know her for the first time, so she seemed like an ordinary woman, and I stopped being just that little bit afraid of her.

Like doctors attending childbirth, added Dora, and now her voice had the hard edge I associated with public meetings and committee rooms. Imagine having to say goodbye to a guaranteed

173

income of annual pregnancies, reliable as clockwork. No wonder they hate us so much. And if the odd one goes wrong, well, they can still send in a bill, discreetly, of course, after the funeral.

Dora's voice broke in the dark, and I knew why. All of us did. We knew she had begun her life's work after her sister, who had a bad heart, died during her first pregnancy at the age of twenty-one.

It broke my mother's heart, Dora told me now, and filled me with such rage, impotent rage, I can't begin to tell you. You see, everyone knew she had a heart condition, but the only advice her doctor would give was that her husband should sleep in a separate room. Well, you know the sort of thing, it's what we hear every day from the women who come to our clinic. Poor darling Flora, so much in love, I don't think she even considered this as a possibility, and afterwards Alfred was shattered, and blamed himself for her death.

But at the time I had no idea how to harness my rage. It was only after my grandmother died, and I came up to the house to clear some of her personal effects, that I first saw the light. The Matriarch was well over ninety when she died, and had lived by herself in that huge house, except for an ageing bevy of servants, for a very long time. For years before her death she had got rather cranky, she lived in the past and would not allow anything to be touched in the house, or changed, except for a little light dusting from the maidservants, who had themselves grown old in her service, and were inclined to grumble if visitors came and upset their routine by asking for a fire in the library or a light meal on a tray. The family knew this, and rarely came, and then only from a sense of duty. For the bedrooms were always damp and my grandmother got extremely crotchety, even angry, if any of her children dared to suggest that the roof needed to be repaired or the boiler was faulty.

Once she had died something had to be done, and I was sent down to get on with it, being a young woman with no other duty in life but to make myself available for such contingencies. It was a formidable task, and I hardly knew where to start. I found cupboards which nobody had opened for years, and by now the servants had forgotten what had become of the keys. When they were found, one cupboard turned out to be full of china ornaments

174

and lace antimacassars, while another on the second landing was crammed full of bedpans, feeding cups, retorts, paraffin lamps and six stone hot water bottles.

It was the same story in the bedrooms. I found dozens of Indian shawls in one chest of drawers, a pile of beaded purses in another, whilst the wardrobes were full of faded crinolines, lilac and pink and ivory, with little satin shoes to match. A cloud of grey moths fluttered out into the room when I first opened the wardrobe door, and the gowns disintegrated almost entirely as soon as they were taken out and touched. Only the black clothes she had been wearing for the last half century were still in good condition, though they smelled of camphor and lavender water. Six wardrobes full of black bombazeen, velvet, silk, and merino, to say nothing of the piles of black lace, feathers, fringes and ornaments of jet. In a drawer was the treble string of black pearls she wore every day of her life as long as I could remember.

It was while I was clearing out her desk in the study that I found it. The drawers were all locked, but I found the key in a blue and white jar of potpourri, under the dried rose leaves. Most of the compartments were full of routine papers, old bills and accounts from local tradesmen, a few letters sent by relatives long dead, my uncle Edward's first school report. It was under an album of pressed flowers, the paper so yellow and brittle that the corners crumbled when I picked it up. *To The Married of Both Sexes in Genteel Life* was the heading, and the first page warned of the consequences when parents had more children than they could afford to maintain and educate in a suitable manner. There was something about the struggle against poverty and despair brought on by a continual increase of children. And then it came, the advice, so simple, so utterly devoid of hocus-pocus, that I could hardly believe my eyes: a piece of soft sponge attached to a narrow ribbon, moistened, and withdrawn after intercourse.

I was bewildered, and then thunderstruck. I read it once, twice, a dozen times. I paced up and down that study for what must have been hours. But there was no getting away from it: this handbill, so simple that a child could understand it, had been locked up for the best part of a century, whilst women died, and suffered, and brought sickly infants into a world which was quite unwilling to

175

house and feed them. Above all I thought of my poor sister, and I was filled with incredulity, and rage.

Of course, added Dora, there was nothing about vinegar or alum solution, but that's just a detail. It was a beginning, and for me too. Until then my future had seemed to offer nothing but a dreary round of social and family duties, mostly shut up in a sick room with my unhappy mother. Pacing that study, thinking about what I had found, I suddenly saw a whole new purpose opening up in front of me. It was glorious, so glorious I started waltzing round that dreary house of mourning, knocking over whatnots, tipping over firescreens, pulling back drapes and opening windows, till the doddery maidservants began to protest that sunlight would fade the upholstery of the chairs and sofas. Let it fade, I shouted, banging a chaise-longue, which gave out a cloud of dust. And I decided we should hold one last bazaar in the grounds of the house to get rid of this detritus, and fund my new venture.

The sale was not a success. News had got round the neighbourhood that I was not planning to extirpate poverty among the urban poor with blankets, coal tickets and biblical tracts, but with free medical advice in the use of alum, quinine and sulphate of zinc. Nobody came, or at least no one with money to spend, and I heard afterwards that the local doctor and vicar had spread the word between them that no self-respecting person should attend such a function. A few grubby children drifted in from the village, and having no use for my grandmother's old finery laid out on the stalls, and with no buyers in sight, I ended up giving most of it to them, and for years after that, when I came back to the house, and drove through the village from the station, I would see children playing games with bits of lace on their heads, or outdated bonnets, trailing skirts far too long for them in the dusty street, in a solemn pantomime of make believe.

But the black pearls had been left to me in her will, and they fetched a king's ransom. I can't remember a time when she did not wear them, and I often wonder what the old girl would have thought of my selling them, and using the proceeds to open my first clinic. Like the rest of my cousins, I also received a small investment income, but it was those black pearls, those three strands so large and heavy in their uniformity that they seemed to

176

weigh down her head and neck, giving her that peculiar stoop I remember towards the end of her life, which gave me the initial capital to get things going.

And that's where I first met Dora, Granny Martin told us. Those two little rooms in a back alley with everything painted white, an examination couch in the back room and a row of frightened women in the front. And they had good cause to be frightened, I can tell you, for the window of the waiting room had a brick heaved through it regular as clockwork, and some of them risked a right beating up when they got home. As I said, we took to opening up after dark for those that were too scared to come in by daylight, but that was risky, since the neighbourhood was rough, and the police turned a blind eye when a gang of men stood jeering outside or threw rotten vegetables.

But I was a hardened case by that time, I can tell you. I'd seen such things as a district nurse as would make your hair stand on end. Women dying bit by bit, and their children too, in rooms half the size of this one, with no heat, no running water, except perhaps through the roof, no nothing. And always another child on the way. It turned me into a bit of a revolutionary, for a while. But I soon found politics was not the answer. I went to one political meeting, and I actually found the courage to get up and speak, though my hands were shaking and the blood drumming in my ears so hard I could hardly hear myself. But anger and urgency gave me courage: I told them what I had seen with my own eyes, women with too many sickly mouths to feed, worn out and dying within a few short years. And then some men at the back began to jeer, and the man on the platform banged his gavel on the table, shouting order, order, so I could not go on, and when the hubbub had died down a bit he told me, ever so kindly, that family limitation was a bourgeois conspiracy to limit the numbers of the working class who would bring about a revolution. There was a burst of applause, and when it was over he added that we must all beware of pernicious attempts to undermine solidarity by fostering the self-help and individual idealism involved in restricting the family, and that a worker properly rewarded for his labour could support any number of children. This raised prolonged cheering, and much stamping of feet, and I thought I would never get out of that hall, with my face flushed and tears in my eyes, and as I got to the end of the row of chairs I heard someone laugh, and remark: just like a woman.

That was my only brush with politics, and to tell you the truth I hadn't a lot of patience with the women who were making such a fuss at the time about getting the vote. But Miss Dora said I was wrong, and that even though some of them did not support us, we should admire what they were doing. We used to argue about it sometimes, in that back room, and when I said that most of the women we knew had more use for a rubber pessary than having a vote, she laughed and said: why not have both? I couldn't argue with that. I suppose it was just that I'd been put right off politics by finding out that the people who were supposed to be our friends were just as bad as the other side. Worse, in a way, since they should have understood.

But, when it came right down to it, Dora was right. For as far as the police were concerned we were all women, and women of a certain sort, and whether it was rubber goods or sticks of dynamite we had on us as we went through the streets was all one to them, as they bundled us into a police van that night. I'll never forget it, all the shop fronts seemed to be tinkling with the sound of broken glass, and pillar boxes were shooting up in flames at every street corner. Alarm bells were ringing, police whistles blowing, and then for a moment I saw her, Christabel, with her gold blonde hair piled on her head and the light of a thousand fires in her startling blue eyes, standing on a soapbox with a megaphone in her hand before several policemen bundled her off to a van parked by the kerb. I recognised her at once by the firm cut of her jaw and those remarkable eyes, having seen them often enough on police posters and in newspaper cartoons, and my heart leaped right into my mouth with the excitement of seeing her.

We tried to get to the clinic, carrying a box of alum and cocoa butter between us, shuffling through shards of broken glass and the sky blazing as though it was Guy Fawkes night. Every now and then another pillar box would explode, making us jump half out of our skins and sending a shower of envelopes floating up into the night sky like a snow storm. Several coach horses reared and took fright, so crossing from one kerb to the other was also hazardous. And then a police van drew up and simply bundled us in, since we did not look like prostitutes, I suppose, and it was respectable women they were picking up that night. We must have looked a real sight, me with my bonnet askew, and Dora arguing to the last, and a lady in black with an armful of tracts who kept saying she was only on her way to conduct a prayer meeting, and she did not hold with suffrage of any kind, since it was not in the Bible.

Granny Martin laughed. They were rare old times, when I think about them now, though they didn't seem so funny at the time.

It was quite dark in the room, except for a glimmer of moonlight.

My goodness, she said. I've quite forgotten the time. I'd better fix the black-out, and you'd best run off to bed or your mother'll be after me.

Tell us about prison, begged Ada.

But at that moment an explosion shook the walls, rattling the cups on the Welsh dresser.

They're trying for the airfield again, said Granny Martin. You'd both better stay here for a bit.

Oh but I want to see, said Ada excitedly, and rushed out before anyone could stop her.

I was starting to feel a bit sick, and my legs shook the way they used to do back home when the siren sounded. But this time there had been no alert, which was more frightening.

Come back, child, my grandmother called out, and started to go after her, but the whistling sound had her grabbing me by the neck as she flung us both to the floor, with herself almost on top of me. I was deaf for a bit, after the explosion, and granny had to pick bits of broken glass out of her hair, and mine.

My God, she said suddenly. Where's Ada?

Seven

Night draws in a little sooner each evening. The summer is over, I can feel it in my bones. Though the sun shines out of a clear sky during this Indian summer, it lacks conviction, and the nights are cold. The thinning trees turn to bronze in the golden light, and a fine black tracery of branches begins to stand out against the sky. Rows of brown stubble show the lie of the land, how it swells and dips and hollows, how it spreads itself to unkempt edges of dried grass and brittle cow parsley. And always the smell of burning in the air, faint, acrid, of dead leaves and dry twigs, the heaps raked together in back gardens, of stubble and husks and burrs, of ghosts and things that are gone dispersing into the misty air.

The mist clings to the branches of trees in the early morning, lies in the hollows at dawn. I open my windows and doors and see the outline of things past superimposed on the here and now. Part of growing old, I suppose. I see them even in the living: a glint of reddish gold in Sally's hair, though not so dark as Ada's, Kate using her hands with precisely the same gesture as Granny Martin, and Emily looking out of my mother's eyes.

How long ago it was, I thought, noticing the old man's beard threading the hedgerows one more time, but nearer than yesterday. How distant, and yet so close, the same bright red hips we collected on school rambles to make syrup for babies, those wartime babies. We were always collecting things for the war effort, milk bottle tops, silver paper, books and newspapers. Once we took a burnt-out kettle and two bent pans to add to a pile of old saucepans by the village war memorial, so the aluminium could be used to make fighter planes.

I drive past the war memorial with the names of two of Granny Martin's brothers cut into the granite and point out the spot where the saucepans were piled up to Emily, who likes listening to my stories. She has made herself a necklace of red rosehips and filled every jar and vase in the house with dried leaves collected on our walks. I showed her how to paint the inside of beechnut husks so they look like flowers. Women used to wear them as costume jewellery during the war, I told her, and Emily is delighted. She is making a bunch for Sally's birthday, and it is a great secret between us.

My mother took me straight back to London after the funeral, and by the time I came back the war was over and my childhood had turned to uneasy adolescence. I tried to tell Sally about it the other night, but she seemed preoccupied, and I stopped after a bit, since she obviously was not listening. She has developed a tendency to brood, I notice, which I put down to her unwanted pregnancy this summer, followed by a mild depression, but I may be wrong: perhaps she is just getting older too, as we all do. Whatever it is, I sense a change in her, something dark, a bit sad. On the plus side, she visits me more often, and I feel somehow closer to her, even if she does not want to listen to me yakking on about the past. And who knows, perhaps she has heard it all before, and I am becoming a repetitive old bore, telling the same old stories, just as my mother did in her final years.

I took Emily round the big house on an open day and told her how it had been used as a hospital for convalescent soldiers in the first world war, and that during the second war it had been full of evacuee children. She is growing up fast. Adam is still a chubby toddler, but Emily has the thin features, the legs and arms suddenly coltish and just a bit too long, which go with rapid growth. I also showed her the box of old photographs which Granny Martin gave me after the war, just before she died. Whilst Sally was bathing Adam upstairs I took out snapshots of aunt Doris on her wedding day, of Ada and me sitting cross-legged on the front lawn with a large ball between us, one of Granny Martin's brothers in his army uniform, and the sepia ones of older, forgotten faces which I had been told about so long ago and recollected only vaguely. Your great-great-grandmother, I said, pointing to a child in the second row outside the old schoolhouse, which is now used as a community centre. How do you know? asked Emily, peering closely at the brownish print. To her it is just one child of many in identical boots and pinafores. Because I do, I answered. Anyhow, can't you see that she looks like you?

The days are getting shorter. More trees stand bare against the sky, and the hedgerows are dry and brittle. I hear the raucous cawing of rooks in high trees, and sometimes the sound of gunshots echoing over bare brown fields. The old airfield is being fenced off, and rumours of various kinds have been rumbling round the village since the contractors arrived to put cement posts and high wire round the perimeter.

It was Sally who first got wind of the truth. She has been moving in new circles lately, and it was her friend Amabel who ferreted out the information. Amabel, it seems, has a friend of a friend who worked at the Ministry of Defence, and she had looked up the file. That it was a girl, quite a humble typist or filing clerk, I only found out much later, when she was charged under the Official Secrets Act. At the time, when the first charges of leaks at the Ministry began to be reported, the suggestion was always that the person involved must be a senior civil servant.

I remember how it started. It was just after the abortion, and Sally was obviously feeling rather low when she rang.

How are you feeling? I asked.

Oh fine, she said in an offhand voice. After all, this is no world to bring kids into, is it?

And she began to tell me what she had heard about the airfield.

I listened to her for a long time, and for once I could not argue with anything she had to say. I thought: she's changed, my daughter, grown older and wiser. And then I thought, perhaps it's not as simple as that, and it is me who is old and foolish, dozing blindly at my own fireside, increasingly unaware. Whatever the reason, I was learning from her, humbly. I asked her to keep me informed, and I said she could count on me to do whatever I could.

I felt a weight inside me when I put the receiver down, and stared out of the window for a long time, where dusk was settling over the black land. I have not felt so depressed for a long time, but at the same time something else was stirring. I was involved, I was alive, my so-called retirement was over. Kate had been right when she said she could not see me burying myself alive in this cottage indefinitely, waiting to die.

No world to bring kids into, I thought, hearing Sally's voice in my head. Through the window I could see a new moon rising beyond the black shadow of the hillside, and its beauty turned in me like a knife. No world to bring kids into: I had heard my mother saying much the same thing to aunt Doris, and when she bundled me into an air raid shelter night after night. I had said it myself when I saw the first mushroom clouds burst on the television screen in the living room and began to store canned milk for Kate in case the Strontium 90 reached danger level. No doubt mothers had been saying it down the ages, right through to the dark ages.

But each birth had brought hope. This time there would be no hope. The cold new moon would rise on a lunar landscape, as stark and dead as itself. None of the old familiar landmarks, hillside and wood, and seasons changing. No sudden beauty to make the heart ache. No lesser celandine breaking through winter in hedge bank and wood, and no eye to see it even if it should do so.

Amabel has bright blue eyes and fair hair tied up in pigtails, and when she comes to the house for a much-needed bath she is usually wearing dungarees or some sort of boiler suit. The girls have been camping outside the base for three weeks now, and Sally is down there most of the time. So far there have been no arrests, only a certain amount of harassment from the police. My own job is to help provide some sort of back-up service; I drive down with fresh supplies of food, take in children for short periods of time, and provide endless hot water for baths. I also sit with them round their camp fire quite a lot, but I don't feel up to sleeping under canvas, and nobody has suggested that I should.

Although there is no recognised leader in the group, there is no doubt in my mind that Amabel is a guiding spirit. She is very sensible, extremely determined, and seems to know instinctively how to cope with each and every crisis, which she does with great good humour and a lack of fuss that calms and reassures everybody involved.

The nights are getting colder, and the girls sleep in anoraks and layers of clothing. Sally sleeps with them, but I insist on taking Adam and Emily home with me at night, though we sit late at the camp fire sometimes, drinking cups of smoky tea and singing. *Can't kill the spirit* is their theme song, I hear it echo through the dark valley and the distant hills as I drive home in the blackness, with the two children dozing on the back seat. My neighbours have become taciturn, a few openly hostile, since they regard the women's peace camp as a local nuisance. There are mutterings about litter and lack of hygiene, and a rather badly attended meeting at the community centre voted in favour of the missile base, since it would provide employment and boost trade at the local shops. This is awkward at times, since some of these same people are in a group who asked for my help in getting crop spraying stopped, after several children in the village developed mysterious skin rashes and eye infections. But some of the young people come up to the camp at week-ends, bringing gifts of cake and fruit. They hang flowers and bits of coloured ribbon on the high wire fence, and join in the singing.

Kate has been down too. She brought several sleeping bags, which I could see were brand-new, and gave Amabel, who is camp treasurer, a cheque. Afterwards I saw her ruffle Sally's hair, and kiss her on the cheek before leaving, and thought I had never seen them so close before.

I have never seen Sally so strong and sure. Suddenly the two of them are equals, and Kate's cool authority no longer riles her, producing those childish tantrums as a bid for my attention. I watch them stand and laugh, suddenly, with one voice, and tears prick my eyes. Another symptom of old age, I find, an easy susceptibility to sentiment. A police officer towers behind them on his brown horse, looking down with a bemused expression under his vizored cap, but to my two girls he seems invisible.

Winter ploughing has begun in some of the lower fields. Scavenging black birds wheel in the wake of the heavy earth furrow. Autumn leaves have turned damp and slippery, and footpaths are muddy. Children stand outside the village store with a stuffed guy in an old pram, collecting for bonfire night. Inside the perimeter fence at the camp is a dead land. I can see the ghosts departing into the grey mists of approaching winter: butterflies that once flew above gorse and thistle, the shadows of courting couples lying in long grass, small boys hunting blackberries. They had begun to drift back once the war was over, but now the last trace of them has gone for ever. The clocks have been turned back for winter and it is almost dark at five. An earth-digging machine is just visible far off through the wire.

The girls sit under their little tents, with their groundsheets, and cooking stoves, and waterproof clothing. They sing songs to keep their spirits up when it gets dark at five o'clock. Emily knows the words now, and joins in. It could be a game, but it is no such thing. The nights grow darker, the temperature falls, the moon is obscured by cloud. A few desultory fireworks light up the sky. Beyond the wire fence I see the black shadow of the old barrow, the mound where Edwin the warlord lies buried. If the fire comes, it will come from there.